Orthogonal Procedures

Adam Rothstein

Arche Press

This is A008 and it has an ISBN of 978-1-63023-056-2.

Library of Congress Control Number: 2017947879

This book was printed in the United States of America, and it is published by Arche Press, an imprint of Resurrection House (Sumner, WA).

Therefore, we must sometimes, so to speak, move at a tangent from procedure.

Edited by Mark Teppo
Book Design by Mark Teppo
Copy Edit by Shannon Page

First trade paperback Arche Press edition: October 2017.

Arche Press
www.archepress.com

Orthogonal Procedures

Agencies of the Executive Branch

circa 1970

In the Department of Commerce

The Weather Service
The National Standards Service
The Census Service
The Patent and Trademark Service
The US Geodetic Service
The US Geodetic Service Corps
The National Park Service
The Forest Service
The Smithsonian Cultural Service
The General Land Service
The Fish and Wildlife Service
The Agricultural Service
The Reclamation Service
The Indian Affairs Service

In the Department of Transportation

The Postal Bureau
The Aeronautics and Space Technology Bureau
The Electromagnetic Bureau
The Mass Transit Bureau
The National Airspace Transit Bureau
The Coast Guard Bureau
The Infrastructure Bureau
The National Automated Transport Safety Bureau
The Advanced Research Projects Bureau

Civics Pop Quiz

Unit 9 - Commercialism and Technocratic Administrationism
Mr. Franklin's 7th Grade Social Studies Class
Jimmy Nesbit
November 8, 1969

1. When did the famous rivalry between Postmaster Roosevelt and Commerce Secretary Wallace begin?

__ 1932 X 1945 (__ 1940) __ 1958

correct

2. What president ended the age of Technocratic Administrationism in 1958, by reforming the Postal Administration, the National Aeronautics Research Administration, the Communication Administration, the Federal Aviation Administration, and the Coast Guard Administration into the new Department of Transportation?

X President Eisenhower   __ President Dewey

__ President Nixon   __ President Landon

3. Who succeeded Postmaster Truman as the titular head of the Federal Government's technological industries?

X Secretary of Transportation Henry Truman

__ Secretary of Commerce Henry Wallace

(__ Secretary of Transportation Quentin Dreyer   *correct*

__ Secretary of Commerce Sinclair Weeks

4. What 1957 event would be the impetus for major changes in the way the Federal Government developed American technology?

__ The URER's development of the hydrogen bomb

X The Electronic Invasion of the Sinai Peninsula

__ The election of President Kennedy

(__ The URER's launch of the first satellite, Sputnik

correct

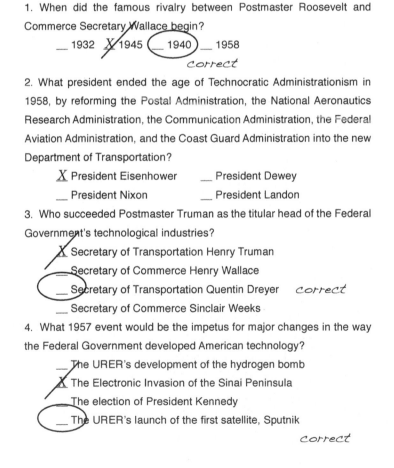

5. According to historian Lisa Gregor, what are the real historical roots of the ideological differences between Technocratic Administrationism and Commercialism?

    X The Civil War

    ___ President Theodore Roosevelt's 1903 creation of the Department of National Commerce   *correct*

    ___ The 1916 Invention of the P-car

    ___ The 1922 Teapot Dome Scandal

Jimmy, you need to study harder. Postmaster Roosevelt died in 1945, so his feud with Wallace could not have begun then! The Administrations became the Department of Transportation. This is basic stuff. Remember that Eisenhower's decision was based on the URER's perceived technological advance, and not only the regional aggressions in the Middle East. And lastly, did you read Question 5 correctly? This unit is about the first half of the 20th Century. Answer A was supposed to be an easy one to eliminate.

Please see me after class. 1/5

1

Parallel
Tangential
Orthogonal

The time is 8:00 AM, Eastern Postal Time. This is the Post News Morning Report for April 17, 1970.

The top story this hour: reports of electronic conflict brewing in Southeast Asia. The South Vietnamese undersea electronic mail cables have been cut again, and while there is currently no evidence, many commentators in the United States are pointing at the United Russian Economic Republics, or their proxies in North Vietnam. Currently the Postal Bureau's overseas assets are responding with electronic countermeasures and defensive jamming in order to allow microwave communications to make up for the loss of undersea bandwidth. Officials estimate that US Postal Bureau-carried traffic between Southeast Asia and Pacific points east will decrease by 9%, and although they refuse to speculate, it's believed that this will allow Russian State Post services to expand further in the region.

Meanwhile, in domestic news, the Infrastructure Bureau had announced new development plans for the five-year period through 1976. The plans, to take effect next year, included a much needed upgrade of elevated trackways in various Midwestern states along the Lincoln Transcontinental Arterial. However, the controversial plans for the Central Baltimore track connection were not included in the over one-thousand-page-long development plan report. It appears that Baltimore neighborhood activists, whose anti-track protests made national news earlier in the year, have gotten a reprieve, at least for now. The activists, focused around the Leakin Park area, had demanded that the tracks be buried in a tunnel rather than cut through the popular park.

SUNLIGHT STREAMED THROUGH THE SMALL WINDOW IN THE TALL office complex of the Electromagnetic Bureau, illuminating the charts and models strewn about the office, piled on the small table and the cabinet against the wall. If Fred Mackey angled his head just right, standing where his engineering degree was framed on the wall, he could just see out the small window past the opposite office buildings, and catch sight of the Potomac over the arterial P-car trackway along the river. It wasn't much of a window. But it was a window that Mackey had earned through hard work and devotion to the Bureau's procedures.

And so ignoring the spring sunlight and the radio quietly playing the morning Postal Bureau News Program, Mackey concentrated on the charts on his desk—the latest data sets from the new interference shielding they had put through its paces last week. It was a decent design, certainly not breaking any records, but just as effective as the shielding on current proximity radar units, and half as heavy and expensive, while twice as physically strong. This was the last stage of testing before the Electromagnetic Bureau's laboratory would give it the stamp of approval and fill out the Part Six certification initiation forms. With any luck, production units would roll out on the rails of the P-car transport system within nine months. He tried to think about the report he would be writing to summarize the data sets—how to summarize the conclusive nature of their findings.

Luckily he had the help of his colleague Lynn Thacker, who was standing across the desk from him, in mid-sentence about propagation pathways around non-ferric metals. She had one of the finest minds in the section, and she knew it. Thankfully, she and Mackey had always had a good working relationship, because it would take the both of them to get through all the figures and explanations on schedule.

Hearing a slight fuzz of static breaking through the normally crystal clear news transmission, Mackey looked up and caught sight of a short, dark-suited figure, standing perfectly center and straight in his doorway. Popping to his feet, Mackey forgot to button his jacket.

The slight woman in the doorway spoke, her quick, commanding voice quickly establishing a stature where her silhouette left off. "I'm sorry...is it Miss Thacker? Yes, Lynn Thacker, author of the recent report on physical contact propagation patterns in micro-helical antennas. Some fine work, Miss Thacker. But I'm sorry to inform you, Mr. Mackey won't be available to help with this Part Six report. I'll be needing him for a special assignment, effective immediately. Mr. Mackey, I am Assistant Secretary of Transportation Grace Hopper."

Miss Thacker was for once thrown off her immaculate poise, even if only for a moment. She stammered, perhaps the first time Mackey had ever heard her speak in such unsure tones. "Yes, Assistant Secretary Hopper, absolutely." Gesturing quickly with the folders in her hands, she spoke quietly to Mackey as she took her leave: "Fred—I'll handle this, and let me know when you are free." And she was gone, with only a slight click of her heels and a whisper of her polyester pantsuit.

There were few government executives who could make Lynn Thacker disappear so quickly and quietly, and one of them was standing in front of Mackey now. Hopper stepped into the office, her business-wear absolutely silent, bereft of any mark or accent, save a small blue Department of Transportation lapel pin. Her flat shoes had thick heels of some sort of rubberized polymer, audibly invisible across the tiled Bureau floor. She wore a trilby over her short brown hair, the headgear only slightly feminized, a black so dark it seemed to absorb light, perfectly matching her suit. Her glasses held thick frames, separating the woman of sixty-four years of age from the room. And yet, she peered through them at everything before her, actively, as if she were a pilot surveying the landscape from a jet cockpit. She did not remove her hat as she approached Mackey. "You know who I am, Mr. Mackey." It was not a question.

Mackey finally remembered to button his jacket. "Yes, ma'am. Of course, ma'am. How can I be of help to the office of the Secretary of Transportation?"

Grace Hopper, Assistant Secretary for Innovation, and special deputy to the Secretary of Transportation, shut the door with an agile, backward swipe of her arm. Almost shockingly agile. As if completed by a person half her age. As if rehearsed a dozen times, until the exact placement and weight of the door had been memorized by her arm muscles.

She continued the quick pace of her elocution, not taking pains for the listener in the slightest. "I know who I am and where I work as well, but thank you all the same. You, for your part, work in the Electromagnetic Bureau, Domestic Interference Engineering Section, one of the many diverse areas of our illustrious Department of Transportation. You work on P-car sensor upgrades and the like. Nothing military grade, as you have no security clearances. You make the cars run without smashing into each other, preventing the pulverization of the fine citizens of this nation. That is all very good, and important work. But I see here from your file," she held nothing in her hands, "that you are also rated Level G in Bureaucratic Literacy. Is that so?"

It was a fact his co-workers often teased him about. "The G-Man" was their adopted name for the unglamorous bureaucratic distinction. Some government employees worked in the Electronic Combat Reserve forces, or had training in off-track vehicle operation for remote installations. Mackey's specialization included weekly time in a basement office suite for training and updates, reading through a manual that took up several shelves.

But the extra training he had undergone for the certification had its benefits, besides the pay bump. His supervisors enjoyed having someone in-section fill out particular forms and certify cross-Department reports, which ordinarily required bureaucratic specialists. Mackey, always happy to take on extra responsibility, would add these tasks to his engineering workload, to the delight of his managers. And there was the spectacular memory for the faces of executives, which certainly never hurt. Being popular with his bosses had never hurt him before.

He was wondering what sort of trouble it had landed him in now.

"Yes, ma'am." His Level G certificate hung framed on the wall next to his engineering degree, but he thought better of directing her towards it.

"And you are also the closest Level G engineer to my office, and that is why I've come to borrow you. I like working with engineers better than career bureaucrats. I used to be an engineer, you know, and still am one on occasion. I've cleared things with Minot, your Bureau's Secretary. I need you to come with me on a special assignment. Someone has been messing with my computers, and we're going to find out who."

Normally if he was being taken up to the Department level from the Bureau level, there would be a Form T561 from the Office of Personnel Management, signed by his immediate superior. Hopper did not appear to have one on her. That was Level A bureaucratic training procedure, and Hopper would know he knew that. He decided not to bring it up at this time.

"What—seems to be the trouble?" he asked instead.

Assistant Secretary Hopper took a step towards his desk and smiled. It was that disarming smile, the one she was famous for. There were more stories and rumors about Hopper than anyone in all the Bureaus of the Department of Transportation. She appeared like any other administrator in a sharp suit. Far younger looking than her years, her short frame hiding an inner power, running off of an unknown energy. Beneath her exterior was a core of intrigue and strategy, as if she was constantly reverse-engineering a person through the window of her thick glasses frames.

Despite whatever official position she had held, she was known as a problem solver—first working for the Office of the Postmaster General since the days of World War Two, and then for the Secretary of Transportation after the great reorganization in 1958. The fact that she had survived the 1958 reorganization and was still in the top echelons of the Department belied how important she was.

Mackey had heard a story about how she once openly threatened an Admiral, after naval ships were causing provocations over an important electronic mail cable route. Another story said she once ordered an Air Mail jet to ditch into the sea, rather than risk flying through a compromised electronic warfare zone. And there was even a story that she had commanded a Postal Bureau combat orbiter. A conspicuous lack of details about when, and against whom, in that last story. But these factors just helped the rumors spread wider and wilder.

But now, in Mackey's office, Secretary Hopper casually brushed aside this veil of mystery as she dived into the technical specifics of her computer system. "It's really quite simple. We've been slowly connecting the computer systems of the various departments, using a sort of telephone box called an Interface Message Processor. Are you familiar with these systems?"

The phrase was familiar, but he couldn't quite place what the device was. "Is that part of the new ASPIC protocol?"

"No, this is fully digitized signal transfer, not analog. The IMPs were developed by the Advanced Research Projects Bureau agency of the Department of Transportation. The project is called ARPNET. At Level G you should be receiving the Canonical Acronym Naming Office Notice bulletins."

Mackey did, per his training, memorize the new CANON list every month when it arrived in his inbox. But even though ARPNET lit up a part of his memory, cross-referenced to the ARPB, he had no idea what it actually was. And the details were likely classified, anyway.

"The gist, Mackey, is that the IMP breaks computer data into packets before transmission across the telephone lines, which then can be verified one by one upon receipt to make sure no data is lost. Each IMP can interface with all the others, to bounce the packets around a number of connected lines, to get all the packets to their destination. By creating a network of these IMP units, any computer system in-network can send and retrieve data from any other system, without any loss, and low latency. This network is the ARPNET. Are you with me?"

Mackey barely had time to nod.

"Fantastic. Now, the computer system for the Postal Bureau has been compromised. Some person has managed to connect into the ARPNET, and is retrieving information without authorization."

Mackey's eyes went wide. "Someone is messing with the P-car system?"

"No, of course not. The P-car's analog radar group-scoping communicate between cars directly. The track signal systems are maintained by the Mass Transit Bureau, and they certainly aren't allowed to connect to something as experimental as the ARPNET. We aren't idiots, Mackey. If this experimental network crashed any vital signals, we'd have a disaster on our hands. The computer in question merely stores data on Postal customers. But, specifically, data about members of the Department of Transportation. *Our* Department." Hopper placed an unusual emphasis on the last sentence.

"I don't really program computers. I occasionally write routines on our PA/360 for wave modeling. If some sort of private interest or criminal has found a weakness in code developed by ARPB, I'm certainly not the person to look at it."

"I don't require your programming abilities at this time. I need your bureaucratic expertise. You see, I already know where the intrusion is coming from. The footprints are a mile wide, if you know what you're looking for. It's the Weather Service. One of their facilities is accessing the data, and I need you to help me negotiate up the chain to get to the bottom of it. So to speak." She smiled that smile again.

"Why on earth would one of the Services of the Department of Commerce be breaking into one of the Bureaus of the Department of Transportation?"

"They aren't *breaking* in. They are compromising the system controls in order to send and receive unauthorized data. They are—so my young engineers have come to call it—*hacking* in. And we are going to find out precisely why, if we can ever get out of your office."

Hopper walked to the door, opened it, and stepped out into the hallway. Mackey left his work on his desk with anxiety at the many tasks left to be completed and snatched his hat off the hook by the door, attempting to look like he was moving with even more haste than he was.

At the underground entrance to the Electromagnetic Bureau

building, Assistant Secretary Hopper's P-car was already waiting. The car's gullwing doors were open wide, while the parking assistant waited along aside, disappearing back into the parking office as he saw the Assistant Secretary approach.

She stepped in without even bothering to grab onto the chrome handle and waited patiently on her seat for Mackey to clamber in opposite her, awkwardly grasping the handle that was not in the standard place, but appeared to have been modified lower for the Assistant Secretary. After he had finally cleared the entry way and stepped across the wear-resistant carpeting and established himself on the gleaming, black patent-leather bench, Hopper hit the requisite button, and the doors pulled shut with a pneumatic hiss. The P-car rolled forward on the track with a deep, electric hum, exiting the underground area and rejoining the streaming sunlight. Hopper slid a punch card into the console, the navigation system chimed, and the car joined the flow of traffic heading across the river.

The P-car, Mackey couldn't help but notice, was top of the line. Only the best for the highest executives of the Department of Transportation, it seemed. Given how long P-cars tended to last until safety requirements finally forced them into retirement, a new model was something that caught one's eye. The interior was finished with real wood, dark in color, inset with cleverly crafted accents. Mackey's Bureau-issue car's interior was constructed entirely from plastics. Showing through the wood of the Assistant Secretary's car, he saw only the newest in technology.

While the car ran on punch cards, it also had a system for magnetic cartridge addressing systems. It meant that the car had an upgraded atlas memory, storing the current signal maps not just for the metropolitan area, but likely for the entire Eastern Seaboard. And yet the small size of the navigation console gave away just how new it was, and the limited space it required allowed a number of other features and systems that Mackey couldn't quite identify. There was a multi-band radio, a radio phone, and also a number of other control surfaces that weren't immediately identifiable, but also didn't seem to be quite at home in an everyday means of transportation.

The radio snapped on automatically, and continued the same news program that had been playing in Mackey's office.

Despite the brewing conflict in Southeast Asia, President Nixon's trade visit to the URER was a success, and it was announced that the Postal Bureau would begin manufacturing P-car systems for the further expanses of the Central and East Asia system, to complement the Russian models.

A minor satellite malfunction disrupted radio simulcasts across Eastern North America this morning. The Aeronautics and Space Technology Bureau reported that the disruption, coupled with sunspot activity, might decrease broadcast audio quality throughout the day until backup satellites could be positioned in orbit.

The Assistant Secretary sat silently, enjoying the view of the memorials along the Tidal Basin as the car negotiated the track switches onto the George Washington Memorial Arterial, heading northwest along the Virginia side of the Potomac. Mackey could see where the angular plan of L'Enfant's District of Columbia still showed through the banked curves and whorls of the concrete tracks. Like translucent engineering vellum, the present-day capital of the United States lay overtop of the founders' Federal City.

Through this superimposed layer, traced with the humming pen strokes of bureaucrats' speeding electric P-cars, April sunlight managed to filter down to the historically maintained pedestrian blocks below, some still paved in nothing but lumpy cobblestone, the aggregate collection of the nation's history visible beneath its current state of the art machinery. From this side of the capital the towering federal skyscrapers were dark blocky masses caught in the silhouette of the morning sun, which gleamed bright even through the tinting of the car's rounded Perspex shell.

Downtown Washington DC was a range of architectural styles, the panoply collecting over the decades as new buildings were updated and added, torn down, and built taller. The singular impression was density. Rising levels of integrated office floor, stacked close together, drawing the various hives of government into close proximity with each other.

Or, at least a bifurcated proximity. South of the Mall was Federal Center, home of most central offices of the Department of Transportation. North of the Mall was the Commercial District, the location of many of the Department of Commerce buildings. For one instant, as the car shot north along the elevated, multi-lane track, he could see directly down the Mall past the Capitol, with these two halves of government neatly divided.

The radio broadcast transitioned into a musical interlude. A Bach concerto, played on an electronic synthesizer. As they rode amongst the congested midday traffic passing Arlington National Cemetery the P-car linked with several others in formation, coming to stasis at their rubberized pivot points at the nose and tail of the stainless steel tubular frame. The other cars, evidently heading in the same direction, made almost imperceptible contact as the radar systems brought them into close, inertially overlapping vectors. As the cars just barely did not touch, Hopper began to speak as if on cue.

"How much do you know about the history of the Department of Transportation?"

Mackey considered the question in the brief silence. Silence, except for the steady whir of the electric motors beneath the P-car, and the slight hiss of passing slipstream as they cut through the humid air of the capital area. One of the cars in the rear of their formation departed, taking the exit track to the Fairbanks Track Research Center, a facility of the Department of Transportation's Infrastructure Bureau. Mackey didn't know what he was expected to say to an executive of this stature, and decided to defer. "Certainly, I don't know as much about Transportation as you do."

Hopper rolled her eyes slightly behind the frames of her glasses across the span of the car from him. Mackey only just realized that although the P-cars could travel in either direction equally, she had managed to sit on the side of the car so that she would be facing forward, toward their destination, while he had his back to the direction of travel.

"This isn't a test, Mr. Mackey. I need to know what you know."

"I suppose I know the history of the Department as well as anyone my age. Plus, the requisite Level G knowledge about specific Departmental and Executive Branch protocols."

Hopper checked her wristwatch. Outside the window, the Potomac rolled on, a bit quicker now. The P-cars began to accelerate as traffic relented a bit through McLean. Out the window, Mackey could look down from the raised track and see the briefest glimpse of pedestrian malls, filled with early morning shoppers. Not individual people, just a blur of humanity visible from the speeding car. A mass of people, recognizable only by the space they were in. Hopper removed her glasses and began to polish them. The action alerted Mackey to a slight smudge on his own lenses, and he desperately wanted to clean his as well, but dared not do it at the same time as the Assistant Secretary.

"What," asked Hopper, leaving a noticeable pause, "do you know about Parallel Executive Procedures?"

Mackey took a glance out the window, reaching back into his Level G training for the definition. Nothing in bureaucracy was very complex—it just required a strong memory to recall the exact interpretations of the various terms and mechanisms, and the appropriate pathways between the myriad places on the organizational chart. "Parallel Procedures define the means by which different Executive Departments can pursue similar ends. To ensure no overlap of jurisdiction and to prevent waste and redundancy, each identical or symmetric activity must be specifically justified within the statutory mission of the Bureau, Service, or Department."

"If I wanted it by the book, I might have brought a copy." Hopper sighed and replaced her glasses. "Okay, Mr. Mackey, let's be frank. You are in the personal car of the Assistant Secretary for Innovation of the Department of Transportation. I could have built this P-car. I have, in fact, had it taken apart and put back together again, under my direct supervision, several times. There are no recording devices in this space. Your superiors and co-workers are not present. No one can hear you but me. Now what—" she leaned back into the patent leather, and gave him her friendly smile, "do you know about the relationship between the Department of Transportation and the Department of Commerce?"

Mackey could see plainly he wasn't answering the questions to her satisfaction, and so decided to play along.

"About as much as anyone, I suppose? I did well in Civics." He looked at Hopper, who was still waiting for him to respond, so he continued speaking. "Old rivalries die hard. And certainly, many people still have opinions about the pros and cons of one way of running a Department over the other. Commercialist versus Technocratic. Just on the radio this morning, I heard a political debate featuring a representative of each viewpoint. But those are just partisan politics. Part of the great American political tradition, stemming back to Jefferson and Madison."

He waited for her to ask him another question, but Hopper said nothing. Suddenly, the engineering elements of Mackey's mind began to take over, and he started assembling the pieces on his own. The Weather Service was one of the oldest agencies within the Department of Commerce. The Weather Service was the origin of Hopper's hacking event.

"Wait a minute." He spoke slowly as he fitted it together in his mind. "Are you saying that the Weather Service invaded— or *hacked*, if that's the term—Department of Transportation computers because of a decades-old inter-agency rivalry?"

Hopper said nothing, but continued to allow Mackey's brain to gnaw on the idea.

"But what good would Postal information about Department of Transportation employees be to the Weather Service, rivalry or not? If they were stealing data about some sort of project, or spying on some sort of Top Secret Postal research, that would perhaps make sense. Or if it was private industry, trying to glean for insight on staff and organization for lobbying purposes. But what would the Weather Service do with personal information?"

The P-car was cruising now, at speeds approaching two hundred miles an hour. They were well on their way to Reston, as Mackey saw from the information screen in the car console. Traffic had decreased enough that the car was no longer in formation with others, their unknown fellow travelers long since departed this track, continuing on their way to wherever they had been going. Mackey and Hopper rode along on their lonesome, or so it always felt to Mackey whenever he was traveling in an area uncrowded enough that there was no formation. P-cars were designed to form a chain if at all possible, to decrease air resistance and stress on the electric motors. Like the cars themselves desired the company, even if their human occupants did not. He continued pondering, now unable to drop the puzzle pieces he was fingering in his head.

"If the Weather Service was going to access the experimental network at the Advanced Research Projects Bureau, wouldn't it make more sense for them to steal ARPB project information? It's an advanced project, information on the network itself might have been useful. Oh, except—" Mackey began to get it, "they already know all about the ARPNET, because they had to, in order to have hacked it. They already have their own Interface Message Processors, or they wouldn't have been able to connect at all. Otherwise they couldn't have requested or received the data packets. That means—" Hopper raised her eyes in anticipation of his P-car of thought arriving at the platform. "That means they have their own ARPNET, which they built under terms of Parallel Executive Procedures."

Hopper smiled, seemingly glad that her choice of personnel seemed to be working out.

Mackey's mind was not done yet. "But why," he asked, "did they use the ARPNET to access the Postal Bureau? Wouldn't they have had more access to Postal Bureau information via some other less experimental means?"

"We think they used the ARPNET because they figured we'd never suspect an intrusion into our own advanced, closed network. If we are the only ones who have the technology to form the network, how could there be anyone on it but us? However, they weren't counting on my engineers, who sleep with one eye on their mainframe clocks.

"As for why they want this information, we don't know. But it must have been important, because we didn't know about their ARPNET, or whatever they are calling their version, before they broke in. One of the cardinal rules of executive branch maneuvering is not to tip your hand. Work quietly, until the time is right. Whatever its use, the data must have been important enough for them to take a risk. They, like us now, must be on a deadline."

"But how could you not know about their ARPNET? Under the terms of the Parallel Procedures an inter-Departmental liaison must be established between the offices of the parallel Departmental Secretaries, or the offices of the redundant Bureau and Service Secretaries."

"This is why I need you. Not only are you an engineer, but you are an engineer who can clearly cut through the muddle of bureaucracy, to see what is really happening." The Assistant Secretary looked as blasé as her intensely sharpened personality could approximate. "Now—do you know what a Form 1286 is?"

He swallowed unconsciously, and took a moment to finally clean the smudge from his glasses. He knew exactly what the form was. "That's a form for receipt of materials classified Top Secret."

"That's right. And I'm not holding one, because I'm not giving you any materials. There are no written materials that relate to the Top Secret information I am about to tell you. And therefore, there will be no Form 1286.

"You may be surprised to learn that there are elements of our bureaucracy, Mackey, that are not written down. They are not committed to paper. I know quite a few. I am about to tell you about one of them. But believe me, despite its lack of paper trail, it is Top Secret. You know what happens when people fail to follow the procedures of a Form 1286. You might be able to guess that what happens when they fail to follow my unwritten procedures is fairly similar. Only there is significantly less paperwork to be filled out."

She made direct eye contact, and held it. Mackey returned her gaze while she spoke. "Parallel Procedures are justified by the statutory mission of the Department. When the very basic rationale for the Department's existence requires it, redundancy is allowed. There is nothing more crucial, nothing more important to any bureaucratic Department, than its statutory mission, its reason for existence.

"There comes a time when the statutory mission of this Department—*our* Department's entire reason for existence—takes precedence over the established procedures. In the same way that a Department might duplicate another's activities if its statutory basis requires it, our Department might abandon procedure if our statutory basis requires it. It's like a threat to life. When an animal's life is threatened, its behavior becomes extraordinary. Because if that animal fails to survive, it will exhibit no more behavior at all, ever again.

"Therefore, we must sometimes, so to speak, move at a tangent from procedure. And sometimes, that tangent will be not parallel to other Departments, but orthogonal. Just as there are times when we might duplicate the goals of other Departments, there comes a time when we must act directly against the goals of other Departments. These are known, secretly within the Department of Transportation, as Orthogonal Procedures."

As Hopper spoke, the P-car passed within sight of the terminal building of Dulles International Airport, switched tracks, and accelerated again as it continued west, on a lonely, straight track cutting across farm fields. The occasional P-car passed, heading in the opposite direction. Swishing past in a blink of an eye, the vehicles' combined relative speed topped 500 miles per hour. The buffeting slipstream sounded like a dull thud against the Perspex.

"The original, affectionately named 'Pierstorff cars' were introduced by what was then the Post Office in 1916. Originally meant to deliver mail, the combination rail and road vehicles began to take on passengers. As any schoolchild can tell you, this was one of the most important technological events of the century, and our society has been built upon this foundation.

"By 1920, the Post Office plants manufacturing P-cars were some of the largest employers in the country. By 1924, the newly reorganized Postal Administration was more or less running the railroads with this new form of transportation, after the rail networks were left in shambles by the inbred, patrician monopolists who built them. In 1928, Roosevelt became Postmaster. Then followed the 1930s, and the heyday of the Administrations. Those were the days, my friend. You think you engineer things now, but you should have seen us! Things no one had ever dreamed of were flying off the drawing boards, out into the world." Behind the frames of the Assistant Secretary's glasses, Mackey could almost detect the faint presence of a gleam.

"We ran radio, we ran aeronautics, we ran the highways while we converted them to P-car tracks. Once we got radar in the thirties, we had the P-cars running themselves on the tracks, while we just ran the switchboards. Vail Labs invented us the transistor, and the switchboards became computers.

"In 1950, we got integrated circuits, and the computers were small enough to go in the P-cars. Everything in America was controlled by electric circuits. And the Administrations controlled anything with an electric circuit. Everything and anything that moved, from Alabama to Wyoming. We completed the national track arterial network in the early 1960s. Today, kids think a 'road' is some sort of donkey path. We made that history, and we turned it into this present. There is not one part of this new world that we did not touch. The world we live in today was made by the Administrations out of whole cloth.

"A lot of people will tell you that the ideology of Technocratic Administrationism means this or that, whatever political soapbox of the month they can invent and broadcast on the airwaves. But there is one rule, Mackey, that overrides all other statutory jurisdictions, and bureaucratic procedure: don't let anything stand in the way of technological progress.

"That is our law. That is how Roosevelt won the war. That is what the national security of this country depends on. Without that one rule, that one idea behind everything that we do, this country blows its fuse. It no longer moves from Alabama to Wyoming, and it no longer moves between places much higher in the national priorities.

"It doesn't matter which Administration was responsible for what technology, it doesn't matter what Bureau you work for, or that the Secretary is a Cabinet man now. We follow our procedure. Whether that takes us parallel, tangential, or orthogonal to anyone else."

Mackey nodded. The Assistant Secretary was putting it in far harsher terms than how it was written in books or spoken on the news, but she was more or less right. The public trusted technology, and they trusted the Technocrats, or the Transportation bureaucrats, or whatever one wanted to call the people who ran the technology. The public trusted them, because the Technocrats' only responsibility was to make the technology work. And as long as the technology worked, the Technocrats could do anything they wanted, and let Congress hold the hearings later. And, he reasoned, that could certainly include sabotaging other government agencies, if they believed there was a need.

"May I ask a question, Secretary Hopper?"

"Yes, Mr. Mackey."

"If Transportation has secret 'Orthogonal Procedures,' and Commerce has Parallel Procedures to ours that include secretly duplicating the ARPNET technology—does that mean that we ought to suppose that they also have their own version of Orthogonal Procedures? A parallel of our Orthogonal Procedures? Some sort of protocol that they are secretly using against Transportation, in furtherance of what they believe their own statutory mission to be?"

"You're beginning to tune in the picture, Mr. Mackey."

Mackey looked at Hopper and tried to read just how big this puzzle was meant to be. The Assistant Secretary checked her watch again, then gazed out the Perspex at the farm fields, flipping past like the cells of a microfilm. When his co-workers spoke about Hopper's work as 'a problem solver,' they either meant it literally in an engineering sense, or referring to her well-known clandestine service to the Administrations during World War Two. But surely, if she had worked with Postmaster Roosevelt, she must have been party to some of the episodes of his feud with the Secretary of Commerce. Not everything could be known to history. There were always conversations held in back rooms.

Mackey tried to imagine the Assistant Secretary in 1928, in her early twenties. That sharp attention to detail, the quick wit, the immaculate presentation and precise movements—all of these traits, forty-two years earlier, could have been deadly. Figuratively or literally. Had she been a spy? Or some other sort of shadow, black bag man? Black bag woman, that is.

He imagined her taking assignments from the Postmaster. What sort of task made up their strategy? Jockeying against Commerce and the War Department for access to President Landon, competing for wartime resources, poaching key technological personnel. Roosevelt had coordinated the technological projects of all the Administrations into a giant war machine. They had invented the cruise missile. They had invented electronic warfare. They had invented the atomic bomb.

Some of Hopper's problem solving would have clearly overlapped between the war zone and the homefront. It was common knowledge that by the time the atomic bomb fell on Berlin in 1942, Roosevelt had been secretly recruiting German scientists to defect to the United States for years. What was Hopper doing during that time? What were her contemporaries in Commerce doing? Was Secretary Wallace just guarding the homefront, waiting for the Administrations to gain every technical advance and scientist they could? What did Hopper know about Commerce in those days? What had she seen since?

Lost in thought, Mackey suddenly turned around in his seat to find hazy green mountains ahead of them. Wherever they were, it was beyond the atlas memory of Mackey's P-car. He had never traveled so far from the District in a single car trip before.

"Where are we going? The Advanced Research Projects Bureau is in Arlington. We're way past Chantilly by now."

Hopper smiled, in the manner with which Mackey was fast becoming familiar, and gave a little nod. "Mr. Mackey, we are going to go break into a mountain, and see what the weather is like inside."

"Good evening, I'm Frank Mathers, and this is National Issues, your nightly Postal Bureau program about the most important political topics of the day.

"Tonight our topic is lunar development. We have with us in the studio Dr. John Brauer, Deputy Assistant Secretary for Lunar Planning of the Aeronautics and Space Technology Bureau in the Department of Transportation, and Miss Jane Alton, Assistant Secretary for Off-Planet Geology at the General Land Service of the Department of Commerce.

"Miss Alton, if I might direct my first question at you: The ASTB pioneered the technology that took the United States to the moon, and established the first long-term research facilities on the surface. They, along with the Postal Bureau, operate the shuttles that go regularly between lunar and earth orbit. Given their clear accomplishments in the field of lunar development, why is it that the Commerce Department feels that private industry should be allowed to lead the development of the earth's lucrative satellite?"

"First let me say, Frank, it is a pleasure to be here with you and in the esteemed company of Dr. Brauer, the studio audience, and those folks watching at home. At the Commerce Department, we know well and respect the fact that the Department of Transportation has developed the technologies that allow us to explore the moon and its resources. This is their mandate from the President, and their job, on behalf of the American people. But as we all know, Technocratic Administrationism was an experiment that worked well for a while, and then had to be phased out. The Transportation Department is not in the business of enriching itself, but in the business of aiding the business of the private citizenry. They have developed the technologies that transport us to the moon, and now it is time to get out of the way and allow private industry to make use of that technology."

"Dr. Brauer, do you agree with this view?"

"Thank you, Frank, Miss Alton, National Issues viewers. While I certainly agree that the mandate of the ATSB and the Transportation Department is to develop the means for accessing the moon, it does not stop there. Consider the P-car system, to take a basic example. Having built a connection from, say, Chicago to Detroit, we cannot just give it to the American people and expect them to care for this highly technological system. That wouldn't be fair to the public, and it wouldn't be fair to the technology. The reason that American technology is the envy of the world is not simply because we invented it, but because we have the systems in place to maintain it. Traveling to the moon is not like taking a P-car to your local pedestrian mall. We work extensively with private partners in order to produce and deliver many of the Department of Transportation's products, to the public's benefit, but we cannot just take American citizens to the moon and drop them off there. It would be a disaster of unprecedented proportions. To think that—"

"If I might interrupt, Dr. Brauer, I think that your phrasing of the situation is not accurate, if you are saying that . . ."

2

Under the Weather

As the P-car slowed and exited the main track, Mackey turned in his seat to look down the narrow track through the woods. The console next to Hopper flashed with a red warning light, and she reached over to quickly type an override command.

Mackey read the screen aloud. "Mount Weather Facility, Weather Service. Facility closed. Why is it closed?"

Hopper opened the storage compartment beneath the bench seat on which she sat, and withdrew a black attaché case. She clicked it open, facing away from Mackey, and removed a number of items. "It is not closed. They've only set the track signals to say that it is closed."

She handed him a badge, which he instinctively attached to the front of his suit jacket. Only then did he look at the information on the front of it. It was his photograph, but the text read "Frank Lanagan, General Land Service." Hopper attached a badge to her suit, reading "Laura Flanagan, National Park Service."

Before Mackey could open his mouth, Hopper pre-empted him. "Mr. Mackey, I'm going to need you to play along here. Naturally, I could have had a Section 25 Approval for Interdepartmental Cooperation in my hand in the time between when I left my office chair and when I reached my office door. But that would have precipitated a series of phone calls that would have reached this facility before I could even come down to the Electromagnetic Bureau and collect you. In the interest of Orthogonal Procedures, we are proceeding a bit unconventionally."

Forging a governmental ID was a felony, Assistant Secretary or not. A lot more than just his professional career was now in Hopper's hands. She handed him a file folder marked "Climate Projections, 1972-1986" and smiled.

"We have an appointment to discuss the land price fluctuations that can be expected due to expected drought conditions across California over the next decade."

The engineering part of Mackey's personality was intrigued for a moment, until he realized that of course they would not be discussing any climate predictions. "F. Lanagan and L. Flanagan? We couldn't get better cover names? You don't think that's a just a bit suspicious?"

"They're real names, if you can believe it. A strange glitch of reality. Stranger even than the fact that their files were merged with ours over at the Office of Personnel Management during a routine tape backup, and so we received their new Identification Cards, affixed with our photographs. The Personnel Management Identification Office is going to have a devil of a time figuring out how those wires got crossed in their database. Someone will be under a stack of paper three inches thick over that mishap."

The buried facility appeared as if planted in the middle of the forest, which was currently sprouting with the season's new green leaves. The P-car pulled up to the gate, innocuous enough in chain link and barbed wire, stretching out through the woods in both directions as far as anyone could see. The car stopped as the electricity was automatically cut. The security officer inspected their badges, as well as the form that Hopper handed over through the car's document portal. The electricity switched on, and the car continued along the rail past the gate and descended into a tunnel within a concrete shroud, curving down into the mountain.

"What is this facility?"

"Originally, it was just a weather station. But weather is on the surface. They've been building downward into the mountain since the 1950s, gradually increasing the size of the complex. We estimate there's somewhere in the neighborhood of 5,000 Weather Service employees inside Mount Weather."

"That's a lot of meteorologists in offices without windows."

"Indeed."

The parking area was not dissimilar from the parking area of the Electromagnetic Bureau, or any underground employee car park at any governmental site, for that matter. The car stopped at the entrance to the complex, and as they exited, Hopper inserted an auto-park card. Once they closed the door, the car moved off of its own accord, the signals directing the car towards a free space. There was no attendant here, just an automated parking terminal that printed a punched claim card, which Hopper accepted and stowed in her pocket.

And then they were off, making an illegal entry into a government facility. It was mundane enough of an activity in practice, simply walking in the door. Mackey stifled his nervousness at the significance of the act as he tried to keep up with Hopper's brisk pace.

The facility was nice, but nondescript. The walls on the entry level were paneled in dull orange, with a small plaque molded with the Weather Service emblem—a lightning bolt striking across a dark sky—the only sign of where they were and whom they were supposed to be. Hopper proceeded past the automated directory down the hallway, making one dull orange turn and then another, past fluorescent-lit offices and dark concrete stairwells descending further into the earth. Mackey tried not to make eye contact with any of the Weather Service employees they passed in the hallway. Luckily, the Assistant Secretary's gait caused most to step aside demurely, out of the path of someone with clear executive purpose.

She whispered to him as they walked. "If you worked in something called the Predictive Analysis Office, what sort of clout would that bring in the Weather Service?"

Mackey considered what he knew about the Weather Service organizational scheme. "Well, that would be fairly high level, if we were talking about a Transportation agency. Future-forward, operations strategy, that sort of thing. But in the Weather Service, it's all models and prediction, isn't it? So if it is work they specifically call 'Predictive Analysis,' it would have to differ from standard weather modelling. Some other kinds of agency number crunching, or second-level analytics. That means progress reports, and data entry. I'd say bottom rungs, first or second tier services, depending on how tied Predictive Analysis is to current priority projects."

They entered an elevator and Hopper considered the buttons. They were marked Level 1 through Level 9, with 9 on the bottom of the stack.

"Just a couple floors above facilities management then." Hopper punched Level 7, and the stainless steel doors banged shut.

When they opened again, they revealed a similar hallway, linoleum tiled, this time with walls in off-yellow paint. Several more of the overhead fluorescent bulbs were dark than on the floor above. Hopper exited, a bit more cautiously now, looking around her for any signs of Weather Service employees, but still walking straight ahead down the hallway.

"Should we check an office directory?" Mackey whispered.

"It's not listed."

Most of the offices were dark, blinds drawn across the reinforced window glass that partitioned them from the hallway, doors shut. Each office was marked with a designation, consisting of numbers and letters, but no signs, names, or titles. They rounded a corner, and the labyrinth continued.

Mackey stopped to examine one room designation marker. They slid out of narrow metal tracks along the doorframe, apparently meant to be swapped. The designation in question read AF-7-1. He checked the neighboring designations as they proceeded down the hall.

AF-7-2, AF-7-3, RS-7-1, RS-7-2, PS-7-1.

On the dusty linoleum floor, Mackey saw a piece of paper, creased as if it had been folded in three, to be placed in an envelope. He picked it up.

It was an internal order form for office supplies, signed by a D. Setzler. Setzler had ordered three D-45 pads and a box of hanging folders. The form was dated three months previous. Unwilling to place litter back on the ground, he tucked the piece of paper inside the folder of climate predictions that he carried.

"Time to prove your usefulness, Mackey," Hopper prompted. "What have you got for me?"

"It's the Predictive Analysis Office, not the Predictive Analysis Division?" Mackey asked.

Hopper looked at him, trying to read in his eyes what he was reading in the signs. "Yes, that's it. Why?"

"Commerce has two separate hierarchical levels designated 'Office.' One is equivalent to a 'Section' in Transportation, in other words, a large, high-level group: what we might call a major Office. But they also call what we label a 'Station,' the small-est-level grouping, an 'Office.' A minor Office, one might say. In that case, an Office is bottom of the chart, two to ten employees maximum. If we are assuming that Predictive Analysis isn't a big project for the Weather Service, then it isn't a major Office. I could envision it classified as Division level within the Service, which is the next distinction, below major Office. But if you're sure it's explicitly an Office, then it would have to be minor. So it's likely not an area that we're looking for, so much as a particular room."

Mackey gestured at the signs. "These are removable. So they can reassign the rooms. I don't know what PS and RS are, but I would be willing to bet Predictive Analysis is a PA."

Hopper smiled. "I'll take that bet."

They continued down the dark hallway, seeing no one. The faint murmur of office conversation echoed from distant directions. Mackey tried to make out where it might be coming from. All the offices on the hall seemed to be empty, dark, closed. Somewhere, far away, a telephone rang. Was he just imagining the sounds one would expect to hear from a hallway full of offices? The hiss of HVAC had a way of masking sounds, and rendering them directionless.

They turned a corner, and down the off-yellow hallway, there was a bright spot some thirty yards away. All the fluorescent bulbs there were brightly lit, new and gleaming, with fresh starters to eliminate the flickering that was scattered across the rest of the level, like drooping, twitching eyes amid an office in need of a coffee break. Mackey would have approached this unnaturally bright spot hesitantly, like a baited trap. Hopper did no such thing, walking briskly towards it, and stopping. When Mackey caught up, he saw a large steel door with a complex security console mounted in the wall next to it.

"Our badges won't work on that, will they?"

Hopper didn't answer, instead looking at the darkened office across the passage: PA-7-1. She gestured at it to Mackey, using just the angle of her head. "I have a badge to open this one."

From a small tab on the edge of her briefcase, she pulled out a thin black metal bar, concealed within the reinforced bottom of the case. Pulling on the door handle and inserting the bar along the jamb, she quickly pushed, and the door popped. She disappeared inside, and with a fervent hope that this would be over as soon as possible, Mackey followed, removing his hat by habit as he stepped inside.

The room was completely dark except for a slight red glow from the indicator lamps of hissing machinery along the wall, and a bit of the bright fluorescent light filtering in around the edges of the blinds, pulled down across the window onto the hallway. The office was not very large, but it was quite warm, and full of everpresent hum. It was the sound of fans, the buzzing of electromagnets coursing with current, the small vibrations given off by the motors that otherwise silently rotated reels, drives, and mechanical feed trays. There was no question that the small, dark office was stacked with computers.

Hopper produced a flashlight and scanned their surroundings. Indeed, an entire wall of the small office appeared in the brilliant beam, filled with a computer cabinets, noisy although idle, powered on but not currently processing. The printer was still, magnetic tapes motionless, and console screen dark. Opposite the machine was a small desk, covered in files. Hopper's light was drawn to a low table on one side of the desk, empty, with thick cables leading to the computer. She leaned in for a closer look. Mackey looked over her shoulder, unsure of what she was looking for. Hopper traced the cable back towards the machine. In the ambient light of her torch, Mackey examined the desk, looking for a nameplate or a business card.

"This is it," she announced, after examining a wall plate. "This is how they connected their IMP between the phone line in the wall and the computer. They accessed the data from this office." Hopper gestured at the magnetic tapes with the flashlight. "No doubt they've recorded the data they were after and removed it by now, but this is where it happened. The cables are virtually identical to what we built at ARPB." She turned her attention to the desk. "What have you got over here?"

Mackey shrugged. "No nameplate, no personal office belongings at all. Just a stack of dossiers, aerial photos of some kind."

Hopper leaned over the desk, paging through the files. She passed the flashlight to Mackey, who held it and directed it at the desk. She held up a photo attached by paperclip to a typewritten page. As she turned it back and forth in the light, the paper slipped off the photograph and descended to the desk below. Mackey picked it up idly and began reading.

"This isn't an aerial photograph," Hopper pronounced solemnly. "It's a satellite photograph. There's no oblique on the buildings. It is taken from orbit."

Mackey squinted through his glasses in the dark. "What are these strange diagrams here? This seems like a standard personnel form, except for these circles with the lines through them."

He held it in the light for Hopper to see. It was a ring with a bunch of symbols inscribed around the outer edge. The ring was drawn into twelve segments, like the hours of a clock. In the center was a smaller circle, cut across by lines at various irregular angles, and a multitude of smaller symbols. They weren't like any engineering symbols or foreign alphabet that Mackey have ever seen.

"I believe those are astrological birth charts. What do you mean, a personnel form?"

"It says here Milton Landry. There's a date of birth, mailing address, and federal employment history. He works for the Postal Bureau."

"What Section?"

"Doesn't say."

"Who else is here?"

Mackey shuffled through the dossiers, looking for names. "A bunch of mid-level bureaucrats here, from the looks of it. Barbara Johnson, Mass Transit Bureau; Pedro Silva, Infrastructure Bureau; Michael Brewer, National Automated Transport Safety Bureau; George Halbersham, Postal Bureau. William Alexander . . . I know William Alexander. Yes, William X. Alexander, that's Bill Alexander, an engineer in the Radio Communications Section, Electromagnetic Bureau. Why is there a file on him here in the Weather Service, with an astrological chart on it? Clipped to a satellite photograph?"

"Your guess is as good as mine, Mr. Mackey. Gather a few of those up for me, would you? Not all together, a sampling from the stack—"

Hopper was interrupted by a noise outside the office, across the hallway. Her light clicked off immediately, and she silently moved to the window to peer out the edge of the blinds. Mackey stood behind her, trying to see. Luckily, the Assistant Secretary was a head shorter than he was. A man in a suit had just exited the steel door and was walking down the hall, back in the direction of the elevator.

"Mackey! Let's go, grab the files."

He quickly raked a number of folders together and stuffed them under his arm, along with the Climate Projections file which, it suddenly and unreasonably occurred to him, probably didn't contain anything of the sort. Hopper turned the doorknob silently, watching the steel door slowly swing towards shut, as the man in the suit proceeded down the hall.

"Now!" she whispered.

The Assistant Secretary stepped silently out the door. Mackey was right on her heels, jamming his hat back on his head. He pulled the door shut as quickly and quietly as he could and turned, just as Hopper was about to put her hand in the path of the closing steel door.

Suddenly, the man in front of them stopped, as if forgetting something, and turned on his heel. Without missing a beat,

Hopper turned her sleeve, as if merely stretching her extended arm, and kept walking. The steel door clicked shut.

Mackey tried not to move awkwardly, but was sure that he did. He walked behind Hopper, trying not to look directly at the man who was now heading back, staring at them, unable to ignore their sudden appearance in the hallway behind him. Out of the corner of his eye, Mackey caught the man's face. He recognized him. The large brow, the balding hair, the expensive but slightly unfashionable suit. He had met him before. But when?

Hopper walked past, her steps as efficient and single-minded as ever. Mackey thought about flipping casually through the files he was carrying, but thought better of it, instead digging into his interior coat pocket as if looking for his glasses, which were already on his face. The man passed them, giving them a long look, and stood in front of the steel door, pausing. Mackey didn't dare look back, but waited to hear the sounds of the security console. He heard nothing. Hopper turned the corner of the off-yellow hallway, and Mackey followed her.

"Quickly now, let's beat it!" she whispered as soon as they were out of sight, and began moving as fast as possible without breaking into a run. Footsteps sounded on the tile behind them as they rounded the corners, until suddenly they were confronted with a dead end.

"What do we do?" hissed Mackey, his pulse pounding in his ears.

"Against the wall, back in the corner! Stay as flat against the wall as you can, and say nothing, no matter what happens!"

Hopper shoved him hard, with incredible strength for her size, and wedged him into the corner beside the last door in the hallway. From inside her suit jacket she removed a long, thin metal strip with odd, scalloped ridges and, unfolding it on silent metal rivets, increased its length four times.

She slapped it vertically against the wall between them and the corridor where the strangely familiar man would no doubt appear in his pursuit, within seconds. It stuck as if magnetized, and then sizzled in the air, glowing, as a small veil of smoke emanated from the long strip, as tall as Mackey himself. There was a slight breeze, and Mackey saw the smoke swirl in an odd, vertical vortex, several inches from the exothermic metal.

Hopper pressed her back up against the wall behind the strip, as if she was attempting to hide behind a lamp post. Mackey, unable to think of anything else useful to do, imitated her.

The man appeared, and stopped, staring down the hallway at them. He turned, looked the other way, and hurried off, as if still in pursuit of two interlopers, down another passage.

Hopper exhaled but remained against the wall. After thirty seconds, she gingerly grabbed the strip from the wall and shook it to cool it down, then quickly wrapped it into a coil, bending the metal into a small whorl which she stowed in her jacket.

"Let's go. Quietly, back to the elevator."

They doubled back, sneaking quietly around all corners until they arrived at the elevator.

"What just happened? Why didn't he see us?"

"I used a *Fata Morgana*. Exothermic compound generates heat, and channeled convection currents create a duct, which along with a bit of haze creates an atmospheric lens effect, bending the light around us. He saw nothing but the end of the hallway."

"A Fata . . ."

"*Morgana*. Similar principle to a mirage. Named after the Arthurian sorceress. Sailors used to say that she would create floating castles over the sea, to lure men to their deaths." Hopper smiled wryly, and opened her briefcase.

"Put all the files in here, Mackey." She held it out to him. Inside were a number of manila envelopes, a pencil, a gas mask, a spool of thin black wire, a radio handset, and a handgun, made entirely from what appeared to be white plastic.

"The tools of the trade," she said, snapping it shut. Mackey turned around quietly, his pulse finally catching up with his adrenaline.

They quickly made it back to the parking area without incident, and Hopper recalled the car from the terminal. It arrived in just a couple of minutes, and they quickly boarded.

The Assistant Secretary then reached into the pocket of her jacket and withdrew a new punch card, popping it into the navigational console of the vehicle. The car began to whir up and out of the tunnel back into the daylight, but Mackey couldn't relax until they were out of the main gate and heading down the road under the enveloping canopy of forest above their heads. And then, finally, his memory clicked into place. Like well-oiled tumblers in a lock, names and titles spun into place, and a mental dossier assembled itself in his consciousness.

"I know that man. The one from the corridor outside the door."

Hopper turned her head slightly. "Who is he?"

"Alfred Gregory. He's the Assistant Director of Data Management, at the Census Service. I saw him give a speech at a bureaucratic conference several years back. Bright fellow. Methods of records digitization was the topic. Benefits of magnetic storage over punch cards, and so forth. We spoke, briefly anyway. I wonder if he recognized me."

"He's not G-rated, is he?"

"No—at least he wasn't. B level, if I recall."

"Then he doesn't have the cognitive mnemonics training that you do. He'd likely be hard pressed to remember all of his administrative staff, let alone a cross-Department engineer from years back. Well done, Mr. Mackey. I knew you would come in handy today."

Mackey unclipped the badge from his jacket and turned it over in his hands, reading the awkward name of Frank Lanagan over his photo.

"Back to the Electromagnetic Bureau now?" he asked, attempting not to make it sound hopeful.

"Oh my no, Mackey! Our day is just beginning. I'm going to let my bet on you ride, and see if you end up even more useful than you already are. We'll be heading to Dulles now, to a sub-orbital jet. We have some new evidence, a new set of clues that have only made the puzzle more complex. I make use of experts, you understand. Expert skills for expert problems. The expert we need to speak to now is across the country, at the Aeronautics and Space Technology Bureau's Ames Research Center. We're going to Mountain View, California. To the heart of Bureaucrat Valley, where we will see James Webb."

Your vacation destination awaits, in Sunny San Jose, California!

Contact your travel agent now for an all-expenses paid Postal Bureau Vacation to the heart of Bureaucrat Valley, with easy access to beautiful Santa Cruz, redwood forests, historic Moffett Field, and San Francisco!

Book now for a reserved Observation position in a transnational Post train stack! From the comfort of your own P-car loaded onto a Postal Bureau train, watch as the awe-inspiring expanses of America slip by during your quick and comfortable twelve-hour journey from the District of Columbia rolling stock pooling hub. Upon arriving at the San Jose hub, check into fabulous world-class accommodations at any one of the Valley's award-winning hotels, where your P-car will be loaded free of charge with atlas data for Bureaucrat Valley, Coastal California, or San Francisco!

Admire the beauty of nature with a trip to the redwoods and Monterey Bay, some of the most gorgeous and pristine scenery in the whole continent! Travel to San Francisco, taking your P-car across the Golden Gate Bridge!

For a limited time only, spots are available on an exclusive historical tour of the Ames Research Center and Moffett Field!

When Charles Walcott of the Smithsonian Cultural Service founded the National Committee of Aeronautics back in 1915, aviation was only twelve years old, and no one could have imagined how high it would fly!

The story of Moffett Field begins in 1930, when Postmaster Roosevelt brought the Civil Aeronautics Administration and the National Aeronautics Research Administration out of the Commerce Department and let them finally stretch their wings. The top scientists in the world have been hard at work here ever since, developing the wonders of American aviation, including the PC-8, the first Postal passenger jet, and the Matador Missile, Roosevelt's secret weapon launched into the heart of Germany after the invasion of Poland in 1939.

See these wonders and more at the Air Mail Museum, open to the public for a special, limited time. Today, the ASTB scientists are hard at work on new projects, taking the United States to the moon and beyond!

What's next for the Department of Transportation? You'll have to take the tour to get the scoop! Make it part of your family's summer adventure in 1970 . . .

Postal Bureau Vacations: Your Happiness is Our Special Delivery!

3

Sacrifices

His heart was still pounding from their adventure in unauthorized federal facility access, but on the short ride to Dulles, Mackey regained most of his composure. He gripped the edges of the bench seat with both hands, until he decided it looked too much as if he was holding on for dear life, so instead folded his hands, placing them on top of his crossed knees. In this position, he could squeeze his fingers together tightly without it being too obvious. With the restoration of level pulse and breathing, he began to feel slightly embarrassed for his adrenaline. He did not want to let on to Hopper that his stomach was still doing a soft-shoe around his torso.

He had just participated in an illegal entry and theft from a facility of an executive Department. That wasn't something to simply brush off. Mackey had never stolen in his life, at least not on purpose. But he had just walked briskly out of an office in an underground Weather Service complex carrying a stack of files he had no permission to remove, let alone handle, let alone read. He had certainly never contemplated a life of crime, but even if he had, it would not have played out this way. He tried to count the number of procedural violations that had occurred in the span of their visit to Mount Weather. He tried to count the felonies, and then decided not to think about it.

Assistant Secretary Hopper, for her part, seemed entirely unperturbed. She picked up the radio phone from the cabinet beneath the control console in the P-car and made a number of calls, apparently arranging their transit to California. She had been so cool, so collected during the entire intrusion into the Weather Service. Not simply as if this was part of her daily business, but as if she had the utmost confidence that everything would work out. Indeed, in less than forty-five minutes, they had found precisely what she had been looking for. Did that always happen when the Assistant Secretary had set herself to a task? Or had they just been lucky?

Mackey could pick up nothing from the woman's facial expression, as she stared past his head out of the Perspex at the speeding landscape, listening to whatever the voice on the other end of the receiver was telling her. Hopper was acting as if this had been a brief errand at a pedestrian mall. All signs showed this to be a routine day's work for the Assistant Secretary, in her cloak and dagger career with the Department. Orthogonal Procedures, indeed.

Mackey did not know what to call Hopper, other than a spy. That was what he felt like. *This is what spies do, don't they?* If she had spied on the Nazis during World War Two, that would have been an action that was distant, faded, as if in a historical film. A memory of a world that worked differently, that had different rules. But today, in the present, he had witnessed the Assistant Secretary spy on the United States' own government, at the behest of that government. And he had let himself be sucked into the plot. He had spied on the United States' government.

Mackey was an engineer, and rules were his bread and butter. It was his job to understand rules and to design within them, to cut across the distance between two points in the straightest line possible. He was not a rule breaker.

But he was now. He could no more avoid that truth than he could leave the P-car, traveling at high speed down the sunny track towards the airport. Even if he could exit, magically teleport back to his desk at the Electromagnetic Bureau, how would he really escape?

He knew there was no way to dodge the woman with the neat hat and wry smile talking on the radio phone across the car from him. At least not for long, if only part of what he knew about her was true. He had to follow, and hope that all was what she said it was, and she knew what she was doing.

It was her car he was riding in, figuratively as well as literally.

If he was going to follow the Assistant Secretary to California, he didn't want her to think he was nervous, as tough as that might be to hide. There was something about Hopper which didn't exactly inspire confidence so much as demand it. He could tell she expected the best. She used experts, as she had said, and for whatever reason she had chosen Mackey, plucked him from his office among his reports and diagrams, and made him one of them. He felt that he couldn't let her down, any more than he would want to fail in one of his tasks that landed on his own desk. Which, it suddenly occurred to him, were no doubt piling up in his absence. He frowned anxiously at the thought.

The action that the Assistant Secretary could stimulate with a few phone calls certainly inspired a confidence of some kind. Mackey had seen a few such phone calls in his time with the Bureau. But nothing quite like securing jet transportation within half an hour. They were less than ten minutes from the airport, but a Department of Transportation sub-orbital was fueled and ready for them when they arrived.

Hopper sent her car to parking, and they hustled through the terminal, largely empty as it was now midday. Bright fingers of light stretched through the beveled floor-to-ceiling windows, in between the bright white concrete columns canted at an angle not dissimilar from the vertical stabilizers of the Postal Bureau passenger jets out on the flight line. Postal personnel guided them through a special door that took them below the ticket counters, and onto an underground shuttle that took them out across the airport. Coming out of the ground onto the level of the tarmac, they disembarked directly in front of a small sub-orbital, parked in a special hangar for Department of Transportation executive flights. Certainly, the Assistant Secretary was used to moving with speed and a purpose.

The pilot and co-pilot saluted them as they boarded the small sub-orbital, arms at strong angles, like the white swept wings of the aircraft. Hopper nodded, and Mackey did the same, careful to follow her lead. "Welcome aboard, Assistant Secretary," one of the pair said, deferentially.

"Thank you, Major Briggs and Major Drecker," Hopper greeted them, reading their name tags. They were dressed in the uniforms of Postal Bureau pilots. Mackey could see that both were decorated as having served in Electronic Conflicts, and he decoded the colors of their service ribbons. West Africa, Middle East, both in 1959 and 1963, India, Greece, and the Western Pacific. That was quite a bit of service, to now be flying an sub-orbital. But, Mackey supposed, the Assistant Secretary would warrant the best pilots.

He might have expected the lavish, executive features of the interior of the jet, given the pristine technological edge of Hopper's car. Six high-backed, leather upholstered chairs in the cabin, complete with desks, communications consoles for radio and satellite radio phones, as well as video connections. And a kitchenette, although with the rush to depart there was no service staff on hand. As they took their seats, Hopper set her briefcase on her desk.

"Mackey," she turned to him, "I'm sorry to ask, but would you mind heating us a few sandwiches in the galley while I make these calls? And if you don't mind, a few for our pilots as well."

There hadn't been any food preparation training with Mackey's level G bureaucratic literacy rating, but he didn't mind an idle task, his actual skills seemingly not needed for the moment. He had no idea what sort of business would require the Assistant Secretary's attention, and he did not ask. But operating a microwave oven seemed a duty suitable for Mackey's somewhat impressionable head space.

He had only been on a plane a few times before, and certainly any device aboard an executive sub-orbital was equally fascinating and novel to him. The microwave was top of the line, smaller than any unit he had ever seen, complete with a clock display formed with lensed light-emitting diodes printing the time remaining in the cooking cycle in small red text.

All the technology aboard the jet was of a similar grade, jacketed in a chromed steel alloy, rendered both heavy-duty and yet light enough to be packed aboard the sleek jet, making them completely different in appearance from their counterparts on the ground.

Mackey matched the codes of the sandwich packages with the appropriate controls on the cooker console and watched with something like awe and endless curiosity as the digits showed him exactly how much time was still required. With a steady, high-voltage hum the cavity magnetron milled electrons off its cathode, oscillating electromagnetic energy inside the range, stimulating the water molecules of the food in a dancing heat. Perhaps Mackey would have to acquire a microwave range for his kitchen—the process seemed so efficient, so clean.

Preparing and delivering the sandwiches took no time at all, so Mackey quickly returned to his seat after dropping off lunch at the Assistant Secretary's desk and the cockpit. During the flight, Hopper continued scanning the files they had taken from Mount Weather, while Mackey mostly looked out the window as he ate, lost in thought. He couldn't help but continue to review the history of Transportation's feud with Commerce in his head, now that he was drafted into it. He had no idea what the ARPNET hacking and the files they had taken had to do with this ideological split, but his knowledge of the Departments' history was all he had to go on.

Moffett Field was an apt destination. The research center there had been built as Roosevelt's victory lap, after stealing the Air Commerce Service and the National Advisory Committee for Aeronautics away from the Commerce Department. The state-of-the-art research center had been technically built by the new National Aeronautics Research Administration, the renamed and supposedly independent NACA. But it was financed with the Postal Administration's bankroll.

With the massive amount of money that the Postal Administration was making from the expanding Pierstorff car system, combined with their growing popular remit to define the technological direction for the nation, the Postmaster could effectively guide every aspect of Administration activities with the funding provided via Postal Technology Grants.

Roosevelt hand-picked the Administrations' executive staffing, site selection, and even research topics. Sites like Moffett Field were as much part of the Postmaster's expanding political control as they were part of expanding technology. Many of the scientists working with the Committee were backed by the Smithsonian, and had histories with both that Institution and Commerce in general. But only two years after becoming the head of the Postal Administration, Roosevelt had them completely under his personal influence. It was part of what proponents of Commercialism called Roosevelt's "technological dictatorship."

Roosevelt's Postal Administration pulled on long strings: or more literally, the wires, printing presses, broadcast towers, and tracks. The Postal Administration controlled not only the mail but the telephone systems, radio broadcasting, newspapers, and newly invented television. They controlled ground transportation, air mail, and the train systems, nearly the entirety of freight and passenger transportation for the entire continent. From there, they began controlling secondary systems: international shipping, housing development, banking, industrial production and resource management, and even the military, via weapons development. And at the top of all of these infrastructural systems was the Postmaster, wielding this control as if he was directing an orchestra. Roosevelt, the former Naval administrator, sailed the Administrations into the future like an admiral with a fleet.

Mackey had no real part in this feud, and yet he was in the middle of it: both thrust into this episode, that was no doubt one in a series of encounters, and caught between the ideas that the split represented. Both ways of thinking had their merits, and he didn't see why the Departments couldn't pursue their goals simultaneously. Why must things be "Orthogonal," and not simply "Parallel?"

But Mackey kept returning to the fact that he did work for the Electromagnetic Bureau. Whether because of politics, history, or simple personal rivalry, if forces within Commerce were trying to interfere with the Department of Transportation's projects, as an engineer in the Department he was bound to protect it against that interference. It might not be a duty he was bound to on an ideological basis, but it was still important.

Transportation affected the public safety and the political and economic stability of the nation. Hopper had a strong argument there. Without Transportation, the United States would come to a screeching halt.

It was ironic that Mackey worked in the Domestic Interference Section of the Electromagnetic Bureau. By analogy, his engineering responsibilities weren't too different from the current situation. His job at the Bureau was to discover unpredicted conflicts between otherwise compatible technologies. And then to diagnose the issue and engineer a solution around the interference. If there was a conflict between Commerce and Transportation, perhaps he and the Assistant Secretary could engineer a similar, political solution before some sort of harmful interference damaged both Departments.

Additionally, he reasoned, he worked in Domestic Interference, not in the Interference Defense Section. That was weapons-grade work—defending against aggressive interference and electronic attacks, as well as creating sources of jamming and interference for use in offensive action. It was the sort of technology that made headline news as it was deployed in electronic conflicts around the world, pushing belligerent governments off of broadcast pathways and cable routes when they were encroaching upon the Postal Bureau's international data interests. But that was not Mackey's job. He didn't want to attack the Commerce Department. It seemed the wrong sort of strategy, given that they were all supposed to be on the same team. Mackey thought about the gun he had seen in Hopper's briefcase, and wondered about why she carried it. If they hadn't escaped the man inside Mount Weather, what would Hopper have done?

Mackey looked at Hopper now, who was herself intently looking at something out of the window below them. He couldn't see what she was seeing, but checked his window to see if he could get a hint. They were over a span of arid mountains, with nothing much to see below. Nothing to see at all, except another aircraft heading towards them from a short distance. Getting closer. And closer. As it approached, it angled to come alongside them.

Hopper quickly picked up the receiver for the intercom to the cockpit. "Fish and Wildlife Service Interdiction Aircraft, Major Briggs. A pair of them, flanking us."

Mackey could see them easily out of both windows now, only a few hundred feet away on either side. They were short jets, with lower stabilizers descending from the fuselage to rival the upper vertical stabilizers. With short, truncated delta wings and a massive intake under the cockpit, the aircraft looked like an exotic shark species. Both craft were painted with the blue and gold livery of the Fish and Wildlife Service.

Looking down at the landscape, Mackey tried to figure out where they were. His best guess was that they were over Nevada. He tried to suggest a reasonable explanation for the sudden presence of fighter aircraft from one of the divisions of the Department of Commerce, more for his own peace of mind than any actual idea. This couldn't be an intra-Departmental response to their theft at the Weather Service site, could it? Had Alfred Gregory, the man in the hallway, recognized Mackey?

"Maybe we are over National Forest right now, and they just want to—" Mackey was cut off by bright spears of tracer cannon fire darting across the flightpath of the sub-orbital.

Briggs maneuvered quickly, pulling up and to the left. Hopper watched as the jets gave chase, and Mackey dug his fingers into the armrest.

"Rear and to your right, Briggs, four o'clock, coming around!" she barked into the intercom.

"I see them!" Briggs' voice came over the cabin speaker.

Mackey gripped his safety belt with both hands, then grabbed onto the seat, then the belt again. The pilot increased speed, dodging down through the atmosphere towards the desert ground below as Mackey's stomach crawled up his throat. Certainly no maneuvers like this ever happened on one of his business flights.

"Can you outrun or outfly them, Major?" Hopper was gripping her briefcase tightly in one hand, the intercom in the other.

"Can't outrun them—those jets have additional rocket engines, with a top speed over Mach 2. I might be able to outmaneuver them at low altitude."

It wasn't the answer that Mackey was hoping to hear, as his internal organs experienced freefall along with the aircraft. They dropped into a steep dive, rolling left to give Mackey a full, unobscured view of the earth coming up quickly to meet them. The Major pulled up quickly as they arrived on the deck, rising to miss a ridge, and diving again into a winding valley. The terrain pulled quickly to the left, around a mountain peak, and the sub-orbital followed, mere yards from the scrub brush and jagged rocks. Hopper was glued to the window.

"Crossing your six! Mackey, keep them in sight out your side!"

Mackey turned, craning his neck to try and spot the jets, mere glints of blue light against the sun.

"At—seven! Make that eight, now nine o'clock!"

Mackey saw nothing but hillside as Briggs vectored upwards to hop another ridge, and then golden sky, as he came back down to meet the twisted evergreens of the mountains, their gnarled wood and bare snags looking ever so much like wreckage to Mackey's wide eyes.

Despite the Major's breakneck flying, the jets moved closer again, and tracer fire once again arced outward from their noses, passing underneath the thin aluminum fuselage, the thinnest of eggshells protecting them from the bullets zipping past them and the sharp rocks below.

The sub-orbital rolled right, descending into a downhill valley as the pilot looked for some sort of escape route. They hopped a ridge, and then a saddle between two peaks, but still the jets were right behind.

Major Briggs shouted, seemingly unaware that the intercom was still open, "Where's a good box canyon when you need one?"

The valley they were descending opened up to a looping dry river bed flanked by oaks and cottonwoods. In the open terrain, one of the jets overtook them and came down in front, engine wash visible out Mackey's window as it burst past the aircraft, distorting the airflow like the heat of the sun on a rock. The other jet was right behind.

"I think they want you to land, Major Briggs," Hopper calmly suggested into the receiver. "If there is a landing strip you believe they have in mind, we might as well do it, and we'll deal with this on the ground."

He spoke over the intercom. "There's an old strip ahead, which is no doubt the one they mean. Must be a wildfire fighting strip maintained by the Forest Service. I'll make the approach." The Major slowed their speed and lost altitude.

The co-pilot came on. "There's a security compartment, Assistant Secretary, inside the storage locker in the back. Push down to release the panel." Hopper unclipped and took her briefcase towards the rear of the cabin to stash it. Whatever was going to happen, Mackey was glad that the plastic pistol would not be making an appearance.

The Fish and Wildlife jets overflew them as they touched down on the dusty, unoccupied landing strip. Then they each circled in an opposite direction, keeping an eye on the sub-orbital as it came to a halt. The pilot entered the cabin.

"We won't be able to take off again without them shooting us out of the sky," Briggs said.

"What now?" Mackey asked.

The co-pilot, Drecker, came back into the cabin and opened the door, letting the lingering evening sunshine enter the aircraft, along with the dry, fragrant desert air. Amid the noise of the jets keeping station, a dull thumping grew louder. Mackey watched as two large black helicopters came up the valley.

"We wait for the Smokies." Drecker gestured at the approaching aircraft, straightened his jacket, and stepped out onto the hard packed soil. Hopper followed him, as did Briggs. Mackey, suddenly feeling quite alone, unbuckled, rose from his seat, and exited as well.

The squad of Land Service Officers had landed with weapons drawn, handcuffed them, and searched both them and the jet. They did not find Hopper's briefcase, it seemed—although they did find the main control circuit from the power distribution panel, ripping it out and taking it with them, dangling black and red wires. They placed the four on board one of the helicopters and swooped away, leaving the sub-orbital where it was.

The two circling jets also departed, headed for points unknown. Handcuffed, crouched in the back of the helicopter, Mackey couldn't help but feel a sense that his confidence in Hopper had been misplaced. He supposed that they would be taken to some sort of debriefing now, and then a jail cell for some indeterminate stretch of time.

Looking at Hopper's face, he couldn't see any realization of that fact. She appeared just as thoughtfully impassive as when she had been reading the files on board the sub-orbital. Her eyes continued to peer out through her thick glasses, analyzing the passing desert terrain, seeing each individual scrub brush and dry dusty wash, noting the passage of boulders and small hills, considering the occasional barbed wire fence delineating some sort of property boundary. *Was she looking for something*, he wondered. *Or was she just looking?*

After a short flight, the helicopters landed at the bottom of a foothill, ascending upwards into sparse pine trees, with snow-capped mountains beyond. *Must be just inside California*, Mackey thought. Mountains like those could only be the Sierras.

They were left with a group of four Land Service Officers, who marched them up the hill at gunpoint. The helicopters, the rest of the armed Officers, and the Fish and Wildlife aircraft had all departed, leaving them in silence on the hillside.

Looking around them, all Mackey could see were the drab hills, with thin clusters of trees set apart from each other, scattered loosely over the bleached white rock. The hill on which they walked was low, set within a ring of mountains, completely blocking any urban landmark from view. There were no tracks, no air strip. They might have been hundreds of miles from any town. The only thing Mackey could recognize was the bright orange sun, now beginning to set behind the snow-capped mountains, in what must have been the west.

He was breathing hard as he climbed the hill. Handcuffs or not, his morning swimming routine made his heart stronger than this. They must be at a fairly high elevation.

Hopper, Briggs, and Drecker were silent, following the orders of the uniformed officers, and so Mackey followed suit. But his mind raced. What was this? Some sort of scare tactics? Did they know about the breaking and entering at the Weather Service installation, or not? How could they have found them so quickly? Hopper had to know how to deal with this situation. Mackey hoped, with every fiber of his body, that she did know what she was doing.

Towards the crest of the hill, Mackey caught sight of a kind of stone pavilion. It appeared like a rough cabin at first, but as they surmounted the top of the hill, it became clear the structure was much larger, and had taken a great deal more work than a backpacker's shelter. There was a terrace paved in stone slabs, nearly a hundred yards square. The far end of the terrace, which by the sun Mackey figured to be the northern edge, was covered by a stone-built room with a small door. This he had mistaken for a cabin before he had been able to see that it was raised up nearly six feet off the terrace, at the top of a wide flight of stone steps the entire width of the small complex. A roof made with dry, dark timber, extended from the stone room out over the steps and the terrace floor.

It all looked old, weathered, covered in the light white dust that matched the surrounding landscape. There was a pale lichen growing on all the exposed stone surfaces, greenish, scaly, like the desert's replacement for swamp scum. At the base of the stairs, where one would descend from the room to the terrace, there was a large stone slab. The evening wind, sweeping up from below, whistled over the construction on the hilltop. Mackey shivered just a bit, in his suit. His hat, he suddenly realized, had been left aboard the jet. *A fine time to worry about your hat*, he thought.

The four officers moved them to the side of the terrace, allowing them a view of the stone slab some thirty feet away. Two men emerged from the stone room at the top of the steps. One of them wore a dark suit and appeared ancient, face covered in wrinkles in the shadowy twilight. He moved to the side of the doorway as the second man exited. This character was far younger, dark in eyes and hair, wearing a long black robe and carrying a flaming torch that cast light over the darkening terrace. At the edge of the steps he leaned to the ground and used the torch to set alight two pools of oil contained in twin depressions carved in the stone.

Flames leapt up, casting black smoke up into the red and purple sky. The man descended the stairs and lit two similar spots on either side of the slab. As the light splayed outward, Mackey could see a round depression in the center of the slab, stained a dark black, running down the front of it to channels set into the terrace. It suddenly occurred to Mackey, inspired by the addition of oily flames and a man in a long black robe, that the slab looked like an altar.

Hopper was studying the Land Service Officers out of the corner of her eye. The two pilots were simultaneously keeping an eye on her, and on the situation around them. Fred Mackey stood as still as he could, deeply waiting for some indication of what was about to happen next.

"Behold, the rising of the sign of Enki!" the man in the robe boomed out, into the wind. "The time has come to renew the waters!"

He held the torch in one hand and a long dagger in the other. Mackey thought that he would gladly go back to a moment ago, when he still had no idea what might happen.

Two more figures appeared in the doorway of the stone house, at the top of the steps. The first appeared to be a Forest Service Ranger from his characteristic uniform, though he was quite disheveled and clearly beaten up, with his hands tied behind his back. He eyes were lowered, and there was a trickle of blood running down his dark face. Behind him, pushing him forward, was a woman, completely nude except for a horned headdress, carrying a heavy staff made from a luminous metal.

As she shoved the man forward, the ranger tripped and tumbled down the stairs, to collapse at the feet of the man in the robe, behind the altar.

The woman slowly descended after him and walked around to the front of the altar, placing the staff before each of her steps.

The robed man stepped over the fallen ranger, discarding the torch, and motioned to one of the Land Service Officers standing guard. The officer shoved Major Briggs towards the altar, where he was snatched by the neck by the robed man. He hauled Briggs backward, leaning him over the altar, his head above the depression carved in it.

Up the stairs, the aged man in the suit watched, arms folded, silently.

"So it comes to this," muttered Hopper, under her breath.

Mackey did not know what 'this' was, but he was at a loss to see how anything before them could be something that Hopper recognized. They were going to be murdered, he was sure of it. And not only murdered, but killed in some sort of nude religious rite!

Mackey stared imploringly at Hopper, trying to figure out how he could say something to her. She had to have a plan of some kind. She had to have a concealed weapon, or reinforcements, or something. Didn't she?

Using her staff, the woman began drawing a symbol on the terrace, some ten feet wide. A thick black liquid was emanating from the tip of the luminous metal staff, smearing a dark, greasy line upon the ground. She drew the shape of an omega and then, reaching down to the ground, scooped up some of the grease on her hand. She drew the same symbol on her naked stomach.

"Assistant Secretary," Drecker asked aloud. "What is this?" One of the officers gestured towards him with his pistol, to tell him to keep his mouth shut and to stand back. The co-pilot's apparent confusion, and the fear in his voice, did not serve to reassure Mackey in the slightest.

Meanwhile, the woman lay down underneath the front of the altar, her body across the pinnacle of the symbol she had constructed. Arching her back, she yelled out a series of words in a tongue Mackey could not identify, and suddenly the large omega symbol on the ground burst into flames.

On her stomach, in the deepening dusk, the smaller figure she had drawn began to glow blue, the shade of an electric arc. In the rising cloud of smoke, for just one second, Mackey thought he saw the shape of a face appear—but it dissipated. It must have been just a trick of the twilight, or maybe the adrenaline now surging through his body.

The robed man screamed into the flames, "The life of these five people will flow like the semen of Enki, into the womb of Ninkharsag!" He lifted his dagger above Major Briggs.

Drecker shot forward, rushing towards the altar, screaming. Two of the armed men moved towards him, reaching out to grab him by the shoulders and haul him back. The knife came down upon Briggs' neck, piercing through the backbone and out his windpipe, sending a cascading spray of blood down onto the altar, filling the cut channels in its stone surface.

As the blood ran down, dripping from the altar channels onto the stomach of the nude woman, Hopper picked her moment to act.

She launched forward, jumping in the air towards the two officers restraining Drecker, landing on the back of the leg of one of the officers as he bent forward into a step. The leg crumbled from underneath him, and Mackey heard a sickening crack over the wind rushing around the hilltop. As the second officer twisted around to see what was happening, Hopper placed a second kick on the outside of his knee, whirling sideways from her crouching position. There was no sound of broken bone this time, but the officer utter a scream to rival a beast of hell as he went down hard onto the stones.

Hopper moved staggeringly fast, running towards the flames. The two officers near Mackey, still with use of their legs, aimed their guns at Hopper but did not fire, not wanting to shoot towards the robed man and the nude woman who were now in the same line of fire as the charging Assistant Secretary.

The man at the altar was not focused on Hopper's attack, as he was busy dropping the lifeless body of Major Briggs onto the terrace, and was now reaching down behind him to drag the collapsed ranger to his feet.

The woman had seen Hopper and climbed to her feet, the symbol on her stomach glowing as brightly as ever, eyes alight with rage.

At the top of the stairs, the old man approached the edge to see what was going on. Now, in the light of flames billowing up from the steps, Mackey realized he recognized the old man.

From the depths of himself, from a place he could not have identified, Mackey suddenly turned towards the Land Service Officer closest to him, lowered his head, screamed, and charged. Mackey's muscular shoulder impacted the man's solar plexus, driving all the air from his lungs in a sudden, involuntary rush. His pistol fired aimlessly in reflex as he crumbled, tumbling backward off the stone terrace, into the dark brush below.

Mackey turned quickly but off balance only to find the last officer beside him, with his gun against the side of his head. The metal was cold, and he could smell the gun oil, it was so close. He wondered if he would hear the sound of the gunshot or not.

Above the wind, there was a roar. With a blinding light, a dragon appeared over the ridge, swooping low over the stone pavilion with a groaning rage from the pit of its green scales. Except, Mackey quickly realized, it was not a dragon at all, but a strange, thin-bodied helicopter, with a bulbous cockpit in the front and spindly thin legs jutting outward at right angles from its stick-figure spine, like a lizard perched on a rock.

The Land Service Officer, who had stepped back in surprise at the noise of the helicopter, got Mackey in his sights again.

Mackey heard the shot. The chest of the officer opened up, spraying a fine mist of blood across Mackey's suit. And then he was gone, tumbled to the ground, body lifeless and heavy.

He turned and saw Hopper crouched on one knee, holding a pistol in her chained hands. Drecker stood near her holding the other pistol, covering the naked woman and the robed man. One of his arms sagged limp, apparently hit by the shot from the officer Mackey had charged. It hung weakly, chained to the hand holding the gun.

The robed man now held his dagger at the throat of the captive ranger, and was edging towards the edge of the terrace with his hostage.

The murderous priest or magician appeared unfazed, and called to the woman monosyllabically. Slowly, she backed away from Drecker, still dripping with Briggs' blood, taking her staff with her.

When she was behind him, the robed man threw the ranger forward towards the flaming liquid at the edge of the altar, and they both dashed off into the trees. Struggling to find his balance, the ranger tumbled on his feet towards the fire.

Hopper dropped her gun and leapt forward, throwing her small body against the ranger to counter his inertia. They both collapsed in a heap a yard from the fire. Mackey looked for the old man, but he had disappeared.

The helicopter appeared again, shining its spotlight onto the terrace, now almost completely dark except for the dying flames. It came in for a landing in the exposed half of the paved square, its massive rotor blades extinguishing the fires completely as they all crouched low in the rotor downwash.

From the cockpit jumped an older woman in navy blue tactical slacks and a flight jacket, wearing combat boots, with an exotic looking sub-machine gun on a sling around her shoulder.

Hopper looked up from the ground, and immediately broke out into a wide grin. "Mary!" she called. "Your timing, as always—impeccable!"

Mackey pulled the ranger to his feet and was dusting him off as best he could, for what good it would have done.

Using a bit of wire from the helicopter pilot, Hopper quickly removed their handcuffs. Hopper looked Mackey in the eyes as she freed him. "You all right there, Mr. Mackey? That was a nice shoulder check. You continue to validate my choice in personnel with your resourcefulness."

He nodded. "Thanks for being a good shot."

She shrugged it off.

"How's that arm, Major Drecker?"

"I'll live." He was still covering the two officers on the ground with the pistol, both disabled with broken legs. But Drecker was looking at Briggs' body, collapsed on the stone terrace.

Hopper moved to the body and checked for a pulse, but there was none. The blood that had previously flowed through his veins was now covering the terrace, as it trickled off the stone altar structure. Mackey was still processing what he was seeing. There was really no other way to describe it: this was a sacrifice. What else would it be called?

Hopper closed Briggs' still eyes and moved to the Forest Service ranger.

"Well, friend? Who are you and how did you manage to get into this torrid affair?"

The ranger rubbed his wrists, and then his face, where some bruises were forming. "The name is Thompson, Gene Thompson. I don't know quite what happened, to be honest. I was on patrol in this unit of the National Forest. I came up to the old hill lodge, because I saw some folks up here, and we've had trouble with poachers hunting out of season.

"Next thing I know they had hit me on the head, and there was a woman taking her clothes off, and they told me my blood was needed to stave off the drought or some such nonsense." He rubbed his closely-cropped head and smiled, revealing a row of straight, white teeth. "Who are all of you? Whoever you are, I sure am glad you showed up because it looked like curtains for me."

"All of that in due time," Hopper said. "But for now, I think you ought to come with us. I think the Forest Service might not be the safest place for you right now, until we get a few things sorted."

He nodded.

"Is that wise?" Mackey asked her gently. "Between our encounters with the Weather Service, Census, Fish and Wildlife, and the General Land Service today, I'm thinking that anyone from a Commerce agency might not be the most trustworthy companion right now."

Hopper touched her hat to ensure it was still there, and cleared the Land Service pistol's chamber before stashing it inside her jacket. "I have a good feeling about this one, Mackey. I think he'll be useful." She smiled. "Unless you know something about him I don't."

Mackey shook his head. "Forest Service ranger is too low-level to be included in any staffing circulars. But I did know one of the people from that terrible scene. The old man who was standing at the top of the stairs."

Hopper glanced at the ranger, and then back to Mackey. "Who was he?"

"Nicholas Roerich. I'm sure it was Roerich. But that would make him something like ninety-six years old."

Hopper stared at the remains of the scene. "Roerich," she repeated. "Interesting indeed."

The helicopter pilot interrupted. "I would love to stand and chat, but your man here has a fairly serious gunshot wound, and there might be some sort of regroup happening below us in the dark as we speak."

Hopper turned to the two disabled officers on the terrace. "Surely your comrades will come back for you, won't they?" The men said nothing, and Hopper turned away without another word. The helicopter pilot kept her cold eyes on them, her weapon pointed lightly and yet seriously as the Assistant Secretary gave orders to prepare Briggs to be moved.

They piled into the small crew cabin of the helicopter, along with Briggs' body, which Gene Thompson and Mackey secured in the rear. The two were pressed together, and shook hands in the crowded space, as much to introduce themselves as to mentally bypass the fact that they were riding with a corpse. "What kind of helicopter is this?" Mackey asked.

"It's a skycrane," answered Hopper. "And a good thing you brought it too, Mary. Our jet was disabled and we'll have to pick it up on the way, if that's not too much trouble."

"Not at all." The pilot smiled as she stashed her weapon. "That's why I brought the big beast when Moffett got the call your sub-orbital had been 'delayed.'"

Call your Congressmen, and tell them to vote YES on HR-17849!

It is more important than ever that public P-car access to the transnational lines be assured, by passing the Rail Passenger Service Act!

Commercial interests across the country want to create private trains on the transnational lines, reserved for paid freight. They would have the ability to deny P-car access, or to place passengers in crowded group carriages, charging rates set based on their own greedy market manipulation.

Since the Postal Administration introduced their transnational P-car carriers, the public's access to ride across the country in the comfort of their own P-cars has been a fundamental part of the American lifestyle. Every year, tens of thousands of Americans get to see their country from the comfort and privacy of their own vehicles, conveniently delivered from point to point.

HR-17849 would enshrine this tradition in law. It would ensure that any private carrier operating on transnational lines offer the same P-car carrier access as available on competing Postal routes.

In America, we believe in competition. It is how we got to where we are. So let's let private industry compete on a level playing field, by holding them to the same high standards of our public industries.

Tell your Congressmen to vote YES on HR-17849. It's what's fair, competitive, and AMERICAN.

4
Crystals

THE HEAVILY LOADED HELICOPTER THUMPED OVER THE DARKENED hills, and in the steady wave of noise, Mackey attempted to wrangle with what had just happened.

In the course of an afternoon, he had gone from breaking into a federal facility, to riding in an executive jet with an Assistant Secretary of Transportation, to an intercontinental appointment with the Secretary of the ASTB, to being a passenger in an aerial dogfight, to being threatened with death in some sort of a blood sacrifice, to now riding in a helicopter next to the body of a man he'd seen murdered, with a full sub-orbital jet slung underneath the reptilian body of the flying machine.

It all put the break-in at Mount Weather in perspective. After what he had witnessed this afternoon, Mackey's last care in the world was whatever sort of disciplinary action or jail time the theft of a few files might bring.

His eyes traveled around the small helicopter cabin, vibrating with the rhythmic, pounding lift of the massive rotary-wings above them. Drecker had been shot, and seen his partner killed before his eyes. He looked dazed, holding pressure to his wound with his good hand, on Mackey's left. Perhaps the pain was taking his mind off the shock of the experience. Thompson, the Forest Service ranger, seemed remarkably well put together given that he had been beaten and had a knife against his throat. Despite his superficial injuries, he was feeling well enough to offer to sit between Mackey and Major Briggs' body, a suggestion Mackey thankfully accepted.

The pilot, who Mackey did not know other than as Mary, was concentrating on the aircraft. But she seemed very serious, in control. As she took her seat in the helicopter she had let her weapon retract under her flight jacket on some sort of automatic sling, even as she continued to eye the injured Land Service Officers on the ground, as if daring them to make a move. The way she moved, the way she was dressed, the way she analyzed events happening around her with a sort of cool detachment— it was all very reminiscent of the way Hopper acted. It was no surprise that they seemed to know each other well. They seemed about the same age. Likely she was one of Hopper's "experts."

As for the Assistant Secretary herself, she was as in command as ever, conversing with the pilot over a pair of headphones, relaying information back and forth that Mackey could not hear over the noise. Perhaps this was how she remained so calm and collected. When you saw terrible things, it made everything else diminish in contrast. So long as someone was not being stabbed through the neck, then things were going relatively well.

The helicopter swept quickly across the darkened delta of the Sacramento and San Joaquin Rivers, crossing over dark islands and transiting ships lit by only red and green running lights, passing over the suspension bridges illuminated by architectural lights to form the rear gateways of the San Francisco Bay. The brilliant cityscape quickly rose up to meet them.

Mackey peered down, watching the light from the bridges and skyscrapers glint off the Perspex of cars zipping to and fro across the twenty parallel tracks of the Bay Bridge. He admired the tall buildings of San Francisco and Oakland: blocky, Deco-cut transistors, studding the circuit board pathways of looping tracks criss-crossing the twin-horned metropolis.

As the helicopter flew south over the San Francisco Bay, Mackey wondered if any of the passengers below looked up to see the odd sight of a large, insect-like helicopter gripping a small sub-orbital jet in its angled legs. Recalling all the P-car journeys he'd made in his life, he decided probably not. Although he stared out the window plenty, he always tended to push his vision outward, and ahead. There was hardly ever anything to see looking upward.

Crossing shipping facilities and salt marshes lining the southern banks of the bay, he reflected upon that. To the world of cars below, he was "up," above the traffic, with the view of the larger scene. A good view perhaps, but not exactly the luxurious vantage point he had thought the sub-orbital to be. He could see the jet's disabled wings protruding from the cargo sling below, still glistening white, but in silhouette, a dark shadow against the subtle city glow. As the bulky helicopter with its large load turned into its final approach for landing at Moffett Field on the extreme south end of the bay, Mackey's eyes looked outward again, peering further south, to the lights of the brilliant sprawl extending down Bureaucrat Valley, until the glowing tracklines of express tracks and suburban subdivisions disappeared in the hazy grey night.

They saw Drecker and Briggs' body to the infirmary. Drecker was in bad shape, but the doctors said he would soon be stabilized. Thompson also had a chance to clean up and bandage his wounds. Mackey sat and watched as one of the clinic staff helped clean the shallow cuts on his arms and neck. The man sat very still, not wincing in the slightest at the disinfectant.

Briggs and Drecker, Mackey supposed, would be used to combat situations. Perhaps Briggs never intended to give his life while transporting a Department Assistant Secretary, but the risk of harm would not have been unknown to him. Thompson, the Forest Service ranger, would certainly have been no stranger to the chance of injury, and probably had a good knowledge of field first aid, although perhaps not expecting this kind of violence out in the woods. Hopper and the helicopter pilot—well, he put that out of his mind for now, both of their personal histories falling into the 'very much unknown' category.

But as for himself, Mackey certainly had never risked serious injury in his work, let alone seen the injury or death of any colleague. Was that the right word? Co-worker? Comrade-in-arms? Companion? Who were these people to him, given the situation? What was he supposed to feel now?

The desire for revenge seemed too hackneyed, too much of a conceit for a film or a cheap novel. Justice without punishment was merely an accounting of events. He wanted answers, certainly. But how would that help? What sort of answer, what sort of investigation would make him feel better about what he had just witnessed?

And yet, what his mind was filled with now were not emotions, or the strong will to act, but questions such as these. And questions, to Mackey's mind, could only be satisfied by answers.

Mackey was fine physically, but his suit had been splattered with blood. He and Thompson both received new, standard Bureau suits. Mackey's didn't fit as well as his own suit, but at least it was dark grey. As Mackey tied his full Windsor, he saw that Thompson's suit did fit him, rather well in fact. The man looked quite dapper with a tie, rather than the utilitarian Forest Service uniform. It was a nice improvement.

Mackey fully believed in suits. Certainly they were not practical for the mountains and forest, but back here in bureaucratic territory, everyone looked better dressed in a suit. Thompson retained his Forest Service overcoat, in the cool chill of the bay night.

When they left the infirmary, a shuttle car brought Hopper, Mackey, Thompson, and the helicopter pilot across the dark runways to the administrative office complex.

"Now that we finally have a moment," Hopper said, turning to them in the shuttle, "and Ms. Ross is no longer flying a large cargo aircraft, allow me to introduce you all. Mary G. Ross is one of the finest engineers working for the Aeronautics and Space Technology Bureau, primarily in the field of ballistics and orbital physics. She and I have worked closely together a number of times before. I planned to take a few moments to speak with her while we were out here at Ames, and here she is, having come to us."

Mackey was floored. This was the famous Mary G. Ross! Engineer of some of the first interplanetary rockets, the largest weaponized rocket systems, and countless other projects. Every engineer in the Department, no matter their bureaucratic literacy, knew of Ross.

"You can thank your lapel transponder for my quick arrival," Ross said quietly, smiling. "I just follow the heartbeat tones on the radar screen."

Well, at least that accounted for one of Hopper's mysterious tricks, Mackey thought.

"This is Fred Mackey, a new associate of mine, working in the Electromagnetic Bureau. Mackey is an expert in bureaucracy, and also very handy in a crisis, as I continue to find out. We've only just met Gene Thompson, recently of the Forest Service Rangers, about whom I expect we'll learn more soon enough."

They all shook hands. "This is an honor! Although I must say, I wouldn't have figured that it was you," Mackey said as he shook hands with Ross.

She eyed him coldly, through her unassuming Cherokee features. "And why not?"

Mackey blushed, not anticipating the remark to come off as condescending. "Oh no—I just meant that while I know of a few engineers who fly helicopters, I've never met one who packs a machine gun."

She smiled now, opening her flight jacket and pulling out the weapon, slung under her shoulder on what he now saw to be a clever counter-weighted, self-retracting harness. She released the magazine and pulled out one of the rounds. It was oddly asymmetrical, rectangular, with a cartridge that protruded far below the bullet on the bottom side.

"It's a weapon of my own invention and manufacture, from powder to projectile, from sight to muzzle. I've managed to do some interesting things with the ballistics, but it required a trained hand to master. Can't let just anyone fire a double-charged projectile, or it will come right back at you like a boomerang."

She pushed the cartridge back into the magazine, inserted it into the weapon, and allowed the sling to retract the weapon back under her jacket, swung around to the small of her back. It was completely invisible, revealing no lumps on her frame.

They entered the large glass and steel structure of the central Ames office building, moving at Hopper's usual pace. The construction was brand new, rendered in a magnificent

Depo-Federal style, not revealing the history of the Center in the slightest. Large multi-story windows across the front of the building allowed those in the lobby full views of the glowing lights of the Moffett runway, where a number of odd-looking aircraft, both scientific and standard issue, waited for takeoff. The white steel beams crisscrossed above them, holding open the space in an unusual and breaktaking geometric grid. The lobby looked like a space station, Mackey concluded, trusses and struts that might as easily hold solar panels and habitat modules as the weight of the offices above.

Hopper did not pause to admire the architecture. Her briefcase moved purposefully alongside her, controlled in her right hand. Showing her identification, her real one this time, Hopper led them to an elevator and up to Secretary Webb's office, although the guards took a long look at Thompson, given the Forest Service coat, most likely.

Mackey was more than a bit pleased he was about to meet James Webb—the man in charge of space operations! He checked his new jacket for lint or dust and straightened his tie. His hat was still aboard the sub-orbital, he assumed, forgotten in the confusion. But he still looked fairly presentable. He noted that the Assistant Secretary had managed to keep her hat on her head without incident throughout the entire murderous affair.

But when they arrived at the carpeted outer office, they were met by an Edgar Winslow, Deputy Assistant Secretary, Facility Operations Section. His hair was slicked to one side, and his linen suit was pale yellow. It seemed to Mackey that bureaucratic fashions must be slightly more sunny out here on the West Coast. He was again very glad his suit had come in a standard dark grey.

"I'm sorry, Director Webb was called into a confidential meeting this evening, and I can't disturb him at this time. Perhaps there is something I can help you with?"

Hopper paused, as if considering her response. Winslow waited patiently in front of the four of them, arms clasped behind his back. There was something odd about this man, but Mackey couldn't quite place it. But the tumblers of his mnemetic lock were turning. The phone back in Webb's office rang, and Winslow went to go answer it. Then suddenly, it hit Mackey who Winslow was.

He quickly leaned and whispered to Hopper, "He is Commerce—well, formerly. He used to be with the Census Service, up until last year. He was the Assistant Director of Personnel Management. I don't know why he left, but I saw the directory change announced in a circular. And not only that— he and Alfred Gregory, the man from Mount Weather, worked together. A number of projects in relation to data formats and personnel records."

Hopper nodded. "Interesting. I wonder what caused his change of allegiance? No matter, we won't waste any more time here." She shooed Mackey back with a wave of her finger, as Winslow replaced the receiver and came back out to them.

Hopper gave Winslow her disarming smile. "It's of no great importance, we'll simply try back when he's out of the meeting." She turned and motioned to the rest, and they returned to the elevator. Mackey could feel Winslow's eyes follow them.

Inside the elevator, Hopper shook her head with a smirk—the first such expression Mackey had seen from her. "I specifically told him to be there alone when we arrived! I wonder what sort of malarkey they came up with to distract Webb. Hopefully they didn't have to put anyone's lives in danger."

"Do you think that Winslow and Gregory have something to do with it? Census must be involved somehow . . ." Mackey asked.

"Hard to say. It's certainly a coincidence, but inter-Departmental transfers happen. We'll do this the old-fashioned way, rather than through channels. Thankfully we have Ross here already. And we'll track down Jack. I know he's up at Ames this week."

Back in the lobby, Hopper accessed a directory terminal, handing her briefcase to Mackey with an eye. He held the case tightly in his arms with both hands while she typed.

"It says he's out at the test stand. Let's get a shuttle car." She took her briefcase back, and the odd group of four followed her outside.

The shuttle car, shorter than most P-cars but still with room for the group, had a map of the facility with touch buttons embedded into it. Hopper tapped the button for the test stand area, pushed the magnetic edge of her credentials into the computer, and the car whirred off towards the water of San Francisco Bay, at the north end of the facility.

The primary stand was a massive white gantry structure, but the activity was happening around a nearby trench that terminated at a large concrete wedge at the bay's edge. Hopper showed her identification to the security officer positioned at the shuttle car unloading platform.

They descended a set of stairs cut into the tarmac and entered a double door into an underground bunker. Down a short hallway and up a short set of stairs was a control room with heavily shielded, angled windows bubbling up from the ground level like a wart, with a view onto the blast trench. Technicians were everywhere, hurrying about busily, most wearing tinted goggles. Hopper grabbed four sets from a table near the entrance, and distributed them to her group.

"It appears Dr. Parsons is in the middle of a test." Hopper gestured. "We'll have to wait until we can interrupt him."

So it was Jack Parsons that Hopper was looking for—another engineer of some renown. Mackey had heard some strange stories. He was excitable, eccentric, and entirely self-taught. But a brilliant mind in the field of rocket propulsion.

"Are we ready already?" yelled a man wearing a thin black tie, and a mustache after the same fashion. His jacket was off, his sleeves rolled up, and there appeared to be quite a bit of dust on his shirt. Mackey marveled at this odd character who somehow seemed to be in charge, and assumed that this must be the eccentric figure they had come to find.

Without waiting for a response to his question, the man slammed a red button on the control panel by the windows, and klaxons sounded everywhere, releasing a outburst of activity from the technicians. The Assistant Secretary secured her goggles on deftly, without removing her hat. Mackey, Ross, and Thompson struggled to quickly place theirs over their faces.

"Start it up, Priscilla! Give us 10%!" A young woman in a lab coat with blond hair behind her expansive goggles put her hand on the controls and began throttling upwards. The console screens around the room jumped into life, and white smoke began pouring out of the trench. A mild shaking began resonating through anything not fastened down, including Mackey himself.

"Fuel pressures nominal, thrust approaching 10%!" someone shouted over the din.

The smoke pushed back out of the trench as the wind began following the thrust of the engine back towards the concrete baffle on the bay end of the trench. When the smoke cleared, Mackey could see what the subject of the test was. It was a very small rocket engine, perhaps only the size of a desk chair, but producing a massive amount of flame.

"Bring us up to 40%, when…you know…as soon as you can!" The man with the mustache was focused intensely on the engine in the trench, both hands against the frame of the viewing portal, all his words yelled into the glass.

"Pressure is elevating, 80% design capacity!"

"Bring up the thrust! We have to see if the turbine can handle it!"

The flame from the engine was condensing, focusing into a pencil point of heat. Odd, mechanically-scalloped edges to the engine bell were flexing, pulling in around the flame, molding its shape.

"Pressure is at 100% capacity!"

"Go to 80% thrust!"

Priscilla waved her hands in exasperation at another technician, who hustled over to the man in the mustache. Whispering was impossible over the vibrations of the building, and so the technician had to shout, "Dr. Parsons! Even with the augmented model, this is all it can take!"

He wheeled around, grabbing the technician's coat by the lapel. "I said 80%! You know the timetable we're on!" He leaned out, waving his arms. "Priscilla! Come on!"

Priscilla shook her head, only to herself, and pushed forward on the throttle controls. The extra pairs of goggles on the table vibrated until they clattered to the floor. Paper fastened to the wall drifted down lazily in the chaos. The flame grew intensely bright, even through the darkened glass of the goggles.

"Pressure is at 115%!"

Parsons leaped across the room and gripped a set of controls. "Now watch this! You'll see!"

As the man gently squeezed the levers together, the scalloped edges of the engine bell expanded outward, and the shaking in the room diminished.

"Pressure is down to 105%! Now 95%!"

"Thrust to 100%!" Priscilla pressed down on her throttle.

The flame narrowed, and went nearly invisible, to dark blue. Odd, shimmering pulses became visible in the line of flame. They grew brighter, at a rigid, equal distance from each other, extending down the trench. Little bright blue diamonds, standing out in the flame. Like a lens flare on a photograph, but tight, directed, like lenses in a telescope, like gems set into the blade of a crystal sword.

Parsons laughed in what could only be described as a maniacal voice. "Haha! You see, you see! Stable mach speeds, and no after-burner! Impossible for a rocket hybrid this size, they said!"

There was a sudden lurch in the room, and all the technicians grasped onto something. Suddenly, flame was building at the forward end of the trench.

"Supply line rupture! Emergency shutdown, now!"

A klaxon tone sounded, and Priscilla scrambled to pull back the throttle, but it was too late. Flame leapt up around the engine, and then with a sun-bright flash, the entire thing went up with a solid boom.

"Holy smoke!" said Thompson, to Mackey's general earshot above the noise. Mackey wanted to throw his hands up over his face, but was unable to give up his view of the fascinating destruction. The shockwave bent the visible light as it pushed back on the heavy glass of the windows, and then all was blocked by an expanding cloud of smoke and a rain of debris. Parsons reached overhead and pulled a handle marked "Fire," labeled again in a more vernacular way with a hand-lettered cardboard sign which read "NEVER PULL!" Red lights flashed from the ceiling, and some technicians ran to get out of the tunnel to the tarmac while others simply rubbed their tired faces with their hands, leaning forward onto their consoles.

"I told you," Priscilla said to Parsons, shaking her head.

"The pressure was fine, it was the test stand that blew. The engine works! Or it did—I swear by the gods, I'll have Facilities' ass in the bay for this!"

Parsons removed his goggles as he whirled around towards the stairs, and then caught sight of Hopper. His eyes widened, and the mouth below his mustache broadened into a smile.

"Why, Grace! How lovely of you to stop by. Poor timing, though! Come with me, we need to go pick up the pieces of my engine. And Mary Ross, as I live and breathe!"

Hopper introduced Mackey and Thompson, who both shook hands with the dynamic man as they all briskly walked out the tunnel to the tarmac.

"Dr. Parsons is directing a number of experimental programs for ASTB," Hopper explained. "He's normally down in Los Angeles, or out in the desert somewhere; we're lucky to catch him here."

"I'm no bureaucrat, you understand," Parsons said to Mackey, clapping grubby hands onto the shoulders of his new jacket. "No offense, of course. I just can't stand the desk. But ASTB does have the best toys, so I let them talk me into having an office." Parsons' demeanor was quite off the cuff, but he had a twinkle in his eye that was a bit unplaceable. "And a Forest Service ranger, I presume? What an odd new acquaintance to be joining us at an ASTB rocket fire!" He winked as he shook Thompson's hand. Thompson looked at Mackey, and they both shrugged out of a confused camaraderie.

"If we could just have a few minutes of your time, Jack, I'd very much appreciate it."

Parsons was already forging up the stairway to the tarmac. "I wish I could, Grace! But we've just blown any chance of another test until we get the second unit out of the shop, so I need to head over there with Priscilla—Priscilla Denton, meet Grace Hopper, and—this is . . ."

"Fred Mackey—"

"Fred Mackey, Gene Thompson, and of course, you know Mary Ross. Priscilla, do you know how they are doing over at the shop?"

Priscilla had been keeping pace, clipboard in tow. "Bill said he would call, the last time I called, and told me to tell you to stop having me call him every fifteen minutes."

The party emerged into the California night, darkness expelled outside of a bright dome of emergency floodlighting, bringing an unnatural white gloss sheen onto the scene from a circle of metal towers, along with rotating emergency beacons, flashing red. The previously clear tarmac was showered with pieces of metal from the exploded engine. A fire crew had almost finished spraying down the trench with foam. The shuttle car that they had left on the nearby track not five minutes ago had a twisted piece of pipe lodged in the roof, piercing the splintered Perspex bubble. The security officer at the track platform was apparently engaged in saving his checkpoint shack, which was currently on fire.

Parsons bent down and picked up a thin band of metal from between his feet. "D'ya think Bill wants me to send this back to the shop?"

He dropped it to the pavement with a clank and turned to Hopper. "Look, Grace. I'd love to chat, but my engine is now distributed over four acres of parking lot. Could we postpone?"

Hopper held her palm open to Parsons, for him to look into it. In the chaos of the test lot, no one saw her hand except for Parsons, Mackey, Thompson, and Ross. Mackey could see a ring on her finger, turned inward, but still glinting in the strong light. He hadn't noticed her wearing it before. He was about to lean closer to try and see what was on the ornament, but she snapped her hand shut and looked Parsons in the eye. Thompson looked as intrigued as Mackey, but Ross seemed to be willfully ignoring the exchange.

Parsons now returned Hopper's serious gaze. "I see. Well, I suppose we'd better go to my office. Let's grab a shuttle. Not that one, though." He gestured to their previous vehicle, then turned to Priscilla. "See that they salvage as much as they can. And keep bothering Bill! I'll call you in a bit."

Priscilla seemed relieved to see him go, and hurried off.

In a new, undamaged shuttle car, Parsons squeezed on the seat across from Ross and Hopper, sitting between Thompson and Mackey, his arms thrown up across the seat back behind them both. "Orthogonal Procedures, is it? I am a bit surprised you're coming to me, given the climate at the Secretary's office lately."

Hopper seemed slightly less authoritative in front of Parsons, but that certainly didn't change her commanding stare and disarming smile. "Webb was busy. Some underling tried to step in."

Parsons stroked his thin mustache with a smile. He was clear into his fifties, with slight wrinkles around his eyes and mouth that complemented the scar running just down the underside of his chin. His face had just a shade of stubble upon it, completing the image of a man who had experienced a fair bit of life, but had not yet given up on his attractive mystique. Nor would it give up on him. His dusty clothing was a bit disarming, however, and it caused Mackey to want to brush himself off, though he couldn't on the crowded seat. On the arm behind Mackey on the seat back, underneath the rolled-up sleeve, were visible the dark bands of a tattoo, just out of sight beneath the fabric.

Conscious that Mackey was looking at him, Parsons turned to the man and gave him a grin and a wink, which caused Mackey to immediately direct his attention out the window, to the massive research center buildings they were passing. Turning to Hopper, Parsons said quietly, "Yes, I think there was some satellite combat. Unpiloted, no casualties. But several intrusions across the LEO frontier will generate long meetings. As for the underling, you must mean Winslow, that slick daffodil. He'll be the one to hear from me about the dangerous lapses in facility maintenance that burned up my engine. So don't you worry, I'll see to him."

In the Design building, the group followed Parsons' stuttering pace as he alternately ran ahead, then turned around and stood still to lecture about the finer points of his new hybrid rocket-jet engine system. He only paused speaking when they arrived at a door marked J. Parsons. With a smirking smile and a little too much gusto, he threw open the door, whispering, "Welcome to my chambers."

The office was anything but standard Bureau issue. The room was dark as they stepped inside, thick red velvet drapes blocking the windows. Parsons threw a overwrought knife-switch on the desk, and orange filament bulbs in a variety of brass lamps and candelabras burst into electric life. They illuminated a vast painting behind the desk of a horned man ascending the side of a stepped pyramid. The desk itself was covered in papers, some of them engineering blueprints, some of them much older, like parchment.

As Mackey nervously entered further, half afraid that spiders would descend upon his head from the ceiling, he saw a lighted cabinet, carved from dark mahogany, at the side of the office. Inside were all manner of curiosities—a collection of short swords, old books bound in wrinkled leather, a rack of small glass bottles containing colored, misty contents, and in the very center, a human skull. The top of the cabinet was decorated with a wooden shield, upon which was painted an obscure symbol in brilliant metallic silver paint. Mackey was drawn into it, tracing its graceful curves with his eyes.

When he focused again, Hopper was seated in a high-backed chair opposite the desk, and Parsons had settled into the leather seat behind it, his feet on top. Ross and Thompson pulled up chairs from the edge of the room, Thompson grabbing one for Mackey as well. Hopper's briefcase was on her lap, with her hands on top of it. Mackey noticed that the odd ring she had shown Parsons was no longer on her finger.

"Do close the door, would you, Fred? And then have a seat," Parsons purred.

Mackey hurried to do so, gladly. He had a sense that he didn't particularly want to be seen inside Parsons' office, for some reason. It seemed a chamber of odd, awkward secrets.

"What have we got, Grace?"

Hopper snapped open her briefcase and removed the dossiers they had retrieved from Mount Weather. Opening to the photos, she placed them on the desk. Parsons quickly snapped them up and leaned back in his chair to study the images, while Hopper briefly explained their source at the Weather Service and the connection to the ARPNET, though leaving out the intrusion at Mount Weather. Ross leaned forward and picked up a set as well.

"Not aerial images. Satellite," Ross noted.

Hopper gave a single, curt nod.

"Not ASTB, either," chimed Parsons.

"I don't imagine so."

Ross scrutinized the image, nodding her head in agreement. Parsons removed a magnifying lens from a desk drawer and leaned closer to the nearest light bulb for a better look.

"This banding here, over the grassy area." Hopper and Ross stood to see what he was referring to. "That isn't agricultural. They are scan lines."

He leaned back in his chair again. "That means it's electro-optical, and that means it is NRS."

Mackey looked at Hopper, and Hopper looked at Parsons, waiting for him to continue. After an appropriately dramatic pause, he continued.

"Mary could tell you this as well as I could, as she's been a part of the ASTB studies on the technology. The satellites are called Crystals, as far as we can tell. Only rumors, really, as it's all Top Secret. Officially, the National Reconnaissance Service doesn't even exist. But when some of the best orbital and imagery scientists are all supposedly working for the US Geodetic Service, and yet they officially don't have an office number in the directory, it's pretty easy to make guesses."

Ross gave Parsons a look that questioned, quite clearly, his lack of discretion. Parsons glanced at Mackey and Thompson, then continued.

"I imagine that as Grace doesn't have you two at gunpoint already, we can talk about this. A benefit of the fact that I don't officially know about it is that I'm not officially sworn to secrecy either.

"It went like this: in 1961, the military wanted a permanent agency in charge of all Top Secret satellite imagery. It couldn't be in any of the branches of the armed forces or the CIA, because of all the convoluted rivalries in the military and intelligence community. ASTB put out a secret bid for it, and so did the USGS. Commerce got it rather than Transportation, it was developed under the USGS, and that was the last anyone heard of it."

"Why," Mackey hesitated, but having already spoken up, continued to ask his question, "would they give the task to a new agency, when the ASTB already has jurisdiction over satellites?"

Parsons shrugged. "The dark mysteries of Parallel Procedures, coupled with some sort of backhanded maneuvers that I don't know about." He glanced at Hopper. "You win some, you lose some. Commerce won that one, and a new secret Service was born. But what I do know is that they have developed some sort of method of transferring imagery captured by electric crystal back to earth via radio waves. ASTB satellites use film, retrieved by Postal Bureau aircraft after the recovery capsule re-enters the atmosphere. We've been working on an electro-optical method, but it isn't quite ready yet. The National Reconnaissance Service has the only Crystal birds in the world, and they would likely produce scan lines on the imagery just like this."

"What are Parallel Procedures?" Thompson whispered to Mackey.

Mackey was trying to follow the conversation, and answered him quickly, under his breath: "When Departments do something they aren't supposed to do, because they have to do it. More or less." Thompson looked confused, but nodded anyway.

Parsons flipped the satellite photo to the side, to read the rest of the dossier.

"My, my, my—what is this?" He showed it to Ross, who traced the lines of one of the astrological charts with her fingertip.

Hopper smiled. "That was my second question for you."

Parsons studied the odd, circular diagram, again picking up the magnifying glass, and also grabbing a pencil and paper, upon which he jotted some notes. "They appear to be astrological birth charts."

Hopper tapped her fingers idly on the edge of her briefcase. Mackey leaned forward and opened his mouth to ask another question, but Parsons interrupted him, continuing to scrutinize the diagram.

"Birth charts, Fred, describe the exact apparent locations of the planets and zodiac at the moment and place in which you are born. Or at any particular moment in time and space, really. At any time and place, the relative locations of the stars and planets in the sky will be unique. From there, one can analyze the planets astrologically, and come to conclusions about the person in question."

"So, the Weather Service was reading their horoscopes?"

Parsons jumped up and dashed across the room to retrieve a large leather-bound volume from a shelf. He returned to the desk and then, as if trying to remember something, put a finger to his lips. Dodging over and digging into a cabinet, he removed a cartridge reel of magnetic tape, held it to the light to check the label, and then dashed over to a curtain on the wall. Jerking it back, Parsons revealed a computer console with all the showmanship of a stage magician.

"What is he doing?" Thompson whispered again.

"If my guess is correct," Ross said, "he's going to do an analysis of the planetary positions in the charts, to try and see what dates and times they might indicate."

Parsons hit the switches and allowed the machine to spin up, the front panel becoming an incandescent blaze of indicator lamps. Opening the tape drive drawer, he inserted the cartridge and latched it home. Returning to his desk, Parsons snatched up his notes, and then drew up a stool to the card puncher, pecking the keys rapidly, pausing occasionally to refer to the giant leather tome he held open on his lap. Ross stood behind him, looking over his shoulder and double-checking his work. As soon as he was done, he handed the cards to Ross, who loaded them into the reader and hit the button. Clattering away, the constellations of lamps on the console danced incandescently and the printer whirred into life. Tearing away the printout, Parsons returned to his desk, and Ross drew her chair up alongside.

Parsons' brow furrowed as he compared the printout to the charts in the dossiers.

"Who are these people in these files?"

"We haven't had time for any deep analysis. Mackey says that they appear to be a number of mid-level Transportation bureaucrats, from no specific Bureaus or Sections," Hopper told him.

Parsons picked up a pen and circled some areas of the printout. He pointed, and Ross nodded. "These aren't birth charts. Or, at least the astronomical positions aren't equivalent to the birth dates and places listed on the dossiers. According to the program, these astronomical positions are current—within the last six months. All places within the United States."

Ross handed the paper across the desk. Hopper looked at the printout, considering the dates that Parsons had circled. Parsons leaned back, placing his pen to his lips, thinking. "There's a . . . possibility."

Hopper looked through her glasses at the man, whose mustache was now curling into a smile. "Do tell, Jack."

"Census are all astrology nuts, right? That's the missing link between the Weather Service and the Geodetic Service. The Weather Service has a parallel version of your ARPNET. The Geodetic Service has the Crystals. To match up celestial navigation data and personnel records, they use birth charts created by Census as a format, because the Census Service has the most extensive database of Transportation staff in all of the Department of Commerce. Census is the nexus uniting the purloined files with the photographs, the hub between the parallel ARPNET at Weather and the Crystals at Geodetic. And the birth charts prove it."

Hopper returned his wry gaze. "So, it seems like we have at least three Commerce agencies involved. Good thing I didn't speak to formerly-of-the-Census-Service Winslow about it, then."

Mackey was hopelessly lost in this chain of reasoning. "Census, sure—there's Winslow and Gregory of the Census Service, who both seem connected to this. But what do you mean by saying that Census loves astrology? Why would birth charts indicate the Census Service?"

Thompson nodded, the same question on his mind.

Parsons turned in his seat, quizzically placing his fingers under his chin as he eyed Mackey. "No one likes to talk about it," he shot a look at Hopper, "but most of the Bureaus and Services have—occult interests."

Thompson folded his arms across his chest, as if he was trying to figure out if this was a joke. Mackey's mouth was open. He noticed, and closed it.

"Typically for code names of missions, research projects, and the like. It's an inside joke, really," Hopper attempted to explain. But Parsons cut her off.

"It's no joke. Each agency has always gravitated towards a particular field of occult research. The Census focuses on astrology, the Weather Service catalogs strange atmospheric phenomena, the Land Service's interests are in dowsing, and the USGS researches ley lines. Here at ATSB we take more of an interest in—"

"Transportation Bureaus, just like the various Services of the Department of Commerce, are all strictly science-based," Ross interrupted. "We didn't get to the moon using flying daggers and philosopher's stones."

Parsons chuckled. "You'd be surprised how much alchemy goes into building a Saturn rocket."

Hopper ignored the remark and turned to Mackey. "Every agency remembers its pre-scientific roots in different ways. As you can see from Dr. Parsons' natural history museum"— she gestured at the cabinet—"he prefers props as his method of paying homage to the occult foundations of chemistry and physics. Other scientists prefer to honor their progenitors via project names, like the Apollo spacecraft or the Aquarian System."

Parsons smiled, fingers rubbing his chin. "Put up a skeptical front if you must, Grace. While the 20th century's historians like to pretend that the current federal government has left its occult origins behind, the 20th century's history tells a different story."

Mackey didn't know what to make of this. He couldn't tell who was trying to kid him, or if all of them were. Instead, he moved on. "Celestial navigation—that's like . . ."

"Telemetry systems that use star tracking rather than ground-point tracking, usually coupled with an inertial system," Ross broke in. "In the same way that birth charts are unique for every time and place, a traveling ship, aircraft, or spacecraft can tell exactly where it is from looking at the stars."

"We must figure out the purpose of these charts. USGS is just up the road in Menlo Park," Hopper said. "I think it might be best if we just go—" she smiled, "ask them directly."

Parsons waved his hands, shaking his head. "Grace! Why break in when we have the best mind in orbital telemetry right here in the room?"

They both looked over at Ross. Thompson and Mackey did as well, waiting to see how she would respond.

She nodded slowly. "We can do a deeper analysis of the charts, but I'll need the orbital computers back at Plant 42 to do it. If this is celestial navigation data linked to the images, we should be able work backwards and find the NRS satellites. Then, from the orbits, we might be able to see what they are looking at now."

"Plant 42, in the Mojave." Hopper thought out loud. "It would be preferable, certainly, to conduct further studies from a secure facility, after our recent misadventure. And you're sure your programs can deliver, Ross?"

"I believe so, Assistant Secretary. We use the same programs to track the telemetry of everything that the ASTB puts into orbit. The equations are quite trustworthy."

"Like the stars themselves." Parsons smiled, and gestured towards the heavens with both hands. "But aren't we forgetting a key piece of this puzzle?"

"What part?" Mackey asked.

"Well," Parsons mused, leaning back in his chair again. "You, Fred, are an engineer with highly specialized knowledge of Commerce's bureaucratic structures, and I suppose that explains your accompanying Grace well enough. She always travels with an entourage of engineers, if she can." Hopper did not take the bait. "But what about—" he gestured to the man in the Forest Service coat, "our friend Ranger Gene here? How does he fit into the puzzle?"

Ross and Hopper relayed the basics of the events in the Sierras to Parsons, who sat forward in interest.

"I certainly didn't wish to be proven correct about my assertions of the occult, through something so awful and unbelievably foolish," he muttered. "Like a two-bit movie set, some low-budget made-for-television schtick. To what deities did they suppose they were sacrificing your pilot?"

"I think they said Enki," Thompson recalled. "And maybe Ninkharsag?"

Parsons shook his head, rolling his eyes skyward. "Some half-chewed Babylonian imitation—it's insulting to all of us, Enki most of all. They no doubt read about it on the back of a cereal box."

"The flames and blood seemed real enough," Mackey said, morosely. "There was this symbol, painted in some sort of grease, and it started to...I mean I thought I saw it—"

"Charlatans. Witless, spineless, common carnival imitators, cheap stage hacks with pocket pyrotechnics. Those kinds think a little bit of blood is enough to please the gods, as if they haven't seen enough blood from uncreative cutthroats over the millennia. I always have half a mind to let those gutless impostors try and defile the womb of Ninkharsag with mortal blood, and see what that gets them. They'll be begging to be shot by the time the goddess is through with them!"

Mackey was not very relieved by this response. "Is this common? Government agencies committing blood rituals?"

Parsons dismissed the notion. "Even the Department of Transportation's worst bureaucrats have more sense than that. What you saw was not a ritual. Nothing but vaseline and saltpeter. As pedestrian as a television cooking program. A blood-based cooking program perhaps. You know the kind. Another microwave roast, another bland concoction of potatoes and onions slathered with cream sauce. The myriad inevitabilities of au gratin." They all looked at him. "But with blood," he finished, drawing invisible lines on the desk with his finger.

"The event seems most likely designed to intimidate, or simply to dispose of us," Hopper concluded. "While it was certainly theatrical, I wouldn't give too much attention to the set dressings in this case."

"And it also tells us," Mary added, "that at least five Commerce agencies are involved in this scheme: the Weather Service, the Census Service, the Geodetic Service, the Fish and Wildlife Service, and the Land Service."

Mackey nodded, but he was thinking of the face of Nicholas Roerich, the old wrinkled man, calmly watching the scene. He noted that Hopper had not shared that detail in her telling of the story. Mackey decided it was best to stay quiet about it now.

Hopper gathered up the files from the desk and secured them in her briefcase. "I'll need your phone, Jack, to see when the plane will be ready to fly, or to coax another out of the Secretary's office."

"What, your jet? Forget it! Look, I'll take you myself tomorrow morning in my Vail-22. I'd love to get out of the Valley and see Los Angeles again! All bureaucrat types up here, even at Ames. All career men."

"And career women," Hopper corrected him.

"Yes, yes! No passion, only caring about the job, no interest in discovery! You know what I mean, Fred?"

Parsons snatched a tweed jacket from the floor by his desk and put it on as he moved to the door. "We'll put up in the executive accommodations here at Ames tonight, and fly straight down in the morning."

"That's fine. We could use a night of rest after this eventful evening. But Jack?" Hopper stopped him. "We'll need to destroy those notes you made. And the punch cards."

"Way ahead of you, Grace." Parsons strode over to the cabinet and pulled out a large stone bowl, which he set on the floor in front of it. He retrieved the punch cards and the page of notes, and flicked a number of switches on the computer console. "Wiped the RAM for you too, Assistant Secretary." He winked at Mackey again.

Over the bowl, he shredded the paper and, selecting a jar from the cabinet, sprinkled a bit of dark powder over it. Striking a match, Parsons applied flame to the small pile, which immediately leapt into the air with a burst of green light and a smell of frank-incense as the room filled with grey smoke. Mackey removed his glasses to wipe his eyes against the overpowering fog. Ross and Thompson spluttered and coughed, while Hopper went to open a window behind the curtains. But unable to penetrate the fabric she went towards the hallway, where Parsons was already waiting with the door open as smoke billowed past him into the passageway.

"The Ames rooms aren't spectacular, but they have a great view of the test stands. There's a new engine on Number Three tonight. Maybe we'll get to see another fire!" he declared to no one in particular, charging down the hall towards the elevator, with the rest of them close behind. Mackey turned back and saw a clerk staring open-mouthed, as the smoke dissipated through the hallway. Mackey shrugged, as if to make some sort of attempt at apology for the pollution, and buttoning his jacket, he jogged to keep up.

It wasn't the radio that Fred heard, but his mother. Soft sobs, eyes welling up with tears, the slight panic in her voice as she called for his father. Fred felt the uncertainty that any child of ten would feel when they suddenly realize that their parent is deeply upset, but fail to understand why. Fred Sr. came into the kitchen and saw his wife with tears in her eyes as she leaned over to turn the volume higher.

"Today at 3:35 PM Eastern Postal Time, Postmaster Roosevelt passed away, while at the Air Mail Station just outside of Warm Springs, Georgia. The nation is in shock and mourning, as the greatest technocrat the world has ever known departed, leaving only his legacy, and a grateful world."

Fred's father took his mother into his arms and held her tight.

The next day, ten-year-old Fred was dressed in his Sunday best, and his mother put on a black veil. P-car service was stopped for the day, and so the family walked the mile downtown to the Post Office, where televisions were set up for the funeral broadcast. The residents of Fred's small town stood together in hushed groups. As the broadcast began, Fred Sr. and the other World War Two veterans snapped to attention. Saluting with his right hand, Fred's father held his son's hand tightly in his left.

Fred had been only seven when the war ended, and couldn't remember much except the joy of having his father back at home. But now, a few years older, it began to occur to him where his father had been all that time. More than the veterans' parades and the ceremonies on VE Day, Roosevelt's death elicited something in Fred's father, a foundation in him as a man, something that connected deep to the core of his beliefs.

Walking home from the Post Office together, his father spoke to Fred. "That man, the Postmaster—he saved us all, Fred. He saved this country from the Nazis. We could never have done it without him."

Fred watched the blossoms from the cherry trees swirl in the warm spring breeze, down the quiet streets of the town. He wasn't entirely sure who the Nazis were, except that they were bad and had been far away, but they would have been here in his town if it wasn't for men like his father and the Postmaster. Looking up, he caught just the briefest gleam of a tear in his father's eye.

5

Occult Knowledges

THE ACCOMMODATIONS AT AMES WERE QUITE NICE, IF UNDER-decorated. Each room had a large window, a bed, a desk, and a bathroom. A bit less modern than the central Ames office building, the block of guest rooms stacked into three levels was meant for guest scientists visiting the facility who did not want to be so far from their labs as a hotel in town. As such, the design seemed intended for minds that were fixated on their work at the test stands, which the windows looked out upon. The rooms themselves were bare white, without art or any decor that was not functional. Mackey didn't mind this—it was how he chose to furnish his own apartment. He simply didn't see the need for automatic baseball scoring receivers, tea-making automats, decorative weather radio window boxes, or the other meaningless technological wares that people utilized to fill their homes.

The bed linens and towels were a pale California gold. Mackey was surprised to see that the only sign of any Department or Bureau insignia were on the small water glasses next to the sink. One of them featured the blue, star-emblazoned sphere emblem of the ASTB. The other, unmatched, simply said 'Department of Transportation' in plain type. Thompson's water glasses featured mission emblems. One was for the PX-15 high-altitude rocket aircraft, showing the black, dart-shaped fuselage crossing the boundary between blue atmosphere and dark space. The other was for an unknown project, with no number or name designation given. The logo was a ring of lightning bolts surrounding an image of cirrus clouds in an otherwise empty sky. There was a Latin motto reading: *Interrogare In Terra*. Neither Mackey nor Thompson could make head nor tail of it.

Their rooms were next to each other. Desperate for some sort of a drink to put in one of his Departmental glasses but not knowing where to procure such a thing, Mackey knocked on Thompson's door instead, to see how he was doing. Thompson was similarly at a loss for what to do, so they ended up chatting, Thompson sitting on the edge of his bed, Mackey in the desk chair. They angled themselves, both looking out the window with the lights dim, watching the activity around the various test facilities. While they couldn't understand quite what was being tested, things at least appeared to be going much more slowly and deliberately than Parsons' dramatic test earlier in the evening.

They made small talk, sharing where they had come from. Mackey told about his father's history with the Postal Administration, and his time in engineering school. Thompson's family was from Angola, but he grew up in Idaho, a child of the outdoors. The Forest Service was a career choice more for the lack of office and desk than for any political allegiance.

"So, what do you think of all this?" Mackey asked.

"Which part?" Thompson responded. "The part about almost getting killed, or the part about how our Census Service apparently believes in alchemy?"

"It was astrology," Mackey corrected. "But, yeah. Both, I guess."

"Well, I can't say that anyone has tried to kill me before," Thompson said. "And certainly the Federal Government has never tried to kill me before. Mostly, I suppose, I want to know why. Why me? Why did you happen to come along and save me? Why is any of this happening?"

"That's it, exactly." Mackey nodded, relieved. "I feel like I don't understand anything that's going on anymore. As much as I know about the bureaucracy of the executive branch, none of this has any relation to anything I know. I can't help but feel like it's made up. Like this is all a big lie, some sort of play."

"I can tell you that knife against my neck was real. That much I know." Thompson looked out the window, and then back at

Mackey. "There's no use in trying to dispute what happened. It happened. I guess the only thing to do now is be ready for whatever comes next, and hope that it puts the pieces together, rather than adds more questions."

Mackey smiled. "What is a weird rocket scientist who keeps skulls in a cabinet when not blowing up engines? An answer, or a question?"

Thompson laughed. "It seems like both. He's two questions for every answer."

"Hopper too, and Ross. I mean, they're both significantly less mercurial, but still a bit occluded nevertheless."

"It seems that whatever is going on here, it's something that both of us have never seen before, although it may be more familiar to our new companions. There's going to be a lot of strange questions, and even stranger answers. I figure the only thing that we can do is try to keep up with these strange government folks, and try not to get in the way of any more daggers."

Mackey nodded at him. "Well, I think on that we can agree."

"You want to fly to Los Angeles in that?"

The vehicle shone brightly in the morning sunlight. The fuselage was completely mirrored aluminum, except for the Postal Bureau insignia and number on the tail, which marked it as a personal executive transport. The problem, in Mackey's mind, was that there wasn't much in the way of fuselage at all. Or wings, for that matter. His eyes were fixated on the four massive ducted-fan nacelles, two on either side of the cockpit, and another pair flanking the tail, each positioned horizontal, to blow down onto the ground. It was a vertical-takeoff-and-landing aircraft. Another piece of Parsons' personality just fit into place for Mackey.

Parsons put his arm around Mackey's shoulder, gazing at the machine, clearly smitten with its beautiful, quadruped visage.

"I'll handle the flying, Fred. You just relax and make us all some eye-openers."

"Where did you get this, Jack? I thought Vail Labs had scrapped the program." Hopper's hand lightly rubbed the nacelle, as if to see whether or not it was real.

Vail Labs was one of the advanced Postal Bureau research labs, named after Theodore Vail. Vail was considered the godfather of the Technocratic Administrations, responsible for planning the rollout of the Pierstorff car system by the pre-Administration Post Office. He had died not long after the cars were introduced, but the lab that bore his name had been responsible for some of the biggest technological breakthroughs in the 20th century. They had invented the transistor. They had invented programming languages. Work on the first telecommunications satellite had begun there. That fact made Mackey somewhat more confident about possibly riding in this strange craft. But also, for every brilliant advance a lab turned out, there had to be a hundred duds.

"They did, but I managed to save one from the heap. Took some string-pulling of my own to be sure, but I never did like riding in one of those damned bean pods."

"My real concern," Ross voiced, "is not the aircraft, so much as the pilot."

"Very funny, Mary!" He slapped Thompson on the shoulder, who was staring at the craft fairly impassively.

As Parsons opened the door, folding down a set of stairs, Mackey had to ask, "So—why did they scrap this aircraft?"

Parsons boarded and then climbed up into the pilot's seat as the rest entered. "Oh . . . I don't know. Apparently the lack of ability to glide in the case of engine failure makes it a 'liability.' But nothing to worry about! It's in excellent condition. And so is the bar. Martini for me, Fred." Parsons gestured at the small wet bar at the rear of the cabin.

"Vodka soda, a double," Hopper said, as she fastened the safety belt on one of the cabin's four executive chairs.

Mackey shrugged, and looked to Ross and Thompson for their orders.

"Just orange juice for me," Ross begged off, as she climbed into the co-pilot's seat.

"I'll have whatever you're having," Thompson said. "And I'll give you a hand." They found the small bar in the rear of the cabin to be quite well stocked. When desiring a drink the night before, clearly they should have thought to look in Parsons' personal aircraft. There were bottles and bottles secured to the wall racks by clever spring-loaded restraining bars. Mackey considered that what he probably needed was his morning swim. But given that wasn't possible, he supposed a drink would have to do.

The engines came on with a loud growl, sounding as much like a carnival ride as a vehicle. After coordinating with Moffett Field tower, Parsons throttled back, and the aircraft lifted shakily from the ground. Mackey grasped the edge of the bar as the aircraft rolled slightly on its center axis. He and Thompson jostled shoulders, without any direction of acceleration for them to brace against. As Mackey poured vodka, he made the mistake of glancing out the window, suddenly noticing that he and the bottle were now hovering three hundred feet off the ground.

Parsons angled the nacelles, and as they began moving forward, liquor sloshed onto Mackey's shoes. The rocket scientist leaned forward and snapped on a broadcast radio, sending the sound of Southern California surf rock through the entire cabin before Ross leaned forward and turned it off.

By the time they had some semblance of cocktails assembled, and the glasses locked by their stems into a service tray, they were rocketing down the Valley at four hundred knots. Locked or not, a good deal of beverage spilt onto the tray by the time Mackey made his way forward.

The Assistant Secretary accepted her glass and took a large quaff. Parsons turned completely around in his seat, took his glass, drained it, and then replaced it on the tray. Mackey handed a glass of orange juice to Ross, who thanked him. Mackey nodded back with a silent thanks that she was sitting in front of a control stick.

Secure in his chair, sitting across from Thompson, Mackey gripped his gin, sipping it while looking out the window.

He watched the traffic thousands of feet below, as the bureaucrats that gave the Valley its name swarmed towards their offices on the P-car tracks. Like rectilinear ants, the cars smoothly swarmed around each other, taking the entrance tracks from their points of origin—the sprawling suburban developments of New Almaden, San Martin, Gilroy, and Hollister—before accelerating northward towards the Valley, the peninsula of San Francisco, and the East Bay. The housing developments below them looked like nets of clover, as looping tracks entered one side of a round assemblage of lots and exited the other side, before entering the next leaf. The loops tessellated across the valley, planned perfectly to use all available space, and to minimize the track distance between each whorl of development and the central arterials. Only the peaks of the hills were bare, the few surviving trees an odd bit of chaos outside the order of the interconnected city. This had all been farmland just fifty years ago, Mackey recalled. But as the efficiency of the P-car network conquered physical space, and the buildup of industry and technology manufacture brought new residents, the Valley had shifted harvests, from produce to people.

Parsons banked the aircraft west, away from the sun rising over the golden California mountains. In a few minutes they were over the Pacific Ocean, and then Parsons swung south at an altitude of barely one thousand feet. Ahead of them in the sea haze rose the shoulder of land where Mackey knew Vandenberg Air Force Base must be. One of the fringe benefits of his Bureaucratic Literacy training was that he had a good working knowledge of the geography of government installations.

As if reading his thoughts, Parsons turned and said, "We should have a good view of the 0900 mail rocket launch from Vandenberg out the port side!" Turning to Mackey, he said, "Another cocktail, what do you say, Fred?" With the steadying effect of his gin finally taking hold, Mackey collected the glassware and made his way back to the bar, this time discovering the useful overhead handholds along the cabin ceiling.

Upon returning and redistributing glasses, Mackey watched the gentle arc of the mail rocket's smoke trail as it ascended up towards the Mail Sorting Station in low earth orbit. Mackey wanted to go to space someday. It wasn't a likely destination for a engineer in a testing lab. Space operations personnel tended to be more of the pilot or experienced technician type, having at least some experience in running equipment in the field, not just on the bench. Parsons engaged the autopilot and turned in his chair, his martini glass half full in his hand. Ross gave him a look, but sipped her juice and kept an eye on the instruments.

"Well, Gene, tell us some stories about the Forest Service! What is it like over in the Commerce Department with the enemy?" He winked.

Thompson shrugged and sipped his gin. "I don't know much about Commerce, I suppose. Mostly about hunting and fishing licenses, wildfires, and what to do if you stumble across a bear."

"What do you do?" Mackey asked, suddenly interested in all kinds of life-saving knowledge.

"Yell at it, and don't back down."

Parsons laughed. "Good advice for bureaucrats, too! How about you, Fred? Tell us more about the new engineer!"

"I'm in the Electromagnetic Bureau, Domestic Interference Engineering Section. Currently working on doing Part Six compliance for shielding components. Current batch is meant for P-car sensor arrays. A good crop—composite material. That combined with some phase cancellation circuits, and the new sensors should be nearly impervious to interference from track-side sources. The real genius is, you see—"

Hopper took the liberty of interrupting him. "Mr. Mackey is Level G certified, and it seems that recognizing otherwise faceless bureaucrats is a real specialty of his."

Parsons sipped his cocktail. "I thought you preferred a more direct approach than bureaucratic channels, Grace." He gave her a knowing glance. Mackey suddenly thought of the strange plastic pistol that he assumed was still in the Assistant Secretary's briefcase, currently on the floor between her leg and the cabin wall. Hopper said nothing and took a swig of her drink.

Parsons turned back to Mackey, cocking his head to one side. Mackey was again struck by the notion of how even in his mid-fifties, the man simply beamed an elusive charm. "So, Fred—only Level G? Nothing higher than that?"

Mackey wrinkled his brow a bit. "Level G is the highest rating for Bureaucratic Literacy. Not to say—I certainly could stand some refreshing, I am somewhat rusty on intra-cabinet procedures, and more mnemonic conditioning is always useful—but that is the highest qualification."

Parsons laughed again, throwing his head back against the pilot's seat and taking a sip of martini. As they passed the end of the point, he disengaged the autopilot to throw them into a banking turn to the east between the Santa Barbara coast and the Channel Islands, all while still managing to hold onto his glass by the very end of the stem. Once settled on the new course, he re-engaged the automatic controls, and took another sip.

"That's the highest *non-classified* certification, you mean. My goodness, Grace—operational security aside, you have to let poor Fred here in on some of our secrets if you want him to help out!"

Hopper waved her hand dismissively towards the pilot's seat, although Mackey couldn't tell if it was because Parsons was pulling his leg or because she was dodging the question.

Parsons continued. "You look like a bright young man, Fred. You no doubt know your history, all about the Administrations, and Commerce and Transportation, and how we got to be in the mess we're all in today. But there is more to it than just Technocratic Administrationism ideology, more to it than inter-Departmental feuding. There are secret orders to the world, which although invisible to us, affect our every motion."

The rocket man balanced his elbow on the seat rest, raising his glass and placing his opposite hand casually upon the inside of his balanced elbow. Mackey looked over Parsons' shoulder to make sure Ross was still keeping an eye on things.

"We've known for some time about a secret society out there, pulling strings. Mostly in Commerce. But their agents have infiltrated Transportation as well. Whoever it is, they aren't *entirely* government. The feud, the ideological debate, the history of the Departments, the Administrations: all that is a ruse. It's a distraction, get it? This secret society has their own motivations for directing the course of events, for setting us down this narrative course of 'the Federal Government as a battle between two divided houses.' We don't know what their motivations are, but we know it is far bigger than that. It isn't about ideology at all, you see. It is about the occult knowledges. Ideology is just the surface! It's only two dimensions! Beneath it, invisible to most people, are the larger experiments, where the real urges that move the world exist.

"There's a purpose behind all of it. Like I said, the Census Service researches astrology. The Weather Service, Fortean phenomena and other odd atmospheric occurrences. The Park Service, vortexes. The Forest Service is working on communication with animals," he pointed his drink at Thompson, "in ways other than yelling at them. On our side, the Infrastructure Bureau researches sacred geometry. The ASTB, alchemy and the harmonies of the spheres and angelic hierarchies. Over in the Electromagnetic Bureau, you work on psychic phenomena. And the Postal Bureau has always had a certain fascination with trying to predict the future, whether or not that is actually possible—"

Hopper was rolling her eyes. Catching her expression, Parsons threw up his hands, though not spilling his drink. "Oh come on, Grace!" he implored. "This isn't classified! Just no one ever talks about it."

Mackey responded cautiously, even as his mind was carefully filing this information away. "I'm fairly certain I've never seen any research on psychic phenomena at the Electromagnetic Bureau."

"Of course not! No one can come out and say that is what they are really working on, because then people would want to see results. They'd want proof, and most of the time, that proof doesn't exist. The whole point of the occult structure is that it is hidden, beneath the surface. You say, 'I use alchemy,' and then everyone wants to see you turn lead into gold. But it doesn't work that way. The results aren't so tangible. The results are in the entirety, not in the specific. You yourself are not researching psychic phenomena. Your scientific work at the Bureau, with interference testing and so forth, are the results of the *larger* experiment in psychic phenomena. You follow?"

Mackey looked at Thompson, trying to see how he was taking this in. It was hard to keep up, and Parsons kept going around in circles. Maybe Parsons was just nutty. Some scientists could be like that, he supposed. But then, why wasn't Hopper at all concerned?

"Okay, I'll start with a better example. Take the P-car, for instance. It changed the world, they say, everything in our society is because of the P-car. But what does the P-car run on? The track, of course. But not just that. What about the electricity? What about your radar components, and the apportionment of the electromagnetic spectrum? Where do the motors come from? The computers? What about all the bureaucracy that greases those gears, that keeps the infrastructure functioning from one day to the next? And then if you admit that behind the 'revolutionary invention' of the P-car there are all these other connected systems, what lies behind them?"

Parsons was gazing out of the cockpit windscreen, still speaking back to the cabin, but also speaking to somewhere else, out beyond the aircraft, in the atmosphere. "The conflicts we see in the world are representative of conflicts on the immaterial plane. Amateurish sacrifices, secret spy satellites, maybe even the explosion in the test trench. It's all part of a bigger narrative. As above, so below. Someone, somewhere, wanted us to be at this point, on this route, at this time. We don't know why, and maybe we never will."

"That's a nice speech, Jack," Ross kidded. "Have you been rehearsing it long?"

"All fifty-six years I've been on this earth," he answered, soberly. "Maybe even longer than that."

Hopper finished her vodka soda and placed the glass in a form-fitting holder in the cabin wall. "Don't let Jack's metaphysical tendencies overwhelm you, Mackey. We may not yet know what to make of all of these events, but that's how this business works. It is not a conspiracy—not necessarily. At least not outside of the scope of the everyday conspiracies of government. There are unknowns, and we seek to uncover those unknowns. Whether it is human malice, undiscovered principles of nature, or merely Commerce trying to cover its own ass, we come up with a theory and engineer a solution. Our theory only needs to be the size of the problem at hand, not a full cosmology."

Parsons finished his drink as well and, stowing the glass, prepared to take over the controls as the Vail-22 overflew the oil platforms of the Santa Barbara Channel. "That may be so, but no individual problem is ever separate from the wider view. Back in 1952, I was almost killed by an explosion. Unsolved mystery, according to the Postal Inspectors. The bomb killed another rocketry specialist. A German man, by the name of Von Braun. Recruited by Roosevelt in 1937, he was one of the finest rocketry minds in the world. Better than me, maybe even better than Mary. If it had been me in the Postal Administration lab rather than him, I wouldn't be sitting here today. A freak matter of chance, you might say. You can't second guess the forking paths of fate. But at the same time, who planted the bomb? Who was its target? Did things go according to plan, or did the plan fail? Unsolved, they said. Without any larger theory, it was only an isolated crime, they said. But you can't put the energy back into the bomb. Someone knows what happened. Someone's will had a deadly effect that day. Right or wrong, lucky or unlucky, the microcosm and the macrocosm are always connected."

Mackey couldn't help but wonder what his father would make of all this. The man had flown electronic warfare planes for the Postal Administration during World War Two, and a die-hard Technocrat like his father would blame the Commerce Department for any wrongdoing. There was an enemy in the government all right, according to the senior Mackey. And the Commercialists were it. The notion of the Commerce Department assaulting and murdering members of the Transportation Department fit right in with the old man's worldview.

Orthogonal Procedures was one thing, but what about these occult procedures? Metaphysics, alchemy, and astrology? Fred had never heard his father mention anything like that. And ten years under his belt at the Electromagnetic Bureau, he had never seen anything like that. Until yesterday. Mackey had seen what had happened on the hilltop in the Sierras, and his father had not. How would his father have reacted to such a situation? What was more important to his father—that everything that the Administrations had done made sense according to science, or that the worldview was diametrically opposed to Commercialism? If metaphysical beliefs were ever a public tenet of the Administrations, would his father have accepted them on principle, or would his faith in Technocratic Administrationism have been diminished?

It was interesting to pose these questions, perhaps. Especially after a couple gins, while strapped to an aircraft made from four ceiling fans and piloted by a charming lunatic. But Mackey knew from experience that he could ask himself rhetorical questions all day, but without a lab bench to sit at and begin working out problems, he wouldn't get any further than watching the clouds.

The fact remained that all of Mackey's lab work involved electromagnetic energies, not psychic energies. The equations, the models, the testing procedures, the technology in the field: it all operated according to physical laws, and never had anyone on any level in the department suggested that their work was anything else. Even if it was just a metaphor, as Hopper had said, Mackey had never heard one whisper of it. He tried to imagine the other engineers in his department, like the brilliant Lynn Thacker, talking the way Parsons did. It was antithetical to the entire way the Section and the Bureau functioned. It was completely outside of the mechanism of their bureaucracy to consider such notions.

But maybe that was what Parsons was talking about, when he said that the microcosm and the macrocosm were linked. The mind has to know what the hands are doing, but not the other way around. Parsons was one of the ASTB's top scientists. Hopper, despite her eye-rolling, was one of the top officials of the Department, and certainly had her own secrets. Ross was a ballistics engineer who not only was a pilot but designed her own machine gun. These were important people, the heaviest bureaucrats that Mackey had ever spent time with. And if they spoke this way . . .

The sacrifice in the Sierras was certainly an indicator of something—though Mackey couldn't say exactly what. Maybe there were classified Bureaucratic Literacy levels, or maybe there weren't. Perhaps someone had wanted to sacrifice them to a Babylonian god and goddess, or maybe it was just a plain old murder. Maybe the Commerce Department was planning some sort of scheme against Transportation, or maybe it was all a misunderstanding. But to Mackey, Orthogonal Procedures seemed like it might be its own form of occult belief. It didn't so much matter, he decided, whether one believed in the conspiracy or not. There were still secrets. And there were still murders. Two days ago, at his desk in the Electromagnetic Bureau, he hadn't seen any research into psychic phenomena, but he also wouldn't have believed in anything he'd seen since.

These thoughts bouncing around his head with no resolution, Mackey dropped the inquiry and looked out the window. Coming around the edge of Point Dume, Parsons flew the craft along the coastline, below the peaks of the Santa Monica Mountains. Coming clearer through the marine layer haze, Los Angeles loomed into view. The sprawling city had the most tangled web of P-car interchanges Mackey had ever seen, like the roots of a forest seen from under the ground. Skirting the Los Angeles Airport, Parsons turned north before the cluster of skyscrapers around Century City and joined the aerial traffic lanes following the thick belt of tracks over the mountains. Over the twisted loops of residential tracks and houses ensconced in the narrow canyons, the San Fernando Valley became visible.

A dense net of arterials, laid over the larger freight lines cutting back and forth across the valley, wove the city together like a thick carpet. Along the entrenched tracks below, able to handle formations of freight cars three times the track gauge of a P-car, Mackey saw the immense Postal Bureau factory complexes, stretching in a thick band from Canoga Park to Burbank.

These plants turned out new P-cars, aircraft, spacecraft, and all of the requisite technological pieces by the thousands and millions. Supply trains hauled these wares back and forth between the mammoth plants, and then outward to the rest of the world, returning to drag new raw materials inward and complete the supply chain. Then, once the produced technology was powered up and connected to the system, it all came hurtling back.

Aircraft crisscrossing the sky, carrying express mail and executives of the vast bureaucracy that accounted for every piece. Spacecraft ascending and then returning from orbit like flame-propelled elevators. P-cars whirring, stretching over the surface of the planet on their hairline tracks, transporting the hundreds of thousands of workers in those plants and the offices to their homes, to the grocery stores, to the pedestrian malls, to the cinemas, and to the sports complexes, scattered over the surface of the valley. And the rest, the minor bits, the smaller, less notable technology that filled in gaps to build the interconnected masonry of the modern world: radio earphones, coffee machines, synth organs, parking consoles, electro-books, and bedside clocks.

The city below really was like nothing quite so much as a circuit board. A single plane connecting many specially designed components into a complex circuit, each feature across its compact surface playing a particular role in the function the unit was created to fulfill. Passive components, like housing developments, shopping malls, and factories, each becoming a valve in the system once the current was applied to them. And between this dense tiling of components, Mackey watched the current flow—millions of P-cars, shuttling in every direction along the tracks that completed the system into a functional circuit. And below that, running through the coils of wire that made up the P-car motors, was the actual electricity, not just the metaphorical current. *As Parsons had described*, Mackey conceded.

It was, he realized, a fairly incredible cosmology that technology had created, over the course of only fifty years. From the first rudimentary Pierstorff systems in 1920, to daily rockets to the moon in 1970. It was almost unnerving to try and imagine where they might be in another fifty years. That some sort of occult metaphysics might be behind it was almost too simple of an answer.

Mackey, occupied with his thoughts, did not see a small white dot slide in between the aircraft, tailing them only a few hundred yards back. The trailing craft was small, too small to contain a cockpit, and fit in with the flurry of other aerial traffic transiting the busy paths above the sunny San Fernando Valley such that none of them even saw it amongst the confusing brightness of the Southern California sky.

After Action Report PA-954
Date: February 6, 1941
Action Date: January 30, 1941
Location: Karlsruhe Sector
Map Grid: **[redacted]**
Mission: Acquisition of Technological Prototypes and Personnel
Officer in Command: Postmaster Hansen

Narrative: *Reports of in-bound train carrying prototypes and personnel from* **[redacted]** *containing potentially cutting edge* **[redacted]**. *Upon reviewing intel, P-Col. Grace Hopper argued for permission to lead the mission herself, taking a hand-selected platoon of engineers and other unlisted operatives.*

While the circumstances of the mission becoming compromised are still under investigation by Postal Inspectors and are therefore classified, Hopper's platoon came under heavy fire from fighter aircraft and perhaps as much as a company of regular Wehrmacht troops upon crossing the Rhine, still some miles from their rally point with Echo Company of the 501st Combat Transportation Division. With many of her troops killed or wounded, P-Col. Hopper fought her way through enemy lines single-handedly to capture an armed off-rail transporter.

After commanding her engineers to reprogram several railed transporters to create a distraction, P-Col. Hopper and her unit not only managed to escape the ambush, but also used the off-rail transporter to drag the target rail car with [redacted] *and* [redacted] *three miles down an unmapped siding, where they managed to meet up with Echo Company, using either sheer luck or communication means unknown to arrange the rendezvous.*

For quick thinking and bravery under fire that not only saved the lives of many of her personnel but still managed to accomplish the mission objectives, I submit P-Col. Hopper's name for consideration for the award of Master's Stamp, and Silver Stamps to each of her engineers. Hopper is a credit to the entire Postal Administration, and is an example of exactly the sort of bravery and leadership that we need among all Allied Forces in Europe.

Document Ends.

6
How You Keep A Secret

Hopper had announced on the flight down from Moffett that she would need to use a secure phone line, for reasons she did not disclose. Mackey felt a wave of suspicion rising at the suggestion, but Parsons and Ross took the request in stride, as if such a thing happened all the time. Parsons suggested since they were going to pass through the San Fernando Valley anyway, that they stop off at the Thermosphere Club for lunch. Mackey did his best to hide his excitement. Although he had failed to meet James Webb, lunch at the Thermosphere Club would be an experience no less incredible for a young engineer from the Electromagnetic Bureau.

Parsons took them west across the San Fernando Valley, towards the Postal Bureau Tower in the Simi Hills. Mackey had seen the tower from the instant they had entered the valley, its iconic structure visible in the haze like a painting. The columnar structure rose over 1,500 feet from the arid hills above Brandeis, like a beacon above the other office complexes scattered throughout the hills below. Once, the area had been a remote rocket test facility. But with the increase in manufacturing plants down in the lower valley, administrative offices had been moved up to the isolated hills where there was still room to build. The tower was positioned at the top of a massive, single-serving band of P-car tracks that extended from the valley up to the center of the West Coast offices for the Postal Bureau and many other Transportation agencies.

When the Postal Administration had decided they needed a Los Angeles office tower, they built one befitting the stature of the Administration at the height of its power. It had been the tallest building in the world when completed in 1955, and was the textbook example of the mid-1950s Federal style in every architecture classroom in the world. Some called it 'the rocket,' others called it 'the control tower,' but its iconic power derived not from its name, or even its world-record status, but from the fact it was the most visible seat of power for Technocratic Administrationism. Even after the end of the Postal Administration and the formation of the Department of Transportation, the building's power as hub of technological activity, and as symbol, remained.

The titular headquarters of the Postal Bureau and the Department of Transportation were in DC, and everyone knew that. But the offices of the Postmaster in DC were in a fairly nondescript office building in Federal Center, two buildings down from Mackey's own office. That was no tourist attraction. On the other hand, people all around the world knew the Southern California Postal Bureau Tower by sight.

It was not just a tower, but a complex, with an outer ring of offices rising about one-third of the total height of the central spire. Separated from the ring by a circular air shaft allowing light down into the interior of that outer ring was that central form, like a Technocratic scepter, extending upward into the blue. On the very top was a thick antenna mast, with colored lights that could be seen at night as far away as Pomona, and radio transmitters to which most of Southern California could tune, in order to receive a range of Postal programming and other relay electronic mail channels. The building was a shrouded dark blue, from the reflection of the sky upon the curved facades of window glass plating the construction's exterior circumference.

But while the visible portion was certainly most impressive, Mackey knew that the building also extended several hundred feet below the ground. The space below ground contained internal Bureau communication offices, with internal addresses prefixed with S. It was covered in one of Mackey's first Bureaucratic Literacy courses. If there was a Postal Bureau Section or Lab with an office in California, they more likely than not had a mailing address that's correspondence passed through the underside of that structure.

Parsons slowed the Vail-22 into a hover and brought it down onto the landing platform that doubled as the roof of the outer, lower ring level. It might have been the lower level by comparison to the tower, but the semi-circular ring of offices still rose nearly five hundred feet off the hills in its own right, before giving way and allowing the central tower to break skyward, free of all shackles and supports.

Exiting the aircraft, Mackey was delighted to once again be on solid ground, five hundred feet in the air or not. Thermal breezes swept across the open landing platform, bearing the warm scent of the California hills. The group crossed the skybridge into the tower, over the height of the air shaft between the structures. Down below, at the bottom of the glass and steel canyon, Mackey could make out a lush shaded garden, with a stream flowing through the architecturally oriented rocks.

The level into which they entered the tower was an open gallery several stories high—a second lobby, high in the air. The five ascended the escalators along the outer wall, eyeing the murals painted on the round outer walls segmented by curved plate glass windows looking out across the air shaft onto the landing platform. The pattern continued, murals and windows, the entire circumference of the three-hundred-foot-diameter tower.

"I knew this building was supposed to be big, but it's like nothing I ever imagined!" Thompson spoke in very genuine awe. Mackey could only nod in agreement.

The walls depicted various moments in the history of the Postal Bureau. The founding of Ben Franklin's Post Service in 1775 was there, as well as the formation of the Postal Administration in 1924. A mural in an Administrationist-Realist style depicted a squadron of Postal aircraft flying in the Second World War— PB-82 Double Mustangs, the same that Fred Mackey Sr. piloted. The most recent painting was of the Lunar Post Office landing in 1968, completed in a modern, abstract style.

In the center of the gallery was an interior column, half the diameter of the tower, that contained the elevators and other building systems. It too was painted in murals ringing this center structure. These depicted the various activities of the other Technological Administrations. Mackey caught sight of the Electromagnetic Bureau mural, painted in a 1950s Federal style, depicting a combination scene with era-appropriate Postal Administration aircraft conducting electronic warfare runs, and P-cars speeding to their destinations along the first autonomous tracks connecting Washington and New York. There was a smaller version of the same mural in Mackey's own office building back in DC, but he had to admit a small swell of pride seeing it rendered in full size here, in the actual Postal Bureau Tower.

At the top of the escalator, they walked onto the upper mezzanine to get to the elevators at the center of the tower. At the mezzanine level above the gallery, they could see into windows where Postal employees were working in their offices along the outside edge of the building at the top of the gallery. Like any other bureaucratic office, no doubt—but with the added pomp and circumstance that came with the fact that these workers knew they were part of the display. Their motions were just a bit more formal, the boxes of forms on the corners of desks stacked a bit more neatly, the chairs at a slightly more erect angle. Who knows what it was that those employees were working on in there. It might be no more than a lost property form processing office. But it looked magnificent, spotless, the very image of bureaucracy. It looked like the invisible gears, humming smoothly, each piece of the machine guided by the skilled hands of the bureaucrats sitting at these solid, steel desks within an edifice of technological progress.

They arrived at the express elevator to the Thermosphere Club, marked only with a small discreet sign, and a slightly less discreet security officer, his strong frame barely disguised by the uniform of an elevator attendant. The Club was, naturally, at the very top of the tower. Hopper, Ross, and Parsons all showed their passes, and with only a moment's murmured discussion between the attendant and the Assistant Secretary, received guest passes for Mackey and Thompson. The attendant called the elevator for them, they entered, and it immediately departed without needing any direction from its occupants.

If he had been excited before, now Mackey was a bit solemn, overwhelmed by his surroundings. The elevator was decorated in a much more subtle fashion, screened in wooden lattice work, using a tessellation of geometric shapes that he guessed must have been from the insignia of various space missions. This elevator was, he reminded himself over and over, the private boundary of the Thermosphere Club. To join the Thermosphere Club, one had to have crossed the Karman Line: the official border to space. Hopper, Ross, and Parsons were members. Apparently at least a portion of the rumors about Hopper were true. Mackey thought about how to inquire in the most subtle way possible.

"Has it been long since you all were . . . up? In space?"

Parsons smiled, clearly glad to have the opportunity to brag. "Last was a proving test of micro-jets for orbital maneuvers. Three weeks in LEO, and a few days in lunar. How about you, Mary?"

"Couldn't tell you the number of trips, but it's been a year since my last time up. Just LEO, on a hardware test run, for inter-orbit telemetry navigation computers."

Thompson was still a bit overwhelmed by the luxurious design of the elevator, but Mackey was genuinely curious, as he looked to Hopper for her answer. She spoke quickly. "However long it's been since my last time up is never long enough, frankly. Once you've seen someone bleed out in micro-gravity, the whole excursion seems much less fantastic." She brushed the ornate wood screen with her fingers. "Luckily they grill a fantastic steak here, or I might not even come this close to the orbital fan club of my own volition."

"It's the flavor enhancers they developed for orbital cuisine that make it so good," Parsons enthused. "Flavors of soy, earthy tones—synthesized from seaweed, if I recall. Have you been to the Bathyal Club, Grace? I know it's mostly Coast Guard types, kind of a poor crowd. But whatever they do to the breathable atmosphere down there, it makes absinthe go *wild* in the veins. Highly recommended."

The elevator opened onto a small antechamber, a tall room with a square floor plan, walls rising nearly twenty feet to the ceiling. Inlaid into the wall was abstract technological art depicting arcing contrails, orbital insertion diagrams, the parabolas of ballistic trajectories, and the electrical hieroglyphics of circuit diagrams. Wall sconces of molded brass, shaped like the bells of rocket engines, illuminated the walls up and down. Depicted in intricate mosaics of tile and glass slivers, the images rose into the darkened heights of the chamber, transitioning from an almost classical blue and gold to a deep purple, and finally, in the shadows above, thin traces of white and red on black.

Seeing Mackey and Thompson gawking at the walls, Parsons pointed at a section three-fifths of the way to the ceiling, deep purple whorls with silver accents. "See that there? That's Mary's work. That's the ballistics equations for stage-separation of the first multiple-warhead, indirectly targetable ICBM."

They looked at Ross, who pointed at the opposite corner. "Actually that's it, over there—northeast corner. It was Top Secret at the time, but I guess it's just a piece of art now."

An attendant stood by a pair of bronze doors cast with relief sculptures of various space capsules and vehicles rising the full height of the chamber, wearing a suit of ultra-black astronautical polymer. Seeing their passes, the attendant opened the door immediately. Although the solid metal construction must have weighed multiple tons, it appeared to be hydraulically assisted, and swung open with the attendant's slightest touch.

"Assistant Secretary, Dr. Parsons, Miss Ross, gentlemen—lovely to have you all with us this afternoon."

Hopper and Ross nodded, and Parsons returned the greeting with his flashing smile. "David! Lovely to see you as well."

From the opened door sunlight flooded into the chamber, involuntarily narrowing Mackey's eyes. When his pupils adjusted, he was confronted with a massive dining room. Round tables covered in white linen stretched out to windows on three sides. Polished chrome accents embellished the ceiling light fixtures, the columns, and other fittings. The ceiling mosaic was composed of pure white tile, a slightly grey grout giving the only indication of the patterns contained within, like the plot of logarithmic graph paper, but twisted around the points of the lights recessed into the distant surface. To the left side of the entrance was the expansive bar, cabinets featuring detailed cedar scroll work, cut crystal glass doors showcasing the library of liquors within. The staff wore immaculate matte white uniforms of astronautical-grade material, cut to look like extravehicular space activity undersuits.

But all of this finery was overshadowed by the views to the south, east, and west, outside the wall-to-wall windows—the Los Angeles area in all of its expansive glory, from the factories of San Fernando to the downtown Administration Deco skyscrapers of Century City and Los Angeles across the Santa Monica Mountains, bookended by the Pacific Ocean to the right and the San Gabriel Mountains to the left. And throughout it all, the geographic features were overgrown with the vines of the expansive Southern California P-car arterial system, running from here to all the borders of the United States.

Mackey studied some sort of red light projections cast on the windows, that moved and changed by the second. They highlighted particular aircraft and ground vehicles moving through the vast metropolis. He had never seen a projection system like it. He watched as a red ring of light solidified around the Los Angeles Airport, quickly narrowing to a small oval. And, as if caused by the projection and not the other way around, a sub-orbital lifted off from the runway within the oval, quickly accelerating upwards as it made its way out to sea, tracked continuously on the window surface with the light. "Air Mail 6478," the indicator system printed on the glass in large computerized type, "LAX - ICN, ON TIME."

By the time Mackey gathered his wits, he noticed Parsons waving him over to a table near the window, as Ross and Thompson selected chairs. Hopper had disappeared, no doubt to use the secure phone. Mackey fell into the chair next to Thompson, across from Parsons and Ross, and accepted the gin that the waiter brought him at Parsons' request. He sipped the drink, looking around the room.

He knew a number of faces here, having seen their images on the television, let alone governmental circulars. There was Roger Mangrove, Secretary of the Mass Transit Bureau, eating a club sandwich. That man might well have the entire plan for every P-car track on the continent in his briefcase. On the other side of the room, Mackey saw Norbert Partridge and Herman Duncaster laughing over drinks. They were both Assistant Secretaries of the National Airspace Transit Bureau, in head of Investigations Section and Air Traffic Control Section, respectively. The safety of anyone who flew in an aircraft within the United States were in those men's hands, and they both appeared to be several cocktails in. If he had seen Secretary of Transportation Dreyer at the next table eating corn on the cob, Mackey couldn't have been surprised. It was a bit much to take in. Instead, he let his eyes return to the southern view out the window, the shock of being some 1,500 feet off the ground and watching the midday sun glint over the Pacific being somehow easier to comprehend.

"You all right there, Fred?" Parsons tasted his martini, amply. "You seem a bit piqued."

Mackey straightened his glasses. "It is a bit—" He stopped, and started again. "Bureaucracy, to me, has always been something that I've read about in an organizational chart and committed to memory, or dealt with by form or by phone. Even the great days of the Administrations, stories my dad told me from when he was flying with the Postal Bureau, it all seemed somehow…distant. I know the day to day, forms and procedure, paperwork, and process. I guess I had it in my head that all the mythos, all the pomp and circumstance, was just a story for history books."

Thompson and Ross were listening to him, seemingly quite interested in what he had to say, their own drinks in hand— Gene with a gin, and Mary now happy to accept a Manhattan. Mackey sipped his own drink, realizing how his words must sound to someone who had been within a stone's throw of the moon. "I know, I sound foolish. But I've been traveling with the Assistant Secretary since yesterday morning. You know what happened yesterday. And today I'm in the Thermosphere Club having drinks next to the people who make this country run. It is startling to realize that it all really exists, when often it all just seems like a story made up so that there can be news on the radio in the morning."

Thompson nodded. "I never thought I would be here. A man like me, and in the Forest Service besides? Never in a million years."

Ross shook her head. "Don't let the fine china get to you. None of these people could wash a dish if they tried."

Parsons nodded, looking out over Los Angeles. "It's a touch of both, I suppose. It's both real and not real. It's superficial, and deep. You have to accept it as fact, and at the same time forget about it."

He held up his half-empty martini glass, by way of example. "All of this—our homes, our cars, the aircraft and the rockets, our telephones and electricity, and even a delicious orbital steak—we forget that it all comes from somewhere. There's a system behind it. That system is distant, remote, obscured, invisible perhaps. They are the systems behind the systems. We could dig into them, turn over the rocks, and go back through the service door. We just don't bother, because someone else does that for us. We stay comfortable. We focus on the plate, and ignore the kitchen. And thank goodness, because if we had to build every building we ever entered from scratch, produce every garment we ever wore, invent every idea we ever thought, we'd spend our entire existence in an exhausted state of shock.

"And frankly, a lot of it is not that interesting. You may love your P-car sensors, Fred. Just as I could spend all day fooling around with rockets, and I do. But to most people, it isn't important. And there's little reason it should be. We leave each task to the requisite expert, whether it is generating orbital insertions, or preparing a steak. There's just too much reality to take in, and so we have to reduce it to a flat image. But after staring at it for long enough, we forget it's an image. We think the image is reality. We forget how deep reality actually goes."

He finished his glass, and the table attendant set down a fresh one before Parsons had abandoned the glassware to the tablecloth. He flashed Mackey a grin that Mackey would have almost called suggestive, if he had not repressed the thought.

"This is what I mean—Gene, Fred—when I talk about the occult. There's two types of magic," Parsons continued. "There's a certain amount of superficial hocus pocus, which we can feel free to ignore. It's important to some people, but it's all just image. But just because we ignore the stage show doesn't mean that there's not real magic going on behind the scenes."

He picked at the ornate silverware, gestured to the salt shaker, with the Department of Transportation seal engraved into the perforated metal lid. "Behind all the smoke and mirrors, beneath all the ritual and protocol that we can choose to ignore, there is still belief. These stage magicians, these afternoon amateurs from the pervert pantomime society club who nearly cut Gene's throat—they believe. They believe in the ends justifying the means. Just like all the executives in this room."

Parsons spoke as if the famous faces of the dining room only existed in the one-way medium of television, as if they were on the outside of the window, hanging motionless at 1,500 feet, looking in. "The people of this government believe that they are doing the right thing. That, more than any technology, more than any weapon, is the frightening thing. Because when you believe that you are doing the right thing, that everything you have done or will do is in aid of that right thing, you will do just about anything.

"In all the sound and fury of our world, we must choose to ignore certain mechanisms running underneath the technology, to prevent us from losing our minds. But we ignore the wrong ones. Look at these men." He gestured in the direction of the two Assistant Secretaries of the National Airspace Transit Bureau with a forwardness that made Mackey flush. "This is executive territory, top level. And what do you see? No field experience. No one who's worked their way up through fire and blood like Grace. Not a one among them who could navigate a re-entry capsule burn with a pencil and slide rule if they had to, like Mary. These characters just book a one-day orbital station stop so they get the privilege to eat lunch at the top of the building, where everyone has told them they belong."

He leaned closer, poking Mackey's shoulder across the table. "Have you ever wondered why there isn't a single woman serving as a Bureau Secretary in the entire Department of Transportation? You must have. A man like yourself." He let the comment dangle in the air between them, and Mackey avoided eye contact. "The reason is that 'it is the way it has been done.' No one questions, no one speaks about it publicly. But it underlies every decision made in the Department of Transportation, every decision made within the entire Federal Government. And that's only the most obvious outer crust of the belief structure that runs this whole country."

"I've always thought ideology was an incredibly dangerous thing, no matter what ideology it is," offered Thompson. "People make bad decisions when their only method of decision making is to fall back on their core assumptions. They ignore facts, misconstrue a situation, just so it fits with the story they already believe."

Parsons raised his glass a touch, in agreement. "Not only do they misconstrue situations, but sometimes the entire nature of reality. They spend so much time investing in elaborate secrets and parlor tricks to make the story better, they forget they made them all up to begin with."

Mackey saw Hopper emerge from a door set into the artistry of the wall, which sealed behind her silently, revealing not even a hinge or a crack. She made her way towards the table, pausing to speak a few words with a couple of tables on the way. Parsons signaled the attendant, who arrived with a drink for the Assistant Secretary. Now he caught Mackey's eyes directly. "And they say I am a strange one, because I speak the names of my gods aloud. But there are more ancient, more dangerous gods than mine in the Executive Branch."

Hopper took her seat at the head of the table, and Parsons ordered five orbital ribeyes. As interesting as Parsons' proclamations had been, they felt a bit uncomfortably personal to Mackey, somehow. He tried to move the subject further away from anything that could lead back towards himself. "If there were an occult subtext to the work of various government

Bureaus and Services, wouldn't everyone know? Belief, or trick, or ideology—whatever you want to call it—wouldn't it be visible, somehow, on some level? There are millions upon millions of government employees. How could such a thing, if it was that influential, be kept secret?"

Parsons glanced at Hopper for a moment, and then spoke. "Let me tell you a story. Have you heard of the American Miscellaneous Society?"

Mackey shook his head.

Parsons looked at Hopper again, and as if relenting, she dipped her head with a shrug. Parsons continued his tale. "The Miscellaneous Society was a—group. Not an agency or division of any agency, it was best described as an hybrid entity, formed by the Smithsonian Cultural Service, the Land Service, and the Geodetic Service. Not unlike some of our joint research facilities. Like a smaller, undercover Ames, perhaps. But entirely secret. Strictly for what we might call Orthogonal Procedures."

Thompson whispered to Mackey again. "Is that the same as the Parallel Procedures?"

"Yes," he whispered back. "Well, no. It's the same, but even more secret, and more antagonistic to other agencies."

Parsons continued. "The Miscellaneous Society came up with its own secret project, called Project Mohole. The mission was to drill a hole in the ocean floor, straight through the crust of the earth, into the mantle. Why, you might ask? Well, why not? What could go wrong? All in the pursuit of science, of mining, of the technology of deep-sea drilling, of the potential of discovery or further exploiting the continental shelves and the ocean.

"Meanwhile, the Advanced Research Projects Bureau of the Department of Transportation was developing their own ship, also for the purpose of deep-sea drilling—ostensibly. As it turned out, drilling was only a cover story. The real purpose of the ship was called Project Azorian. The mission of Project Azorian was to secretly recover a sunken Russian submarine from the bottom of the Pacific Ocean. As it turned out, roughly the same technology was needed to stabilize a ship for drilling as for lifting a sunken submarine. Rumor has it, Project Azorian was successful—though no one can say exactly what was recovered from the submarine that was so valuable." Parsons took the opportunity to look at Hopper again, but she ignored him, sipping her drink and looking at the view.

He continued. "When the Miscellaneous Society heard the public Project Azorian cover story, they figured ARPB was trying to beat Project Mohole to the mantle. ARPB didn't actually know about Project Mohole, because it was secret. But Miscellaneous figured they had been discovered, and so they tried to sabotage Project Azorian's ship, completely unaware that its drilling mission was itself a cover for a secret mission. When ARPB discovered the sabotage attempt, that led them to *actually* discovering Project Mohole.

"The secret mission of Project Azorian having been achieved, and having the ship stabilization technology required for deep-sea drilling in its possession, ARPB turned over its ship to its internal top-secret Summa Division, who then used it to beat Mohole into the mantle. What had been the cover story became the actual goal. Partly on principle, and partly because they figured that if Miscellaneous was so aggressively defensive of Mohole, there must be something really important down there. And ARPB wouldn't be left in the dust, by the gods!

"Summa got to the mantle a month before Miscellaneous did. But in this race to the mantle, there were growing whispers about two separate, secret Parallel Procedures being conducted, with lots of subterfuge and sabotage instead of any real explanation of why they were even drilling into the earth in the first place. Plenty of questions were asked behind closed doors in the highest levels of the executive branch, and although the scandal never became public, Miscellaneous ended up dissolved in the controversy. Someone had to take the fall, and because Miscellaneous lost the race to the mantle, it was going to be them. In the end, to save everyone a lot of embarrassment and limit the collateral damage, it was all swept under the rug. Everyone forgot what they knew, all the better to hide their potentially embarrassing secrets.

"But even though few know this, even fewer know the real reason that this competition existed to begin with"—Parsons now broke out into his bemused grin—"the real reason why anyone would want to drill into the earth's mantle. In the effort to forget, no one realized that they never even knew what it was they were looking for down there, deep beneath the earth's crust."

Their steaks arrived, and he used the opportunity to create a dramatic pause as they cut into their food. The meat was excellent, and terribly succulent, quite unlike anything that Mackey had ever tasted. He normally avoided red meat at the advice of his doctor, but if he had flavor like this readily available, he could see delicious and unhealthy dining choices filling the rest of his short life. Astronauts, he supposed, had bigger health problems at hand than hardening of the arteries.

But Mackey also wanted to hear the conclusion to Parsons' story. Finally, after the rocket scientist had savored his meal bite by bite, eyes closed, gripping his knife and the edge of the table in an evocative, almost sensual way, his eyelids snapped open, and he continued.

"The drilling"—another brief moment of thoughtful chewing—"was only the means, not the end. The real purpose was the test of another, more secret device. A sort of telescope, for looking *through* the earth."

They sat in silence for a moment, chewing, Parsons the only one at the table smiling, relishing his role as storyteller. Finally Thompson swallowed and spoke. "What do you mean, looking through the earth? Like into space on the other side?"

"No, looking into the earth. Under the ground."

Once more, Mackey was left confused. "How could you use a telescope to look through solid objects?"

Parsons laughed and finished his cocktail. "That's the kicker, isn't it? The trick of the whole thing."

Ross frowned. "Are you saying the Miscellaneous Society invented a way of seeing through solid matter?"

"Not exactly, and no, not them. If they had invented such a thing, they wouldn't have been dissolved. No one knows who built it. No one knows who controlled it. But it could only look into the earth itself, and that is why Project Mohole existed. If it was a matter of seeing through solid walls, you could test that in your bedroom, in a rock quarry, or wherever. This device could only be tested by drilling through the crust of the earth, to see if what they saw was actually down there. Whoever it was that made the telescope, they seeded the idea of Project Mohole to the Miscellaneous Society in secret, setting off a whole chain of events that resulted in two boreholes through the skin of our planet, and one more skirmish between Commerce and Transportation that almost ended in public scandal."

Hopper brushed a single hair off of her forehead and pushed it up underneath her hat. "A form of low-frequency radar, is what you're talking about?"

Parsons deposited his silverware on the plate, shrugging his shoulders. "No idea how it works, I didn't build it. All I know is what I've heard. But how the telescope works and what they were looking for with it isn't the point."

He turned to Mackey. "You see? There is a nesting effect, with secrets. The people doing the drilling, the people planning Project Mohole, the people planning Project Azorian for both its cover story and its real goal, the people who built the ships, the American Miscellaneous Society, Summa Division, the Russians who lost a submarine, the people trying to uncover a scandal, the people trying to brush away the scandal, and whomever it is that built the underground telescope—all of them think they know a secret. They think it is their job to believe this secret and guard its truth. And because their understanding of the secret matches up with what they think their job is, they do believe it. With all their heart.

"But in reality, they only know a little bit of the secret. The don't know the entire story. Maybe no one knows the entire story. And because they all think they know the entire story, they wouldn't believe the actual story even if they heard it. And that, my friend—is how you truly keep a secret."

"If the story is true, and not fiction," said Hopper, focusing on her meal.

Mackey was looking at the tilework on the ceiling, thinking about what Parsons had said.

"What was it they were looking for with the telescope?"

Parsons made eye contact as he answered with a perfectly straight face. "Alien artifacts, lodged in deep geological strata."

Ross snorted into her Manhattan, and Thompson grinned, assuming it was a joke, though Parsons looked quite serious. Hopper laughed out loud, throwing her head back as she did, attracting a number of eyes from around the dining room.

Parsons merely shrugged. "I merely tell the story as it was told to me. You can believe it or not. The privilege of the human mind is to believe we know the difference between reality and the opposite." He winked at Mackey, coyly. "Well! I would certainly have a"—he tried counting on his fingers, but gave up—"one more drink, but I am flying. What say we hop over the mountains and see what's cooking at the Skunk Works today?"

Waiting for the elevator to arrive, Hopper adjusted her hat ever so slightly, even though it seemed to Mackey that throughout the entire day he hadn't once seen it out of place. Like the briefcase that had been with her constantly without fail, across thousands of miles, except for the brief hiatus in the Sierras. Thompson and Ross were listening to Parsons explain an anecdote about a 16th century English historical figure, by way of part of the patterns on the wall decorations.

Perhaps it was the gin, in far more quantity than Mackey ever imbibed at this hour of the day, that made him willing to hazard a question while the others were engaged by Parsons' tale. "Assistant Secretary Hopper," he began, realizing immediately how awkward it was that he was still addressing her by title, but without any other recourse he proceeded, "I…how should I take all of this? Are there secret occult and metaphysical practices going on? I don't mean to ask about classified information, if that is in fact what it is. But is he"—he nodded his head towards Parsons, still gesturing at the wall, deep in his story—"just pulling our legs? Is it a gag, or is he serious?"

Hopper looked in Parsons' direction. "Well, he's certainly not joking, from his perspective." She turned to face Mackey directly. "I told you before you would be hearing some secret information, a sort of information that was outside the scope of paperwork and procedure. But just because information is secret does not necessarily make it trustworthy. In my business, there are rumors, there are lies, there is misdirection, and there are as many false flags as legitimate banners. What I need you to do, as my assistant in this matter, is to trust your logic and intuition, and apply them to whatever we uncover. You are an engineer—only removed from your laboratory of electromagnetic radiation, and placed into this wider lab of ideas and information. Can you do that?"

When she put it that way, it didn't seem nearly as confusing. Providing executive clarity, Mackey supposed, was the Assistant Secretary's job. "Yes, I believe I can."

She nodded once. "It all does seem a little much at first, I know. And you've already had to witness terrible things, even as we've only just begun. There were times, back in the early days, when—" She shook her head slightly as she paused, then dropped it. "Always remember: focus on our goal. We protect our projects, our Department, our technological progress, and our country. That is what our jobs are about, regardless of what Orthogonal Procedures anyone deploys, and what metaphysical shibboleths someone invents to wrap them and obscure them."

He nodded, even as he recalled what Parsons had said about the efficacy of "the ends and the means" only fifteen minutes earlier in the dining room.

Hopper smiled and gave him a forceful slap on the shoulder.

The elevator door opened, and the group entered together. In another fifteen minutes, they were back in the Vail-22. Mackey took his seat, a bit relieved that there had been no further orders for drinks. Once cleared by the Bureau Tower ATC, Parsons throttled back, and the vehicle lifted up and back from the landing platform. Banking slightly, Parsons angled the nacelles, and moved them forward, heading off due east towards the Verdugo Mountains and the larger San Gabriel Mountains beyond.

They flew in silence for a bit, crossing the busy airspace of the valley, over the tracks and factories below, a small white dot trailing them, sneaking back and forth to alter its position, disguising itself as a trick of the light, a bird, or a fragment of cloud. Parsons and Ross had some sort of brief discussion about course selection. Hopper and Thompson were both looking out the window at the ground below.

Mackey was also distracted by the view as they crossed Northridge, shadowing the freight line. A great train, hundreds of cars long, the size of a small city itself, was heading east. He watched as the containers blinked underneath the track overpasses, cutting up the region into loops and ribbons. Each of those shipping containers was as large as Mackey's apartment, filled with unknown technological materials.

The Vail-22 passed over the thirty-plus track bands of the West Coast Arterial, which trailed up from Mexico, north all the way to Canada. The small lumps of P-cars along it looked like tiny bubbles, carried along a strangely bifurcated mountain stream, rushing in two directions at the same time. They flew over Hansen Dam, a mile-long curved concrete bastion protecting the industry in the valley from the raging winter floodwaters that would occasionally rush down the steppes of the San Gabriels. Then up the dry Tujunga Creek bed through Sunland, gaining altitude to cross the mountains. Below the Vail-22, the looped tracks of housing developments finally gave way to National Forest, dry sparse pines above dry chaparral brush in the valleys and worn crevices.

Mackey thought about this landscape as the baseline, the blank canvas. As if it was what was underneath everything else built on top of it. This wasn't actually true, though. The city, all the technology, dug down so deep into the earth that nothing could live underneath it.

Tell your Congressmen to defeat the unfair, Administrationist proposal of HR-17849!

Our rail lines are a fundamental, basic part of American society. But the partisan Administrationists are stuck in the past, letting their bureaucratic quagmire ruin the pride of American technology.

Private industry could keep us competitive on the world stage, by introducing innovative new means of passenger travel. Increasing efficiency, lowering prices, and increasing consumer choice is what America is all about.

But lifelong bureaucrats stuck in the post-War years are blocking any attempt at private innovation. "That's not the way we do things," they say. They want to keep total control of America's rails to themselves.

HR-17849 would create expensive hurdles for private use of transnational rail lines, creating a de facto government monopoly on passenger travel, and increasing costs for every American.

Call or write your Congressmen today, and tell them that Freedom, Openness, Competitiveness, and Innovation are our core values—not Technocracy and Conservativism.

Tell them to vote no on HR-17849, and send these bureaucrats back to their paperwork, and out of our citizens' lives.

7
Among Other Skirmishes

Descending out of the San Gabriel Mountains, the Vail-22 came in low over the desert city of Palmdale. Dropping through the foothills, the terrain made a stark transition from hillside to flat desert basin, as they crossed over the literal seam in the earth of the San Andreas fault. Almost simultaneously, the aircraft crossed over the less-natural seam of the California Aqueduct, the newly-finished gigantic water distribution project feeding the industrial metropolis of San Fernando and Los Angeles with snow melt from Northern California, shipped by pumps and gravity over 400 miles south. Enough water flowed through the nearly linear course of the concrete-banked trench to qualify it as California's third largest river.

Then, buzzing over the separated residential blocks of Palmdale—most of whose denizens were somehow linked to the plant operations—the Vail crossed State Arterial 14 and entered the airport zone of Postal Bureau Plant 42. The buildings were large, rectangular, with curved roofs in the case of the expansive aircraft hangars, overall very utilitarian. There was little to show off here. At least, from the outside. The inside of these buildings were where the power of Plant 42 lay.

After communicating with the tower and giving the proper executive transport code, Parsons set them down in front of one of the large hangar buildings that Ross pointed out to him.

Mackey knew that Plant 42 contained some of the more secretive Postal Bureau research projects, including the home of the Skunk Works special aviation Section. Here on the edge of the Mojave desert there was limited population other than the plant personnel, which made tests of high-performance aircraft with their frequent sonic booms much easier than in the crowded airspace around the San Fernando Valley. Also, the rural area made security easier as well. Mackey had noted the triple-fence line, topped with barbed wire, below them as they had flown into the complex.

The air was hot as they exited the Vail, dry and dusty, smelling of some sort of desert plant that Mackey couldn't identify, with just the smallest hint of jet fuel. He coughed involuntarily at the dust and lack of humidity. Mackey saw Thompson take a deep breath, drawing the desert air into his lungs. "Refreshing, is it?" he asked the ranger.

"Fantastic! None of the haze of the city. If you ignore the traces of fuel, of course. Sometime, Fred, I should take you out for a better mountain experience than the one on which we met. You're an athletic fellow, I bet you'd love it. Picture it, nothing but a backpack on your back. No P-cars, no strange aircraft, nothing but you and the landscape."

"And the occasional bear," Mackey said. But in truth, the idea had appeal.

They entered the laboratory of Mary Ross, inside one of the many white-arched concrete rectangles, indistinguishable from the other buildings and hangars in the complex. The laboratory room, like the building, like Plant 42 itself, was large beyond most easy comparisons. Certainly the space was big enough that Ross could not utilize the entirety by herself. She must have assistants, secondaries, and collaborators of all kinds sitting at the various tables, running the machinery. T

here was no one here now, and the room was silent, though nevertheless full. Banks of large computers ringed the edges of the space. Scattered throughout were benches covered with disassembled machinery and equipment. Test equipment and tools, of course. But also pieces of aircraft, some large enough to be suspended on wheeled racks, disassembled with dangling wires and exposed hydraulic connections. There were the de-shrouded electronics of what might have been weapons, some large enough to be vehicle mounted, others small enough to be concealed in the hand, and yet others too obscure or deconstructed to be identified specifically. And there were small round canisters—that might have been satellites, except for the fact that Mackey knew satellites were prepared in the facilities' giant clean rooms, away from dust, dirt, and the other hazards that a crowded lab might offer.

The lab was quite cluttered, to a point that would certainly not have passed muster with Mackey's supervisors in the Electromagnetic Bureau. Ross seemed like a very logical, orderly person, and Mackey was a bit surprised at the state of affairs. The lab seemed to be for an odd purpose. It felt as if experimentation and assembly were not the goals here—but vivisection. It was like these technological devices were being searched through, their anatomy riven apart by searching fingers of technicians and scientists, left to fall aside like leaf litter, like fat trimmed from a butchered animal. It was as if they were looking for something within these devices, and unable to find it, had moved on, ceding the carrion to what scavengers might be interested next, and then on to worms, insects, and finally rot itself, a putrefaction of semiconductors, down at the bottom of the chain of technological life. The walls of the room that were not blocked by computer cabinets were covered in blackboards scrawled with obscure symbols which lended to the air of mystery in the lab—but thankfully these were the sort of mathematics symbols that Mackey could recognize.

Ross and Parsons got to work on preparing the data for her computer programs. Meanwhile, Hopper disappeared for another set of phone calls, leaving Mackey and Thompson nothing to do but sit at the large table, which after having cleared it of the disassembled pieces of a portable satellite radio receiver dome, they faced each other across the smooth expanse and chatted.

"So what is your favorite mountain, or range of mountains?" Mackey asked. "That is, where is your favorite place to go?"

Thompson smiled, clearly visualizing the place in his mind. "There is this valley, a sort of steppe. Above it are hills capped with snow, and below there is a small river flowing from a lake.

When you are in this place, you can see it all, no matter where you are. From the grassy fields you can see up to the mountain, and from the mountaintop you can see down into the valley. It is self-contained, a basin, and it feels like a small house, even though it is miles and miles. From the bookcase you can see the stove, and from the stove you can see the bedroom, and from the bedroom, the bookcase again. It feels like home."

"How do you get there? No P-car tracks, I suppose."

"Oh, no. By jeep, or some other Army or farm vehicle. Internal combustion engine, roaring like a wild thing, over the dusty land."

Mackey thought about what that must sound like, rushing in an open-topped vehicle over the bare land, the engine compartment containing an indistinguishable series of explosions. He'd never been in an internal combustion-powered vehicle. He'd been off-track in any number of vehicles with rubberized wheels and manual steering, naturally. And it was easy enough to see farm vehicles when riding a P-car through an agricultural area. But you couldn't hear them, to know if they ran on fuel or electricity. Mackey could only remember hearing the sound of a fuel-burning engine in films.

"I'm a child of the city," Mackey admitted. "Cars, computers, and federal campuses."

"A lot of computers in here," Thompson mused. "Among everything . . . else. Do you know much about computers?"

"A little bit," Mackey said. "I run programs sometimes, simulations of various physics things."

"I'm in awe of that sort of thing, but I can't say I envy you." Thompson shook his head. "All that time with your thoughts inside a box. Thinking about things with no space, no surface. Just ideas, folded up and flowing through circuits."

Mackey shrugged. "That's kind of engineering in general. You can look at the pieces in your hand, but there's always more going on than you can see. There's a lot to keep inside your head. The physics of electricity, electromagnetic waves, the properties of various materials, chemical interactions. All that stuff exists in a different realm, but you have to try and keep it in mind somehow."

"I try to keep it tangible. Even out in the woods, everything has signs. You want to look for animals, you follow the signs. You want to know about what is happening under the surface of the soil, you look at the plants. They always show some kind of sign."

"Technology shows signs, too. Did you know you can hear how complicated a P-car route is by the number of clicks inside the navigational console? Those clicks are the sound of the card reader verifying the location. When you drop the car in the slot, the P-car moves immediately, but the navigation takes a few minutes to decide the route, depending on the atlas data. Every time it makes an alteration to its journeying script during the decision process, it rechecks the destination. If the console clicks only a few times, the route is simple. If it clicks for a few minutes, there are many more track changes."

Thompson smiled. "I didn't know that."

"If you want to hear some out-of-this-world computational noise," Parsons spoke up, "wait until you hear this routine of Mary's running through the feeder. She's thrown in everything but the kitchen sink."

Attaching a magnetic reel to a machine, Ross merely said, "You use quick and dirty code, you get quick and dirty orbits. In ballistics, some try to get results by using a bigger hammer. I could drive in a nail with a needle, as long as I could get it moving fast enough."

Mackey and Thompson were quickly recruited into helping. Collating cards was easy enough, making sure the data was in the proper order and nothing was misplaced. Then, Mackey sat at a coding console while Thompson read to him from a page of notes Ross jotted down, altering a pre-written stretch of code. After Mackey got used to the syntax, it wasn't so difficult, and a few test runs cleared up his minimal errors.

After they had worked on their code for a couple of hours, Hopper returned, just as they were about to begin the program. "It should only take a minute to run and print, once we get it going," Ross reported.

Indeed, after just a minute of clattering from the feeders, whirs from the tape drives, and rapid grating from the printer, the files were spread over the table in front of Ross, where she studied them, alongside her code diagrams.

"Here's what I can tell you, Assistant Secretary. As Dr. Parsons' somewhat rudimentary program showed," she gave him a look, "the so-called birth charts all appear to be indicating places and times in low earth orbit, using celestial navigation. All times over the last six to nine months, and the associated dossier images appear to match the locations—in other words, it seems that they are photos taken looking straight down at the earth from the points given. Our working theory appears correct, and these charts contain places and times to be photographed from orbit.

"From these locations, I've managed to regress a number of likely orbits for what we would assume to be the satellite or satellites taking the photographs. If we assume that there are few orbital maneuvers made between each image—that is, the orbits are constant—we can identify four separate Crystal NRS satellites.

"Now, here is where things get interesting." She flipped the pages, displaying a second set of charts.

"Each dossier contains two birth charts. Jack ran the charts on the first pages of the dossiers at Ames, and those refer to the time and place within the last six months. The second charts from the second pages, however, are different. From these, we learn three notable things. First, all the dates are in the future. Second, they don't regress to any of the identified orbits of the Crystals. Third, and this is the kicker: they are all set for the same time, about twenty-six hours from now."

She paused for that to sink in. "What exact time?" Hopper asked.

Ross showed her on the printout. "All within a five-minute window."

"How many orbits do the future dates utilize?" Parsons asked.

Ross showed an expression of curiosity. "This is the problem: it would have to be as many orbits as there are locations. Each chart indicates the location of a satellite. For the first set, the locations are at different times. So, a satellite could appear in one place and time, and then after orbiting the earth, appear at a different place and time. But for the second set, all locations are at the same time. So two different locations, indicated at the same time, would require two different satellites. There's twelve files here, all showing different locations, so that would require twelve Crystals."

"What if the navigational information isn't for Crystals, but some other type of satellite, in some other orbit?" Hopper asked.

The engineer considered it, flipping her pencil between her fingers. "It could be that they are using the position of a hypothetical Crystal satellite to denote a place on earth that would be photographed by a satellite in such a place, looking straight down. The Crystal, from what we think we know, pretty much takes a image perpendicular to the earth. So any particular position of the Crystal would relate to a particular place on earth below. A single geostationary satellite, in a much higher orbit than the Crystals, could look down on most of the hemisphere at once and see all the places below where a Crystal might have photographed—like standing behind a group of photographers spread out across a room and taking a single photo of all the photographers, as well as all of their subjects. But such a high orbit is too far off for decent photos of any ground structure, using current lens and sensor technology. And it seems like a very awkward method to position satellites by using the hypothetical position of other satellites."

"What about the fact of the charts?" Mackey asked. "Does this odd format tell us anything?"

Ross nodded, leaning back in her chair. "I'm tempted to agree with Dr. Parsons' ideas about the occult reference. Typically, celestial navigation is just written in sets of numbers, altitude and declination, with other information if necessary. The fact that the information is presented in such an odd way would seem to be indicative of something, and the Census Service's passing interest in astrology can't be ignored."

"Census would be the likely origin for any plan of widespread, location-based surveillance," Hopper agreed. "These locations are across the entire country, and Census has the most up-to-date location information of any agency outside of the Postal Bureau."

"I'm sorry, I don't know if it is my place to ask questions here," Thompson spoke up, "but even if we accept some sort of metaphorical purpose for astrology within the agency ideology of the Census Service, what could that really tell us about these satellites?"

Parsons opened his mouth, but before he could speak, Ross answered. "Since we seem to be laying our cards on the table here, and we are now in a secure location, I can perhaps speak to that. A relation to occult and metaphysical beliefs is not just a habit or arcane agency cultural practice. It has long been a signature of classified Federal Government activities, particular of Orthogonal Procedures. This is a tradition that goes all the way back to Operation Paperclip, prior to World War Two."

She continued, brushing her dark hair back over her ears. "Postmaster Roosevelt was aware of the inevitability of war in Europe as early as 1935. In addition to preparing highly advanced technological weapons and planning with France and England for Germany's eventual aggression, the Postal Administration began recruiting scientists from Europe, especially Germany. Agents went to these scientists and clued them in to Roosevelt's suspicions about the coming war, and offered them lucrative jobs with the Administrations if they emigrated beforehand and pursued their research in America. This plan, not exactly secret, but never public in its widespread orchestration, was called Operation Paperclip.

"The influx of scientific talent would change the course of history for this country. But along with it came other cultural influences. It was an exciting time to be a scientist or an engineer. New immigrants, whose names we had only heard of in research papers or headlines, were now setting up labs just down the hall. There was a feeling that anything was possible. And there was a sense that everything was necessary. We were never told specifically, but everyone knew that Roosevelt wanted us on a war footing. He knew we were headed towards the most techno-logically advanced conflict the world had seen up to that point in history. In this mix of languages, cultures, and histories, there was a sense that nothing was out of bounds. Everything was available, and if you had a big idea, no matter how outlandish, there would be someone else who would work with you. It was this culture that brought us the atomic bomb.

"In addition to the difficult ethical issues surrounding that particular weapon, there were other trends among the technological milieu that were not agreeable to all scientists. Eugenics had a fairly wide following, before it became scientifically discredited and linked to the Nazis. And the occult was also in play. I could tell you a story or two about the negative consequences of some of the numerological theories at the National Standards Service. There were rumors of hunts for particular legendary artifacts, which ate up enormous amounts of funding as well as supported some very nationalist ideas. Some of the National Airspace Transit Bureau's projects involving 'cloud spirits' seem like a big waste of time to me, even if not ethically suspect. And the Indian Affairs Service's ongoing appropriation of Native shaman practices is just"—she shook her head, eyes closed—"repugnant."

"It became a foundation," Parsons said to Thompson. "A way of establishing the appropriate scope of research, with an unspoken notion that all was available, and all was required. It was a way of justifying superlative efforts, and ignoring potential consequences."

"I don't know if I would call it an establishment," Ross countered. "All of my tools and theories go back to mathematics principles. The work being done was always with science in mind. That is the establishment of Technocracy. The occult is more like a nostalgic dream. Something for people to return to, something comforting, reminding them of the 'old, wild days,' now lost to bureaucratic history, and built over with Departmental structure. It's what anthropologists might call a myth, or a legend."

"So," Hopper interjected, "when a government agency is pursuing something big, something they feel necessary to their survival, it is not out of character for them to employ occult terms or ideas. They embody the importance of secret knowledge, and underlie the life-or-death nature of the conflict, in their point of view.

"And speaking of points of view," she continued, "Mr. Mackey, why don't you share who you saw during our adventure in the Sierras. There is a very direct tie-in to this conversation, I believe."

The group turned towards him, and he flushed just a bit, straightening his glasses. "I saw Nicholas Roerich, watching the sacrifice. And then he disappeared."

"Roerich, Roerich—how do I know that name?" Parsons rubbed his chin.

"He created the Megatherium Club, with Henry Wallace," Hopper answered.

"Or, reactivated—some say," Ross added.

"What's the Megatherium Club?" asked Thompson, tentatively.

"Henry Wallace became Secretary of Commerce in 1940, after President Landon was re-elected," Mackey said, "just as the war was kicking off. He had previously been Secretary of the Agricultural Service, but was promoted after the election. Many say Landon did this to counter the influence of Roosevelt, who was gaining a lot of power after successfully predicting the outbreak of war. The feud between Wallace and Roosevelt that resulted is legendary, of course. But it wasn't until 1944 that Wallace's friend Roerich, a Russian of odd character, joined the Commerce Department."

Hopper nodded. "That's right. Wallace, for his part, thought that the issue between Roosevelt and Landon was simply a matter of executive politics, and played it as such. When he finally learned about Operation Paperclip, sometime in 1943, he was furious. He took it as a direct affront that Roosevelt would be corralling the best scientific and technological talents in the world, and using them to further his own political power.

"So when he pulled his old confidant Roerich into Commerce, the direct aim of the Megatherium Club was to counteract the recruiting of Paperclip. Paperclip sought to poach talent not just from the Nazis, but from the URER, and from other agencies of the government as well. Megatherium was a secret society of sorts, looking to do the same thing, only even more secretly. It was the first Orthogonal Procedure, we might say. Roerich was the primary architect of Megatherium, and he was leading it when the feud truly reached its heights in 1944."

Mackey spoke up. "I knew about Roerich, but I've never heard about the Megatherium Club. I suppose it makes sense that Commerce would want to counter the influence of Roosevelt by nearly any means possible. But Roosevelt died in 1945. Truman became Postmaster, on much closer terms with Commerce than Roosevelt was, and so the feud ended. Wallace continued to serve as Secretary until he departed under a scandal about some of his religious beliefs in 1952. Eisenhower, just elected, replaced him with Sinclair Weeks."

"You see there," Parsons exclaimed, "it wasn't just 'religious beliefs.' Wallace was as much of an occultnik as any of them, he just let it slip. That's why he had to go."

Mackey shrugged, unsure of the full story and perhaps willing to concede the point, but continuing at any rate. "Roerich stayed on board at Commerce, but retreated from the limelight. Technically, his title has remained the same—Director of Bureaucratic Security. But he hasn't been seen in years. And if in fact it was him that I saw, he would be very old. He ought to be ninety-six by now."

"Well," asked Thompson, suddenly quite focused. "Did you see him? Can you be sure?"

"I would have sworn it was him. I've seen his photograph many times. And he did look old, indeed. His face was aged, his skin was dry and wrinkled. But his body looked younger, as if he moved with no problems of a man that old. It was getting dark by that point. I only saw him by the light of the flames." Mackey looked at the table, feeling sorry that he didn't get a better look at the man, or better yet give chase.

"That's quite all right, Mr. Mackey, you did just fine." Hopper pulled one of the files on the table towards her and glanced at it idly before continuing. "The presence of Roerich, or even just the potential presence, introduces a new theory of this conspiracy we are investigating. Thus far, we've only been considering the Department of Commerce and its various agencies as antagonists. But this activity might be more global in scope, involving the Russians, and the Anti-War."

Thompson shook his head, throwing his arms up in the air. "The occult, Megatheriums, Anti-Wars? What have I gotten myself into?"

Mackey felt bad for the man. He didn't understand much of what was happening, but he felt at least a few steps ahead of Thompson. And yet, once again, he too didn't know what Hopper was talking about.

"The Anti-War," Hopper explained, "is not a war exactly, but the unofficial name for the recent period of increasing tensions between the URER and the United States."

"Space combat," Mackey said aloud, suddenly fitting a piece of the puzzle together.

"Among other skirmishes." She nodded. "Mostly conducted through proxies, downplayed, or described as accidents. The term is being used to distinguish the evolving status of hostilities, out of the realm of electronic conflict.

"Since the end of major hostilities in World War Two, the public has come to view electronic conflict as an essentially 'victimless' form of economic power that can be used to promote the United States' interests abroad. The atomic bomb was one weapon developed during the war, electronic conflict was another. By comparison to the horror unleashed on Berlin, it appears civil and restrained.

"Electronic conflict, conducted directly or by various proxies, often ends up public—take the currently escalating situation in Southeast Asia, for example. This means of warfare doesn't create much of a scandal, so it is deemed vastly preferable to open war. So the Postal Bureau is allowed to conduct jamming, cable cutting, and other forms of informational sabotage as they see fit. Elected officials and if necessary the UN will occasionally intercede, when it seems as if any particular hotspot might lead to physical blows. Until then, undersea cables are cut, hijacked, reclaimed, hardened, and replaced. Interference and jamming are used in electromagnetic space with increasing regularity, to claim particular parts of the spectrum in certain geographies, and to drive others off of it. Navigation beacons, aeronautical instruments, and other necessities of mail and electronic mail routes are defended against tampering and intrusion, as well as assaulted if they are thought to be vulnerable. It's all part of protecting the Postal Bureau's ability to conduct communications activities around the globe, in order to maintain the premier status of American technology, for the nation's greater interest. The Great Electronic Game, if you will.

"In the newfound domain of outer space, it was thought that this hard-won status quo of electromagnetic skirmishes would simply continue. However, the United States and other countries, namely the URER, have begun butting heads in orbital space with increasing frequency. The UN currently has no jurisdiction outside of the atmosphere. As the United States and the URER are supposedly allies, there has been little political will to make the conflict public, which might necessitate some sort of political negotiation or UN resolution on outer space, which in turn might result in either side having to withdraw their current claims. So, as each side tries to get the upper hand, tensions are increasing. Ever since Sputnik, space has been a battleground. The political, economic, and technological effects of surface or atmospheric conflict would be catastrophic on both countries, and so neither side has brought the fight back down to earth. But casualties in space are mounting, now including not just bandwidth, but physical satellite hardware, and on occasion, human beings."

"Anti-War is kind of an odd term for it, if people are dying," Ross said, morosely.

Hopper shrugged. "Unlike some of the other nomenclatures we have, I don't think it was chosen deliberately. It was simply the vernacular term for what wasn't being discussed, for what could never be a war, because war would mean Congress and the President were involved, and the conflict was public. It was a means to describe a Technocratic, Departmental strategy for orbital power projection that would and could not become a war. And then the name stuck."

"But what does Roerich have to do with Anti-War?" Mackey asked.

"There are a number of connections." Hopper leaned back in her chair and let her eyes focus on the ceiling while she thought. "First—Roerich has never been a major figure in the feud between Commerce and the Administrations, although he joined Commerce during the height of the feud. He worked for Wallace, *not* for Commerce. When Wallace left and Roerich stayed, he never showed any vindictive behavior towards the Administrations, or Transportation. He has never led any sort of Orthogonal Procedures against us since then that we've been able to discover. To put it another way, he plays defense, not offense. Therefore, his motivations have always been assumed to be somehow—larger."

Parsons began nodding his head vigorously, and opened his mouth to speak, but Hopper continued.

"Second—although we can't say with any assurance what Roerich's motives are, we do know they lean towards the..." Hopper paused, looking at Parsons as if mentally searching for a better word, but finding none, continued, "occult. He has some peculiar notions about the role of human spirituality. He has odd affinities for particular works of culture—art, music, architecture, and the like—and spends a lot of time in the Smithsonian archives and the Library of Congress. Doing what, we can't say. This is not a direct connection to any of the occult activities we have seen in the last couple days. But, we would be wise to remain open to the idea that things are, as Dr. Parsons might say, 'not always what they seem.'

"Third—if this is not strictly a matter of Department of Commerce Orthogonal Procedures, then one must at least consider the possibility of the Russians. They are the most likely belligerent force to move against Transportation, after Commerce. And while Commerce seems certainly involved, if we are talking about space as a likely venue for some sort of new weapon or surveillance platform, we would be seriously remiss to not at least consider the URER.

"And fourth—Roerich is Russian. While he has been predominantly based in the United States since the late 1930s, it is known that he has many ties back in the URER. These are ties that don't necessarily take the form of family or business. The full extent of these ties is unknown. This has never been a problem in the past. But—and I must stress we do not know anything for sure—it is possible that if there was a continued increase in antagonism between the URER and the United States, Roerich's loyalty to our government might be in question."

"So you're saying," Mackey's mind was reorganizing in light of this new idea, "that this might not be about Commerce moving against Transportation at all, but Roerich using Commerce in a way to make the United States vulnerable to the URER."

"That is a possibility we'll have to consider," Hopper concluded.

Ross arranged her printouts and notes in front of her on the table. "So, Roerich is a player. Satellites have been photographing mid-level members of the Technocratic establishment. And there is likely to be some sort of satellite action happening in the next twenty-six hours, but we don't know what kind, or why. And, the URER is aggressive in space." She turned to Hopper. "What is the next step, Assistant Secretary?"

Hopper folded her hands in front of her. "We absolutely need a better idea of what is happening in order to take action. Until we know the exact nature of the threat, I need you all to stay with me—you are the only ones with knowledge of the situation and your skills may come in handy."

"So, we're a team then." Parsons nudged Ross. "Just like in the old Mojave days with the strategic weapons section, eh Mary?" She smiled, then turned her attention back to Hopper.

"There's someone in DC we need to consult with," Hopper continued. "What is the fastest aircraft currently available here at Plant 42?"

"This consultant, who is he?" Mackey asked.

"Or she?" Ross corrected.

"Actually, it's an 'it.' I'll explain when we arrive." Hopper stood up, and the rest followed suit. "How about that aircraft?"

Ross considered the question. "We have a trial ballistic transport, but it isn't ready to launch, and would take at least four hours to prep. I think the Skunk Works' PE-70 Valkyrie is the fastest thing ready to fly, if you can cut through the supersonic red tape."

"Easily done. Also, given there has already been one serious attempt on our lives, I'm arming our small, impromptu group. Ms. Ross, if you would be so kind as to direct everyone to the Weapons Prototype Section, I will meet you there after arranging for the Valkyrie." And with that, Hopper gathered up her paperwork along with her ever-present briefcase, and was out of the lab.

Ross looked over the rest of them. "Well, I suppose we had better hurry, as I can't imagine she'll take long."

They followed Ross on a winding course through the Plant 42 facility. Parsons walked alongside Ross, cutting an odd twosome between his tweed jacket and her flight jacket and combat boots. They were reminiscing, catching up about names and places all unfamiliar to Mackey.

Mackey and Thompson brought up the rear, while Mackey explained a few points of federal history to the Forest Service ranger. Thompson, for his part, was very attentive, listening and nodding, looking Mackey closely in the eyes while he spoke, no matter how strange or convoluted the things Mackey said were.

Mackey was having a difficult time focusing on his own words, given the labs and test areas they were passing through. It seemed that aeronautics research was not all that was happening at Plant 42. Or at least, the aeronautics research was taking some fairly uncommon forms.

Through thick glass windows that opened onto their passageway, they looked out into an open hangar space, where a central metal tower was creating some sort of swirling cloud around it. It was not smoke, but looked much thicker and blacker than fog. Lightning flashes lit up the hangar with strobes of bright blue light, causing the four to have to look down at their feet as they walked, averting their eyes from the glare. The thunder rolled through the walls and glass like a deep growling, coupled with another low moaning sound, which Mackey hoped was not the metal beams of the building being torn from their rivets.

Moving at a decent pace, they departed that strange internal storm through a set of large doors, and were outside, crossing a tarmac in the late afternoon desert heat towards another similarly giant building. In the space between the edifices, centered within a large circular pad of concrete, a massive sculpture of polished chrome spheres stood, hoisted up upon cantilevered frames, slowly orbiting each other, reflecting the red sunlight. Or at least Mackey assumed it was a sculpture. On the surface of the ground, set into the concrete, were wide metal rings surrounding the sculpture in nine giant arcs.

Mackey wished that he had time to contemplate it, or ask Ross and Parsons what it meant. Even the smallest bits of decoration and the most minor artistic motifs of any Department of Transportation facility were beginning to seem relevant. His curiosity was running at high gear on all this information. He wanted to learn everything, to know as much as he could, and get the widest picture of this world. Mackey was now aware of how much he didn't know, but there were clues to this hidden information all around. The awareness of new, secret knowledge was like alcohol—it made his mind run faster, insatiable for substance to consume, if more recklessly.

In the next building, they trooped down a passageway alongside a howling wind tunnel visible through thick test glass, the river of air screaming like a banshee. They could see a small ellipsoid profile suspended in the raging torrent, forged out of what appeared to be a chromed alloy. The silver egg had small arcing stabilizers on the rear end, and as they pushed in and out of the curved surface it maneuvered back and forth in the rush of wind, wobbling spastically, then suddenly holding precise and steady. As it caught this envelope of stability, a haunting hum began to shake through the building and into their feet. Then suddenly it returned to wobbling and the strange vibration ceased.

Next, they passed through another large open hanga, containing a miniature rocket test stand that drew Parsons' attention at a run before Ross pulled him back by his elbow. He began speaking quickly to her about some sort of booster project, about the tenacity of pressure gradients within micro-jets, or guided rocket nozzles, or something Mackey could not follow.

On the far end was stacked some sort of folding scaffold of vast geometric shapes that caught Mackey and Thompson's attention. Contorted and angled pipes were collapsed in upon themselves, like the joints of an expanding flower coming out of bud. Currently shut down and compacted, the folded arms of the construction obscured whatever technological purpose such a bizarre tangle of metal might hold. An antenna fixture? An expandable space station module? An aerodynamically evolved windmill? Quiet, it sat abandoned in the hangar like the plaything of some gigantic child. That child, now asleep, was no doubt off somewhere, dreaming of new games to play with its marvelous toy sets, as soon as the next day's sunrise arrived.

They arrived at the Weapons Prototype Section at exactly the same time as Hopper. The Assistant Secretary's small departures and arrivals were odd, one more thing that Mackey had yet to understand. The guard allowed them to enter after Hopper showed her pass, although he eyed Thompson's Forest Service coat warily.

Hopper brought them through as if she was familiar with the facility. It consisted of metal racks and shelving extending from floor to ceiling, filled to capacity with metal crates, ammunition boxes, and wooden packing containers stenciled with complex series of paint-encrusted designations. Looking down the rows between the shelves, Mackey could not see the end. Nor any way of sorting this material. It felt mundane, like these containers could house dry biscuits. But it also felt deadly, as if a thermo-nuclear weapon could easily be misfiled within any of these identical shelves.

"Please point me in the direction of the explosives," Parsons said, rubbing his hands together.

"Only what you can carry discreetly on your person," Hopper cautioned. "I'm not carrying a bag full of bombs for you." She wrote out for Parsons a series of designation numbers, and list in hand, began searching the various bin and aisle numbers looking for something dangerous.

Ross went to a nearby cabinet she seemed familiar with, and from one of its gaping mouths produced a second sub-machine gun like the one she carried under her flight jacket. Opening some hand-labeled ammo boxes, she began filling magazines with odd-looking ammunition. "All of my own design," she explained.

Hopper brought Thompson and Mackey over to a smaller bin. "I—don't have much familiarity with weapons," Mackey stammered, suddenly nervous.

"Not a problem," Hopper said, handing each of them a small handgun produced from the padded storage bin. "This is a dazzle pistol. Lasers set for temporary blindness, about three minutes full recovery for most individuals. Aim generally towards the head—and try not to shoot any of us."

She produced a small metal box, six inches long, three inches wide and a half-inch high, attached to a short rod, with a folding metal stock. Underneath was a rudimentary trigger. It looked like a steel mouse trap attached to umbrella handle—not any sort of combat equipment. "This is a electro-blast gun. Ought to wipe any mercury memory, magnetic tape, disk, rope, or charged memory circuit within ten feet of range. Won't do a thing to humans, at least as far as we know. But be careful—it fires in both directions, forward and reverse, due to the radiator's properties. So don't fire it with your back to any data or computer you particularly like."

She handed them each a shoulder holster that comfortably concealed the dazzle pistol and the electro-blast beneath their suit jackets. The leather holster was stamped "Data Enforcement Section," a nonexistent Bureaucratic Level in any Bureau or Service Mackey was familiar with. That was odd, but regardless, Mackey did feel a bit better knowing he wasn't going to be carrying firearms. And yet, no matter how well concealed the weapons were, he felt heavy, encumbered.

For her part, Hopper opened a small, thin crate, and from a bed of packing hay produced a thin metal walking stick with a bulbous black metal knob for a handle. On the knob was a cut design of three lines at equal angles from each other, passing into a circle, and intersecting a single line.

"Is that a transistor symbol?" Mackey asked.

Hopper nodded. "I call it a transistor staff. My own design."

"What does it do?" asked Thompson.

"No time for that now. Hopefully I won't need it." She waved to Ross and Parsons, who made their final selections and came over.

"I would have hoped for more Semtex throwing bars, but I am pleased to see they have some of my new hyper-extrudables on hand," Parsons said, nudging Mackey and showing him a small satchel that he had filled with items. "My own patent." He winked.

Hopper opened a small box and withdrew a number of small round metal rings, each suspended on a length of cord. She handed one to each of them, and took one for herself, putting it around her neck, then tucking it into her suit. Mackey pulled it up to his eye for a better look. On the front were a number of markings—an electronics diagram not immediately recognizable to the engineer. The ring was wrapped in copper wire, and on the back was a small bit of circuitry, though with components smaller than he had ever seen, and completely alien to him.

"The lab has been calling them 'electromagnetic amulets,' but all joking aside, they defend against some weapons effects that I am not at full liberty to discuss."

Parsons put his on, examining it. "That doesn't make me feel much better, Grace."

"Oh, not to worry, Jack! As long as we're wearing them, you should regain full control of your limbs within a year."

Mackey stared, open-mouthed, only to see Hopper grinning. The Assistant Secretary had just told something like a joke. "It's not as bad as all that. But never take it off, for any reason. I am serious about that."

They stood in a small circle, fully equipped. "Should we, I don't know—develop a team motto?" asked Parsons. Ross kicked his ankle with her boot, making him jump.

"Let's just get on board the plane. Johnson should be calling through to it any time now."

The Valkyrie was impossibly large, with white delta wings, thin as a razor blade, shining bright red in the setting desert sun. Polygon intakes large enough to drive a truck through lay underneath the wing form, feeding a cavernously large duct of engines, each nozzle at the end of the craft as large as a person in diameter, six arranged in a single row. Forward from this giant, triangular phoenix of a wing form extended a thin neck of fuselage with a cockpit on the tip, and then reducing to a needle point at the leading edge, like a loaded syringe. On either side of the great bird's throat were small trapezoidal stabilizers.

"Never flown one before," said Parsons, scratching his head, "but I'm willing to give it a shot."

"No you won't," Hopper replied curtly, as Mackey breathed a sigh of relief. "Thankfully, we have a pilot fully trained in supersonic flight to do that task for us. We all need our rest even if flight time is just over an hour, because it will be early morning by the time we land at Dulles, and we have many tasks ahead of us tomorrow."

The neck of the PE-70 had been fitted out with a small executive cabin and a series of six bunks extending down the length of the jet, which one entered from the end, feet first, like a one-person space capsule. Lined up with rounded Perspex portholes, they looked not unlike the row of six supersonic engines at the rear of the plane.

While they taxiied down the runway the call from Roy Johnson, Secretary in Charge of the Advanced Research Projects Bureau, came over the video monitor. The Postal Bureau video phone logo faded into the image with the slightest hint of fuzz, that Mackey read as a sign of circular polarization in the signal—meaning it was being relayed by satellite. The man was thin, angular, with wire-frame glasses, his suit straight and neat, but having the unmistakable look of being worn for more than twenty-four hours.

"What's the situation, Hopper?" he asked, his voice coming through the plane's interior speakers.

"My people say Commerce has at least four Crystal birds, and an unknown number of other satellites. No idea of their purpose or make, but we do know a likely timeline—less than twenty-five hours."

Johnson put his hands on the desk and leaned forward towards the lens. "Well, there's one way to find out. I'm going to call a piloted assault against the Crystals and sweep the outer orbits until we find something. We'll snatch them up, bring them into the space station, and then we'll get to the bottom of it from there."

Hopper raised a finger. "Not yet. That sweep would take time, and would alert them that we know something is up. It might advance their timetable."

The man on the screen pursed his lips. "You have another plan, I take it?"

"I do. An agent I've used before with some success."

Johnson sniffed. "'Some success' is not an option here, Hopper. I'll hold off the assault for now, but you'd better have some more information soon."

The screen clicked to static, and then turned off. The jet accelerated, leaned back, and the ground dropped below them as the triangular wings improbably managed to conjure a physical envelope of pressure and lift, pushing the vast machine against the force of gravity and up into the sky. Spiralling west, the Valkyrie gained altitude, so that it could hit its afterburners and go supersonic.

Hopper distributed heavy goggles, each with a pack of electronics attached over the lenses, and then a small white tablet. "Put these on while you rest. They're for long-haul astronauts, and should get you into REM sleep in under twenty minutes. That, combined with the time-release amphetamine sheathed with switch-engineered melatonin, will help you feel like you've had six hours of sleep in under an hour."

Crawling into the sleep chambers fully dressed, each of the team swallowed the tablet and donned the goggles. Mackey lay back, feeling the subtle accelerations as the jet maneuvered into a vector aimed at the nation's capital. Colored lights spiraled in his vision, and the soft vibrations of current circulating the speakers' electromagnets above his ears filled in the gaps of the roaring engine and slipstream with white noise. It was the sound of riding an ocean wave, cresting on the peak of the collapsing curve. Or more correctly, Mackey knew, a random distribution of wave amplitudes, within a finite range of audible sound frequencies. Somewhere, on the ocean of human-perceptible sound, Fred Mackey roiled up and down from a relative point, hissing in and out of lucid consciousness.

Out over the desert, a rolling boom echoed over the evening sky.

"*In a terrible accident, sixteen people in Denver were killed today when the radar scopes on two P-cars malfunctioned simultaneously, resulting in a horrific collision. Traffic throughout the central Colorado area is backed up as far as Boulder while emergency crews tend to the wounded, and engineers try to estimate the extent of the damage.*

"*Although accidents involving P-cars are rare, in this case a double failure between two different P-cars' radars caused a three-car collision at a relative speed estimated by authorities at sixty miles per hour. Our resident engineer, Dr. Patricia Underwood, explains:*

"'*Under normal conditions, each P-car's computer only controls itself. It relies on the changing radar signal from the cars around it to know what they are doing, and to react to it. If the signal is delayed in any way, or gets distorted, sometimes the cars come together a little fast and bump together, like pedestrians jostling into each other on the sidewalk. It can also happen if a track signal is distorted, and the P-car tries to make a navigational adjustment to switch tracks too fast.*

"'*As you can see in this diagram, the front car is transmitting a radar image to the rear car, augmented to include a bit of extra information. In addition to looking for other cars, it broadcasts information, and listens for other cars broadcasting in turn. Each broadcast is unique, so the receivers can tell them all apart. Its "shape," so to speak, is the adjustment of the broadcast image, augmenting what the other cars "see," if you follow me.*

"'The rear car can sense not only how far away the front car is, and its speed relative to ours, but also whether that car is in a formation with cars ahead of it, and how far it thinks it must travel before its next track switch. The rear car will only get behind it if it is going less distance than it—therefore preventing the entire formation from slowing when it decreases speed to change tracks. The cars behind it will do the same. That way, formations of cars build that can assemble and disassemble without any centralized control.

"'In this case, both cars' passive mode radar failed. The cars could see each other, but they couldn't tell their distance to switching. They both attempted to take a switch at the same time. The rear car hit the front car, and derailed it on the switch, sending it crashing into a third car, here, on the right-hand switch track. Then, the rear car impacted that collision. Debris from the collision caused several other derailments in nearby cars, which then were hit by more cars piling up, unable to stop in time due to the speed and extent of the damage.'

"Thank you, Dr. Underwood. A rare and scary situation indeed, as well as certainly tragic for those in Denver tonight. At this time, the Assistant Secretaries for Safety of the National Automated Transport Safety Bureau, the Mass Transit Bureau, and the Postal Bureau are on the scene of the investigation in Denver, where they will make a combined public statement. We now take you live to Denver . . ."

8
Open To Potentiality

MACKEY AWOKE AS THE WHEELS OF THE VALKYRIE TOUCHED THE runway. Somewhere conductively connected and yet distant to his sleeping body, he felt the harsh friction of ten tires releasing a cloud of rubber smoke into the pre-dawn air. In his prone position, he felt the G-forces increase rapidly along a single vector as the drag chutes popped and the aircraft decelerated. There was no immediate sensation of changing pressure against his skin, no light to be seen. Nothing except the rough metal edge of the electromagnetic amulet Hopper had given him against his chest, as he lay pressed against it at an odd angle, between his skin and the solid mass under the force of inertia.

One by one, like indicator lamps on a console, awarenesses were presented to his consciousness. Location—the capsule in the Valkyrie cabin. The pressure against his chest—that was downward. The heavy inertial vector—forward, the plane slowing along the runway. Time—likely Eastern Postal. Hour—perhaps only an hour into the future, jury still out, sensors still looking for data. Vision—distorted, blaze of colors. Ah, but of course: the REM goggles were still on his face, displaying a soft blue light. Removing them, the rest of his senses returned. He had a body— fatigued, a bit sore, with limbs, head, torso, and skin.

Turning over, Mackey released the stress of the amulet against his chest, and the object, the same temperature as his skin, seemed to disappear. He popped open the capsule door and crawled out into the cabin, along with the rest of the team, smoothing his clothing, making sure he was as dressed as he could possibly be.

He needed a mirror. The reflective glass on the end of the capsule, just glossy enough to give a slight reflection, allowed Mackey to straighten his tie, by habit. And there he was, the familiar image, recalled from memory and substantiated. Fred Mackey, aboard a supersonic Postal Bureau aircraft, amongst a quintet of secretive, possibly occult, engineering-oriented spies.

Ross was rubbing her eyes. "It's not a clean sleep, but it's surprisingly effective."

"I could have used a little bit more amphetamine on the exit," Parsons commented, yawning. "Maybe combined with a bit of serotonin extension, or maybe a light empathogen for added dream sensitivity."

They collected their new, weaponized possessions. Mackey buttoned his jacket over the shoulder holster. Thompson decided to leave his coat on board. It was a warm night, and the Forest Service patches were attracting unnecessary attention among Department of Transportation personnel. They descended to the dark tarmac and entered the deserted terminal.

"That reminds me," Parsons said, taking a deep breath of the early morning air, still cool and crisp, not yet humid. "I had a dream that was possibly relevant. We were in a vast underground labyrinth, struggling to collect the last of a series of sixteen artifacts, each representative of a different goddess from a variety of traditions. I was piloting a mini-sub in a subterranean lake, but the viscosity of the water was being altered by some sort of telepathic octopus. And then Fred said to Gene . . ."

Hopper interrupted the narrative as they approached the parking portal. "We'll head straight to the NATSB, and see if Eliza is awake."

The Assistant Secretary's P-car was waiting, of course, doors open and ready for boarding. They all climbed inside, Ross pulling the doors closed behind them.

Thompson ended up in the middle of the bench next to Mackey, with Ross on the opposite end. Hopper gestured to Parsons, who was next to her, to find the right card in the atlas binder. He inserted it in the slot, and the car took off. "What's the NATSB?" Thompson asked Mackey.

"The National Automated Transport Safety Board," he explained. "The Postal Bureau builds the P-car system, the Infrastructure Bureau runs the track, and the Mass Transit Bureau handles the switches. But the NATSB certifies any technology carrying passengers and handles safety investigations. I've worked with them a number of times, providing some technical analysis in cases where sensors and track signals had interference issues."

"Electromagnetic resonance." Parsons nodded, to himself as much as the others inside the car. "Orthogonal Procedures through wave space. Got to keep that third ear open to the etheric music."

"Complicated stuff," Thompson murmured.

After passing through Tyson, the tracks met the Potomac and swung southeast towards the capital. Mackey looked out at the looped tracks of the suburban developments, glowing slightly under amber lights, pushing up against the tracks and the river. That synthetic Bach track that had been playing on the radio—now almost two days ago, in the Assistant Secretary's P-car—suddenly looped back through Mackey's mind. Quite vivid, almost as if replayed, not as a memory.

The city was dark, almost entirely asleep, and yet with a thin trickle of traffic as if the metropolis was turning over gently in dreams. The city of bureaucrats slept, off-duty, but undergoing that necessarily dormant phase that would enable procedures to begin again at nine o'clock. Any one of the glowing apartment buildings housed people, now in states of rest, who were just like himself. Its citizens traveled in cars from home to office, each and every day, and then back again at night. The whirling loops of tracks were part of the federal circulatory system, and naturally engaged in their own rhythms. The inhalation of the day was countered by the exhalation of night, when those cells were returned to the far-flung organs of the suburbs, allowed to recharge in sleep, exchanging the gases that allowed the very metabolism of government. Were the bureaucrats the blood? Were they the nervous system? Or were they the nation's thoughts themselves, released from the protocols of wakeful identity, to lapse into semi-consciousness for eight hours, retreating to the dreamscape of their apartment towers, before being called back into the more highly regimented, logical systems of the federal bureaucratic consciousness . . .

Mackey wasn't sure what the proper analogy was, if there in fact was a suitable one. He himself had spent the single hour that qualified as 'last night' chemically and physically attached to an astronaut-tech dream machine. In his simulated, augmented, drug-induced sleep, he was restored to a level of function necessary to interface with the schedule of the clandestine Orthogonal agent.

Regardless of the significance of the bureaucrats traveling through the P-car system, he had left that previous classification. He had fallen through that system, into the one below. He was the energy of the car system, released from hydrocarbons in the coal and oil fires of the Infrastructure Bureau's more than five thousand power plants, funneled to the grid as invisible electrons, to course through the tracks and into the copper coils of the motors. Mackey had left behind the natural cycles of day and night and joined the technological system, running on its own artificial periods, like a space station in LEO seeing the sunrise every ninety minutes. He had crossed the country twice in the last forty-eight hours, and on this periodic trajectory had witnessed a side of the government that he never would have seen.

This hidden structure stood out in sharp contrast when one looked from the top of the Postal Bureau Tower. Its grooves and circuits loomed into vision when one speculated about satellites from within a secret desert lab. The cryptic codewords pricked the eyes and ears when one was held at gunpoint by federal agents, before an altar covered with blood. But from his office in the nation's capital, it was invisible.

And this life had apparently carried on without him, the sun rising and setting on several million daily routines. But now he was out of balance. He was in another mental orbit. As he chased the artificial satellite of the District of Columbia at 17,000 miles an hour, his old vantage point was revealed in stark contrast as it emerged from the shadow of the earth into the blinding radiation of sun, unrestrained by atmosphere. Returning to the city in the middle of the night was like stepping outside of himself. As if back in the suburbs, another Mackey was asleep in bed, as this one ought to be.

He tried to blink, and clear his head. Such strange thoughts, stampeding over themselves into his mind! No doubt it was a lingering effect of the sleep-inducing tablet.

Thompson was looking over Mackey, out the window as well. "Sometimes I forget. Growing up in Idaho, where the P-car tracks often dead-end in fields, rather than looping back around. And then spending so much of my time out in the National Forest, without any track at all. I forget it can look like this. No trees. Just buildings, as many as if they were trees."

Mackey nodded silently in agreement, although he had never been to Idaho. There were massive regions of land that they had just flown over, which Mackey had never visited. He had seen similar regions from the air, over the Sierras, over the San Gabriels and the Mojave, the various biomes of California.

It was the lack of rainfall, Mackey supposed, that spaced out the trees in the West, defining their shape, their lack of density, their sparse arrangement together into the overwhelming thing that was the western forest lands. Here, it was the placement of the arterials that arranged the buildings, and the density of the traffic passing through the track networks that wove the suburbs into existence. The buildings crowded up to the river on both sides, clinging to the loops and arterials as if the tracks were their roots, their link to solid ground, the only anchor keeping them from tumbling out over the water itself. As if the apartment buildings were the dark, luminescent forest under a waning western moon. Limited by the urban planning version of a timber line, the constraints of the water and temperature in a forest mimicked by the availability of electricity, population, and tower footprint. A forest, a city, or a human body, each constrained by their needs and the system by which the material to satisfy those needs was made available.

He looked out the window at a group of unfamiliar looking low-slung buildings, only single story, no P-car tracks leading up to them. For half a moment he wondered what sort of building wouldn't have tracks or parking areas, before his supersonically jetlagged mind figured it out. It was a Housing Act complex. The people who lived in them couldn't afford cars, and had to take a rail trolley from a nearby station. He had seen them any number of times around the Washington area, but never at night, he realized. At night they appeared darker, when their concrete forms absorbed the light rather than reflected it. Few streetlights, Mackey noticed. They looked hidden, sunk into the ground compared to the larger buildings around them, caught in a shadow, without the bright lights of the cityscape. The world was woven with mysteries and unknowns.

The car traveled in silence, each occupant seemingly lost in their own thoughts, no sound but the constant whir of the electric motors underneath and the gentle rushing of air passing over the curved, swept form, like a pebble in a stream. The after-effects of chemical-induced sleep echoed silently in the car. A silent effervescence. A chemical afterburn lingering in bloodstreams, phase-matched with the jetlagged syncopation of consciousnesses in parallax. Humans and technology, placed at different angles to the target, angles computationally attuned into a range, hovering at the frontier between uncertainty and certainty.

But soon the machinery interrupted the reflective moment. As it was programmed, as it was designed, and therefore as it could not have failed to do. As the humans had indicated they wished it to do, with the information faithfully provided to the machine, as designed, as programmed. The navigational computer detected the signal of the oncoming exit track it had been set to wait for, and its relays began to click, setting in motion a series of responsive actions.

The P-car slowed, and the formation ahead of it continued onward. The deceleration occurred smoothly, bringing the vehicle down to a speed at which it could engage the switch from the main travel track and slide over to an exit siding track. The deceleration continued, bringing the velocity down to a point at which the car could comfortably make the curved loop of the exit, passing out over the bank of the river before circling back down and under the main track course. Aware that it had successfully maneuvered the exit, the computer began looking for the next expected signal on its internal maps, and found it—the entrance track for the Fairbanks Track Research Center. Equipped with Hopper's radio credentials, the car proceeded through the gate as the guard waved to the occupants inside.

Descending to the parking structure, the P-car's motor tone dropped to a low hum, and finally, gently, came to a stop outside the underground entrance to the main building. It had never really occurred before to Mackey how when arriving at a federal building via car, one never saw the architecture. One had to arrive by aircraft to get the full view.

The door popped open with a pneumatic hiss. And only then did the passengers have to once again act for themselves, collecting their various accoutrements and sliding out onto the steel pedestrian passage. The Assistant Secretary assumed the lead, taking them through a warren of corridors and offices, down escalators and stairs, descending into the complex. Until, after nearly fifteen minutes, they arrived at a lab secured by a thick set of double doors, marked with a handwritten sign reading only "Eliza." Hopper produced a thin plastic card and waved it in front of a console. To Mackey's surprise, the console light turned a pale green without even being touched, and the door popped open. The team trooped inside.

The room was bright red on floor, walls, and ceiling, with a geometric grid in thin white lines embedded on all surfaces. This grid was used to position the room's contents in a recti-linear manner, in rows, aisles, racks and towers. These contents were a vast amount of computer equipment, against the walls and pushed together in islands, some as tall as twenty feet, transforming the room into a thin maze of corridors one grid square across. It was as if a winding limestone cavern had been abstracted into cubes. A technician in a lab coat was working off of a clipboard at one of the many machines. She looked at the arrivals, and stood up straighter when she saw the Assistant Secretary.

"Assistant Secretary Hopper! You should have told me you were coming, I would have—"

"Not to worry, not to worry. We have some information, and some important questions to ask."

"I'm just running diagnostics right now, you picked a good time." The technician looked at the odd group, not sure what to make of them.

"You must be Eliza," said Parsons to the technician, offering his hand. She took it, and was preparing to say something, but Hopper pre-empted her. "This is Dr. Emily Willamette, Eliza's technician. This—" waving her hand at the computer equipment, "is Eliza."

"More accurately," said Willamette, "Eliza is inside of all this. On the magnetic tape, loaded in the memory. Eliza is an artificial intelligence program, and she is currently substantiated on this equipment."

The team looked around the room, seeing reels of tape, punch card feeders, dials and knobs, and row after row of indicator lights. It was difficult to know where to direct one's attention, as the room was simply filled with machinery, warm, echoing with the hum of fans and motors, chittering with the sound of relays scattered underneath the many housings and cabinets.

"Eliza is an advanced research project, housed here at NATSB," Hopper explained. "It began as a natural language processor, meant to simulate conversations, invented by Joseph Weizenbaum at Vail Labs. We acquired that program, and have wrapped it over a series of parallel learning algorithms. The goal was to create a computerized engineer that could analyze information fed from P-car accidents and other technological mishaps, and then generate specific queries in response to generalized queries, until it had enough information to present a full report."

Willamette nodded. "Eliza isn't as quick as human beings with general information. If you ask her whether ketchup goes best with hamburgers or ice cream, she cannot answer. No one has ever told her the answer, and because she doesn't have a sensory system or data on human taste buds, she can't answer questions based on what we would call 'opinion' or 'common impressions.' She lacks the ability to form a 'hunch,' because she doesn't have the history of unspoken inputs that a human being has, such as long-term memory, and the resulting inclinations. She can only work with the data she is provided. But she is very good at asking questions, to try and get the information she needs."

"What we're going to do is give Eliza some information," Hopper announced. "And we're going to see what it wants to know."

Willamette showed them to a number of desks with punch card machines. Hopper divided up the information they had, and the team began writing card sets with the information. Parsons typed up the astrological diagrams from the dossiers, while Ross began readying a set of all known orbital telemetries from ASTB databases. Mackey prepared several sets of cards containing reference information on Department of Transportation employees mentioned in the dossiers, while Thompson helped him collate. Meanwhile, Hopper and Willamette began preparing an ARPNET interface message processor, along with the commands for accessing it, in a form Eliza could understand. Every reference database in the entire Department that was linked into the ARPNET, Eliza would be able to search for information.

In a couple hours, they began feeding information into the computers—the equivalent of spreading information on Eliza's desk. The card readers clicked and whirred as the small cards flew through, their arrangement of punch holes activating or blocking switches, which then converted the marks into digitally stored data. Willamette loaded several new reels of magnetic tape, running the tape through the heads, and then letting them fly, the tape whizzing back and forth at a rate of meters per second, as the computer accessed and organized the information according to Eliza's whim. From the interface message processor, the shrouded sound of a dial tone was heard, followed by a sequence of beeps and clicks, as Eliza began dialing different computers across the country and asking them for information in a tongue provided to her by the IMP.

Finally, after another hour, the machine quieted, the magnetic tapes moving more slowly. The punch card machines stopped. They gathered around a console with a text input screen. Willamette sat in the chair and turned on the monitor, which flickered into life with a dull green glow. A small rectangle flashed at a regular rate in the top left of the display.

Willamette used a keyboard, and as she pressed each letter, the letter appeared where the rectangle had been as it moved across the screen to the right until a sentence was displayed. It was a novel interface, thought Mackey. Like a live sheet of paper.

"Good morning Eliza. Have you reviewed the information?"

Willamette looked up at Hopper, standing over her shoulder. Hopper nodded, and Willamette tapped the 'enter' key. The green rectangle jumped down to the next line, and this time, without any input from Willamette, text printed across the screen.

"Good morning, Emily. Yes, I have reviewed the information. This does not appear to be information regarding a transportation accident. Please let me know your general line of inquiry."

"A future Department of Transportation accident, perhaps," Parsons quipped.

Hopper considered her words carefully, and then spoke. "We want to know the best target for a raid on Commerce, for the purpose of gaining further evidence."

Willamette looked away from the screen, but did not turn around to look at the Assistant Secretary. She thought for a moment, and then began typing.

"What Department of Commerce location would be most likely to hold significant evidence on the subject at hand?"

The green rectangle blinked in the same place. Then it skipped a line, and Eliza's answer came.

"The subject at hand is obscure, and not well identified. Do you agree?"

Now Willamette turned to look at Hopper. The Assistant Secretary nodded.

"I agree," Willamette responded.

Eliza asked another question. "Do you think past events are more relevant, or are events in the future more relevant?"

"The future," Hopper said, and Willamette transcribed.

The rectangle paused.

"Do you think it is more difficult to predict the future, or the past?" Eliza asked.

The humans gathered around the screen looked at each other. "Is that an error, or is it philosophical?" Mackey asked.

Willamette shrugged. "If there's a programming error, we get an error code. But some of her questions do come off as spurious."

"It depends," said Ross, slowly, "whether one wants to be limited to definite truths, or open to potentiality."

Hopper looked at Ross over her glasses. "Are you saying that about Eliza, or is that your answer to her question?"

"You mean like the difference between what exists, versus what might exist?" asked Thompson.

"Sure, I guess. If you are open to a wide range of potentialities, you can say anything about the future. But describing every potentiality of the past is difficult. On the other hand, if you simply want make a definitive, true statement, making pronouncements about the past is easy. You can say just about anything with generalizations. But saying anything with definite certainty about the future is hard."

They thought about that while Willamette typed it out.

Eliza responded with another question. "Are you more interested in actuality or potentiality?"

"Well, she flipped that one right back at us," Mackey noted.

"Serves me right for trying to engage in philosophy with an artificial intelligence." Ross shrugged.

"Potentiality," said Parsons. "We should be open to anything."

"But we do need one specific location to raid," Hopper cautioned. "We can't invade every Commerce facility."

"I think we can say both," Willamette said, as she typed. "Eliza likes multiple variables, even if they can contradict, as they help her focus on a line of inquiry."

The sentence she typed read, "Potentiality, but we need a single answer to our query."

Eliza paused, and then asked another question. "I cannot find the technical specifications documents for the database operations programs involving Postal Identification Number location distancing sequences. Where are they?"

"Well, at least that question isn't philosophical," Thompson mused.

"Anyone have any idea?" Hopper asked.

"We can give her a rough guess even if we don't know for sure," Willamette suggested.

"Most database technical specifications are kept in the Section manuals of those employees who do data entry," Mackey said. "But as far as which Section of what Bureau does location distancing, I have no idea. I'm not even sure what that means."

"I'll try telling her that," Willamette said, and transcribed Mackey's response as best she could.

Eliza seemed to accept it, and asked a new question. "Do prediction models show potential civil unrest for the greater Detroit area during the period of 1972 through 1976?"

"Is that the sort of thing you can model?" Ross asked.

Hopper shrugged. "I'm sure someone has tried, but I have no idea what Bureau or Section, what they might have found, or how accurate it is."

"We can tell her we don't know," Willamette suggested. Hopper acquiesced.

The next question Eliza asked was met with dead silence. "Is Gene Thompson to be trusted?" The rectangle blinked, awaiting their response.

Thompson stood up, startled, looking around the room. "Can she see me?"

"No," Hopper explained. "The program doesn't have a concept of its location. It knows its address in the ARPNET, but it has no idea that it inhabits a room, or that there might be people in that room. But I had to describe the entire narrative of events up until this point. We gave it all the information we have, so it knows about all of us."

Leaning to Willamette, she said, "Write that Assistant Secretary Hopper says yes."

Eliza's next question appeared quickly. "Where is a databased copy of the *Liber Loagaeth*?"

Parsons jerked backward, knocking over a stack of manuals on a nearby table. "That's an Enochian magic text from the 16th century!" he exclaimed.

"Why would Eliza want that? How could Eliza even know that?" Mackey asked.

"Isn't it obvious?" Parsons spoke rapidly, full of excitement. "The underlying occult! She's found it, a link coming through the information somehow. She's divined it, pulled it out of the data! The algorithm is nothing short of oracular!"

Ross looked at him skeptically, and then asked Willamette, "Can you ask why that text is important?"

Willamette did so, and the glowing rectangle took a moment to consider.

"It is referenced in Helmsted, Winton Xavier. 'Glossolalia and Ancient Script,' Library of Congress Classification BV158. H1937."

Mackey rubbed his eyes behind his glasses. "Like many things, I don't know if that makes what is happening more reasonable, or more strange."

Parsons looked slightly disappointed with the answer, but that didn't prevent him from having a response. "There should be a copy on the ASTB Interstellar Rocket Research document repository, under Enochian."

Hopper looked at him quizzically, and gestured to Willamette, who fed the information to Eliza.

The rectangle blinked steadily for five seconds. Ten seconds. Thirty seconds. Then the response appeared.

"The answer to your query is: Project Sanguine Research Site, Republic, Michigan."

They looked at the screen, waiting for more, but there was none.

"Well, I would call that a fairly specific answer," Ross offered.

"I've heard of Project Sanguine," Mackey spoke slowly, trying to recall. "It's an experiment with myriameter radio waves—extremely low frequency. So low that they can penetrate the ocean waves."

"To communicate with submarines at sea," Hopper finished, and Mackey nodded.

"So is that it then?" Thompson asked. "They want to disrupt communications with submarines?"

"Commerce was running the program," Mackey continued. "It was a Geodetic Service project, because it required knowledge of the earth's crust to place it. Underneath the Upper Peninsula of Michigan is the Laurentian Shield, a large expanse of Precambrian rock. The rock is very old—dating back to the early history of earth. But the reason they chose that site is that the rock has very low conductivity, allowing the radio waves to propagate further under the ground."

"Could they be using the myriameter waves to communicate with their satellites without us interfering?" Parsons asked.

Ross shook her head. "Extremely low frequency waves have very little throughput—only a few characters a second. Satellite telemetry and sensor data requires far more bandwidth. And even if you wanted to broadcast myriameter waves to space, you couldn't. Much of the signal at such low frequencies would bounce off charged particles in the ionosphere and come back to earth. That's good if you want to communicate with submarines, but bad for satellites."

"So what does this have to do with anything?" Parsons asked. "Not that I don't love a good red herring, but isn't it possible Eliza has given us an answer that is, as Emily phrased it, spurious?"

"There's not really any way to know quickly, given the question," Willamette said. "We asked for what would be most likely, not a proven logical theory. To unravel Eliza's reasoning would require analyzing thousands and thousands of code executions."

The Assistant Secretary straightened. "In that case, I say that we continue to play this hunch. We are going to raid the Project Sanguine site. Eliza has come through for us in the past, and it's at least a concrete lead."

Parsons shouldered his satchel of explosives. "Well then, what's the fastest transit to Michigan? Back to the Valkyrie?"

Hopper smiled. "It would be even faster if we travel without moving. The NATSB happens to have another tool that may be of help, in a lower laboratory."

She turned to Willamette. "Thanks for your help, Emily, I'll be in touch."

The Assistant Secretary picked up a phone and began dialing, motioning to the others that she would meet them in the corridor.

Camera pans across an unnaturally blue lake, grey, cloud-colored concrete in the form of pedestrian viaducts and P-car tracks, centering on a large Administration Deco apartment block.

This is Greenbelt, Maryland, one of the first model towns of the former Postal Administration's Resettlement Section in the late 1930s. This stylish apartment block is steeped in history, recalling the days in which the Postal Administration was planning the rebuilding of America in harmony with its accelerating technological advances. The Resettlement Section had ceased to exist after 1958, but the legacy of well-planned neighborhoods like Greenbelt inspired the rest of the country. Transferred from governmental management to private ownership in the early 1960s, the managers of Greenbelt maintain the classic Administration Deco style and layout, because that is what brings the tenants: well-paid bureaucrats who commute daily into Washington DC.

Camera shows a modern, high-speed elevator in period Greenbelt style, with inlaid wood paneling in dark swoops accented by polished brass curves, that opens onto a clean garage filled with neatly parked P-cars. Camera switches to views of a large aquatic center, strangely absent of people, but with attractive smoked-glass brick and aqua-tiled stairs augmenting the concrete exterior.

Today, most modern neighborhoods do not have ample park space around a lake, or such community facilities as the residents of Greenbelt. Buildings are far taller and built closer together, leaving only room for track access and pedestrian walks, making areas with dense enough stands of trees to be considered 'park' untenable. As older, early 20th century neighborhoods were slowly demolished in the post-War decade so the P-car tracks could be centralized on loops around new apartment towers, at least a nod was made towards the idea of green space when possible. Not actual park space, but tree lines between the tracks and pedestrian viaducts and similar other landscaping nodded to the idea. For those who make their home in Greenbelt, actually living in an area that was the inspiration for these design elements is indeed quite a luxury.

Scene fades into a shot of small, filthy shacks, crammed together under the concrete footings of a massive arterial overpass. A few poor children kick a ball around in the mud.

But here, not two miles from Greenbelt, we see the dark legacy of the Postal Administration's policies. Tucked underneath the express arterial that delivers the bureaucrats to their office buildings, we find the dilapidated housing known as Roosevilles, bitingly named after the Postmaster that started the wave of re-urbanization some three decades ago. Moved out of their former homes to make way for new highrises, these people build shelter from whatever they can find, stealing electricity from the tracks above in dangerous cable patches that have been known to electrocute people and start fires. When the Infrastructure Bureau finds these settlements, they are supposed to move the residents into a Housing Act development. But as our America: Tonight! reporters have uncovered, there are far too many Roosevilles for the limited Housing Act spaces available. What will happen to these people? Are they a sign that the era of Administrationism was too good to last? Can private development solve the housing crisis?

Find out with America: Tonight! as we show you the stories that the governmental news channels can't and won't cover—8pm Eastern Postal Time, 7pm Central.

9

Multiple Contacts

FOLLOWING HOPPER, THEY BOARDED AN ELEVATOR. THEY DESCENDED further down, into the rock below the surface of Virginia.

"Is this really the best idea?" Ross was asking Hopper. "We have no idea of the basis on which Eliza pointed out the Michigan site. We have no idea what is at the site, or what we're looking for."

"That's a reason to go," Parsons suggested. "We go in and then we see. The only way to know is to go."

"But what if there's nothing there?" Ross protested. "Then we've tipped them off, maybe triggered a Federal incident, and all for nothing, because a computer said so."

"Not a computer, a computerized engineer substantiated by parallel learning algorithms," Hopper corrected. "And the alternative move, at this time, is to let Roy Johnson of ARPB declare open war in low earth orbit. Johnson is a good man, and a good Secretary. But he's working on instinct right now. He wants to shoot first and ask questions later. Eliza, on the other hand, is trying to make our bullets do the asking. Eliza was designed for just these sorts of situations—when we don't know what questions to ask, Eliza figures it out."

Departing the elevator onto an unnamed and unnumbered subterranean level, they proceeded down a white hallway, floored in ceramic tile. At the end of the short passage, Hopper unsealed another security door and led them into a white lab room.

The lab was nearly empty except for ten long tanks, like antiseptic white coffins made of molded thermoplastic, lifted up from the floor on narrow, stainless steel legs. From the underside of each tank glowed blue neon light, wavering off of small rectangular pools of water. Thick white electrical conduits like tendon flesh led from each of the white tanks upwards, into the ceiling of the lab. White spherical pressure vessels were suspended there, like clusters of organelles, or antiseptic, space-age fruit. The setup gave the room the feeling of a health club designed by someone who had just been to the 1964 World's Fair in DC.

On a small table in the center of the room was a ball, larger than two feet in diameter. Upon closer inspection, Mackey saw that it was actually an icosahedron, a polygon of twenty equal-sized triangles, each slightly rounded outward. The triangular panels were white, made from a composite material. In the center of each triangle shone a small black lens.

"This," Parsons swept his arm at the tanks, "is clearly not any sort of aircraft. What sort of transportation is this? Pneumatic tube travel?"

"Our bodies will not be leaving this room," Hopper announced. "Only our minds will travel."

She placed her hand on the icosahedron. "This is a remote unit. They are already prepositioned in various locations across the country. The ones we will use are at the Coast Guard base in Sault Ste. Marie on Lake Superior. I activated the Guard's 261st Hovercraft Division to provide the transportation to the site and to conduct the raid. They'll load the remote units on semi-autonomous hovercraft, so we can go along with them."

Thompson reached out and touched the spherical object. "What does it do?"

The remote unit jumped at his touch, and Thompson quickly withdrew his hand as if it had tried to bite him. The curved triangular sections flapped in and out in turn, using each triangular edge as a hinge to extend the opposite point. Connected to the remote's body at the triangle's center point, by using a servo-actuated piston, each triangular side of the remote had a free range of motion, like flapping scales that opened in all directions.

As these fins flapped, the remote emitted a constant whirring hiss punctuated by chattering, as internal compressors balanced pneumatic pressure and the relays switched the actuators on and off. After all the sides ran through the same startup diagnostic range of motion, each in turn popped outward and retracted forcefully, beginning at the top, continuing in sequence around the shape until the bottom side fired, launching the remote upward a foot in the air before catching itself deftly on the piston-cushioned triangle. The device had to weigh at least fifty pounds, judging from its construction, and yet it bounced itself on its scales as lightly as a personable beach ball.

"The remotes can move by adjusting their scutes, as you see. The lenses in each scute capture video imagery and create a composite, full-axis spherical view. The remote transmits that imagery to the local repeater, which then relays to satellite. That comes here to us, in the tanks. We wear special television helmets, so we can see what happens in real time. We control the remote using neural stimuli nets attached to the helmets and the tank suits. Our control commands are transmitted back through the satellites, to the repeater, to the remotes."

"Well," said Mackey, "of all that I've seen over the last two days, I suppose this is not quite the most outrageous."

"Not at all, Fred," Parsons assured him. "This is just a bit of astral projection, with the help of satellites."

"When you describe it like that, it definitely sounds outrageous," concluded Thompson.

"We'll need to change. Gentlemen, you'll find the equipment in the room there," Hopper indicated a door to one side of the lab, "and Ross and I will suit up in the other room. Try to be quick, the acclimation to the tank takes a few minutes and we don't have much time before the Coast Guard force departs base."

In the small prep room, Parsons, Mackey, and Thompson found white suits made from thick neoprene, and large spherical helmets of thick, dark, nearly opaque glass, riven through with thin white grid lines, like latitude and longitude on a globe.

Mackey tried to look through the helmet. "Like a blind astronaut, lost in outer space," he mused.

"Psychonauts, traveling in inner space." Parsons winked. "The road is inside you."

A useful pictogram on the wall depicted the act of dressing in the suits using step-by-step images of stick figures. Interpreting the images, they deciphered the best means of entry, sealing up the suit, and attaching all the leads between the suit and the helmets. Holding the helmets under their arms, with just enough slack in the wires to do so, they trooped back into the main lab, where Hopper and Ross were also dressed and preparing the tanks.

"These must be saline suspension tanks," Parsons guessed. "Enough salt in the water and you float, allowing a bit of freedom of movement on all sides."

"That's right," Hopper said as she typed commands into a console to bring the system online. "The suspension aids in the ability to put one's mind into the remote, to see what it sees, to feel what it feels. After a few minutes, you'll forget you have a body at all. You'll be entirely in the scene, as depicted to you via the satellite connection." She showed them the inside of the tanks, where they would connect the suit leads to the tank wall using waterproof connectors. "Leave your glasses off, Mackey," she said, removing her own. "The helmet will focus itself to your eyes."

"What is the purpose of this system?" Thompson asked. "I mean, why build it? Is this intended to be a new form of entertainment?"

"The National Automated Transport Safety Bureau developed it in concert with the Mass Transit Bureau to allow remote inspections of tracks, signals, and bridge structures," Hopper responded. "But now they are testing it for more widespread consumer use."

"A tank in every home? I don't really see the appeal."

"Think of it," Ross suggested. "Right now, the P-car system is designed for human bodies. But what if all it had to transport was a tiny ball? Getting humans and their life support systems into space is the majority of the weight in most spacecraft assemblies. If all we had to do was shoot that ball into orbit, costs would plummet."

"Except then we'd spend half our lives in tanks, rather than sitting in cars," Mackey said, morosely. Then, that idea having given him another thought, "What happens to us if the remote unit is killed? I mean, if it falls down a hole, sinks into the sea, or burns up during re-entry, or whatever?"

"It's disorienting for a moment." Hopper shrugged. "But the computer will patch you into another remote, if there's one available." She handed out a small capsule to each of them. "Take this."

Parsons popped it into his mouth and swallowed. "What is it? Tastes like amines."

"It helps with motion sickness. The whole experience can be a bit intense the first time."

With a look at the clock, Hopper ushered them into the tanks, climbing in by way of short sets of steps drawn up to the tank.

"When you are plugged in, put on your helmet and lie back," she commanded. "We should hear each other through the audio channel."

Mackey put on his helmet, shutting out the bright fluorescent lights of the lab. He lay back, feeling as if he were slipping downstream. The capsule he had swallowed made him feel slightly dizzy. He realized that they hadn't eaten anything yet today. Perhaps it had been the amphetamine effect of the pill they had taken during the short, supersonic REM goggle sleep which had kept him from noticing until now.

He heard the Assistant Secretary's voice from behind his head. "Everyone online?" The team chimed in, one at a time. The voices sounded fuzzy and distant, like a telephone call. "The synchronizing program is spinning up. We'll check in again once we're through."

The white grid inside the opaque helmet glass glowed incandescently bright before dimming to a dull luminescence. A test pattern of two interlocked counter-rotating spirals appeared and steadied on the inside of the dome that hemmed in his awareness. Then the logo of the NATSB flashed up—a blue eagle with triangular, inverted delta wings, spread wide with track-like bands encircling it. It faded, and was replaced by a circle, drawn in a thin green line on utter blackness, expanding outward until it was at the limits of his peripheral vision. Fine reticle hashes appeared along the outside of the circle. Mackey counted; there were twelve of them.

"This is the ready pattern," Hopper's voice came into the backs of the helmet. "As soon as the satellite connection comes through, imagery should appear."

Mackey waited, feeling his legs extend further from him, buzzing slightly through either dizziness or hunger. The floating sensation was different than the pool he swam in every morning. It was not wet, because of the suit and helmet. His buoyancy in the saline liquid made him rise high in the tank. He felt like an unloaded barge, almost top-heavy, desiring of ballast or forward motion, wishing he could push against the liquid in his familiar strokes. The green reticle hashes began rotating, slowly, around the green circle in the dark. Mackey began to feel uncomfortable, unstable, vertiginous, as if he was lying on a thin plank, suspended above on unknown height. He thought he heard, through the audio system, very faint sounds of what he was sure was . . . Bach?

"Does anyone hear that?" he asked, to no response. He felt pressure on his arms and chest. Was he lying on his back? Or was he flipped over, head down? His breathing was quick, unsteady.

And then the visual feed appeared in a burst of static, giving way to a grey sea, bouncing quickly, moving rapidly underneath him. He was on the prow of a boat, as if standing erect. Mackey braced himself for the force of the wind that he could hear in his ears, but there was none. He was bouncing with the motion of the vessel, speeding over the waves, but his feet were firmly anchored, like he was a rod of iron connected to the bottom of the ship. He suddenly felt very stable, as if the weight of a heavy blow would simply bounce off of him like a pebble.

Hopper asked for a check-in, and all responded. She informed them of their status. "We're each on board a different hovercraft. You'll see the indicators, which will make it clear who is who. The strike force is moving into position north of Grand Island. We'll cross due south onto the land near Marquette, and advance up the P-car tracks to the southeast until we get to National Mine. Then it will be a short jaunt across country to the Project Sanguine site.

"You are on autopilot until you get your bearings. After about sixty seconds, your vision control will phase in. Try looking about you. Don't turn your head, just think about turning your head, and the cameras' composite image will pan for you. I think you'll find that your adaption to the control system will occur fairly quickly."

Mackey already saw his vision drifting, and seized control, looking down to try and see what his legs were standing on. The image pivoted rapidly, so quickly that Mackey forgot about trying to move his chin, and just used his eyes. Looking down, he saw the black rubber skirt bouncing just above the waves. But he could not see his legs—obviously, he thought. But he wondered, then, what was he exactly? A large camera-studded ball, strapped to the deck?

Mackey tried to turn about and look behind him, and did so easily. There was a slight delay, but by only gingerly changing direction, he was able to control his vision angle fairly well. The hovercraft extended behind him, dark green, with the Coast Guard's orange and white livery stripe and blue Transportation eagle insignia visible along the side of the angular, darkened crew housing. The craft was about forty feet long, capped on the end by two massive fan nacelles, which reminded him of Parsons' Vail aircraft. On top of the crew housing, glistening black in the thin rays of sun that were passing through the partly cloudy sky, were a pair of multi-barreled machine gun turrets.

Looking off to the starboard side, Mackey saw a long line of hovercraft, all identical. Above each was a hovering green indicator in the shape of a downward pointing triangle, accompanied by a string of unparsable numbers and letters. Four of them resolved, flipping digits until they decoded to read Hopper, Parsons, Ross, and Thompson, respectively. On the bow of each of these craft he saw a short post with a white ball on the end. That must be what he was looking through—one of the remote units, fixed to the boat. But all the hovercraft, not just those four, had the remote posts on the bow. The other indicators did not resolve, remaining a scrambled string of text. Who, he wondered, might be viewing through those remotes?

"We have multiple contacts, bearing 290. Range, six miles," an unfamiliar voice announced through the sound system.

Hopper responded immediately. "Hostile, Commander?"

"Likely out of Ashland Harbor," the voice replied. "That would be a USGS Corps rapid response. Radar makes ten ships, fast cutters. 110 feet. Each armed with 25 mm autocannons."

Mackey heard Ross' voice cut through. "Can't we just outrun them?"

Hopper responded. "We're faster than them, but they are cutting us off. Looks like we're going to have to engage."

"How do I control this thing?" It was Parsons, naturally. "How do I shoot?"

"Radar autopilot is still engaged," explained Hopper. "You'll need to get acclimated to the difference between visual and physical control. It can be awkward at first. We'll spread out the formation before turning over to remote control. The last thing we need is to all crash into each other."

"No one said anything about driving a hovercraft," Mackey interrupted. "I've never piloted anything larger than a bicycle in my life."

"Seize the moment, Fred!" Parsons shouted through the channel, encouragingly. "Nothing like the heat of combat to teach you!"

"Can't the autopilot do the fighting?" asked Thompson, not really fearful, but clearly a bit reticent as well.

"No," Hopper said quickly. "The radar keeps the craft on course, and prevents it from hitting anything. But combat takes human foresight and quick thinking. I'm afraid that's the way it is, and there's no time to argue. Commander, give the order for a combat spread. They might outgun us, but we're faster than them. If we can draw them out and circle them at high speed, hopefully we can disable a few of them and encourage them to pack it in."

"Yes, Assistant Secretary," the commander replied. "Initiating combat spread, four groups."

The hovercraft began spreading apart, diverging from each other in wide turns until there were four groups heading in different directions. Mackey's boat turned sharply to the left, and he saw the boats marked Hopper, Ross, and Parsons join other groups, while Thompson followed his. There were five in his group, including Thompson. A green indicator text lit up in the corner of his vision, reading 'Delta Group.' *At least I know my group name*, Mackey thought.

He looked out into the distance, wondering in which direction the enemy ships lay. Suddenly, a compass heading appeared in green at the top of his vision. He turned until he saw 290 degrees appear, but he could not make anything out through the haze. He squinted to try and see further. He was surprised to see the view flicker and magnify, flicker and magnify again. The lenses on the remote camera system must be changing in response to his thoughts.

Then he saw them—grey ships, seemingly towering above the water, though still far away. They were breaking formation as well, cutting into courses out towards them in groups of twos and threes.

"You will start to feel manual control kick in," Hopper announced. "Test it out. Just think about moving in the direction you want, and learn how the system responds."

His vision resetting to normal lensing, Mackey felt his hover-craft decrease in speed, and the other craft in his group began to overtake him. Not wanting to be left behind, he thought 'faster.' Not of the word itself, but of the idea—the desire to catch up, not be left behind. The craft accelerated as the massive rotor blades kicked into high speed, and he pulled up behind the group. He thought about moving left, and then right, and watched as the hovercraft waggled slightly, tail heavy, as the rudders behind the ducted fans adjusted according to his whim. There appeared to be some sort of computer-assisted steering going on. A craft as awkwardly propelled as a hovercraft couldn't be so simple to control naturally. *Okay*, he thought. *Maybe this isn't so bad after all.*

"Your weapons will be armed when I give the order to engage," Hopper explained. "You have two Vulcan 15 mm chain-guns. They aren't as big or as long range as the autocannons the USGS are packing. But they spit out 6,000 armor-piercing rounds a minute, compared to their 200. Use short bursts, or you'll burn through all your ammunition. Aim above the waterline, two-thirds of the way back, below the funnel. We'll try and disable their engines.

"Your targeting system is online, although the weapons are not. Try it out. Each gun is controlled independently. The best way I can describe it is to extend the index finger of each hand. That should bring up the reticle. When you want to fire, squeeze. Do it with your mind, not with your hand."

Mackey gave it a try, and once again he was surprised by how easy it seemed. As he barely formed the idea of extending his fingers, two small green circles popped up into the sky. He squinted towards the distance, and his vision magnified until he could see the two ships speeding in their direction. He moved the circles until they both lined up on the superstructure of the leading vessel. Shocked at how easy it was, he relaxed, and the circles disappeared.

Were there human beings on those ships? Were there, for that matter, any human beings on the hovercraft he was controlling? He supposed that his boat was uncrewed—or certainly they would have given command of it to anyone other than him. But were there USGS Corps sailors on board those ships bearing down on them now? Would they fire at him? Was he really defending himself, if he was actually floating in a tank nearly one thousand miles away?

The USGS ships were growing larger now, and Mackey looked around to get a sense of what his group was doing. They had extended in a long line, single file, attempting to cut across the path of the leading cutter, increasing the relative motion between themselves and the USGS as much as possible. Mackey looked out and saw puffs of smoke erupt from the bows of both ships. Were they on fire? Had they been hit already?

And then the sea erupted on the opposite side of the line of hovercrafts, jets of spray soaking the decks of the lead boat. They were being fired upon! The hovercraft ahead of Mackey began oscillating, jockeying back and forth across the waves as they turned, changing heading to avoid the gunners' corrections. He did likewise, wondering what a 20 mm shell would do to the small, flimsy craft and its nacelles.

Looking out at the USGS ships, he saw them bending to the side, turning at high speed to alter course and follow them. The hovercraft were too fast, and were still closing distance, even while taking a wide, clockwise arc around the larger ships. Mackey saw the ships open fire again. This time shells landed in a staggered line across the arc of hovercrafts. A shell hit one of the hovercrafts ahead of Mackey and exploded, shattering the hull. It veered to port, quickly losing speed, and then flipping. He watched in horror as he saw several helmeted figures dressed in combat fatigues catapulted from the wreckage, hitting the water with a hard, twisting motion.

There were people on board! Were they on board his craft as well? Was he about to get an unknown group of Coast Guard sailors flung into the water or blown up with shells, all over some unknown inter-Departmental intrigue?

"We're taking fire, one boat was destroyed!" Mackey shouted. "There are—there were people on board! We're risking lives here! What are we doing?"

Hopper's voice came over the speaker. "Get ahold of yourself, Mackey. We know what we're doing. Stay in control."

"We're all part of the same government, aren't we? Why is this happening?"

"I can't answer that, because I don't know. But as you can see, they are going to keep shooting. If we want to know why, we have to disable those ships."

Mackey felt a hovercraft slide up along his starboard side. He looked, and it was Thompson. He heard the ranger's voice over the communication link. "I know what you're feeling, Fred. But it's like on that hillside, when you leapt at that officer. He was holding a gun. You didn't know why, but you knew you had to act. Let's do this. Let's take out their engines, and then we'll find out why."

He wished he could have seen Thompson's face when he said it, but all he saw was a dark green hovercraft, identical to his own. "All right, Gene. All right. Let's put an end to it." Mackey accelerated, turning sharply in towards the ships, skewing his craft tail-outward with the force of the turn. Thompson cut in behind him, following tight on his port side.

"Good lad, Mackey." Hopper's voice reassured him from the back of his helmet. "You're only half a click from entering range. Your weapons are now hot. Break group, and circle in opposite directions to draw their fire. Look out for crossfire as you complete the arc."

In front, the first two remaining hovercraft broke towards starboard, circling out to get around the pair of ships counter-clockwise. Mackey and Thompson continued, heading straight on, before dodging towards port to circle clockwise. The USGS gunners, confused over which to follow, stopped firing for a moment. This gave the hovercraft a chance to break in towards the tall grey hulls.

Mackey pulled up the reticles, now a deep crimson. He put them over the hull of the closest ship, and when the ship was turned perpendicular to him, he thought of squeezing. With a jolt, his hovercraft pushed back across the waves as a roaring sound filled his ears. On the side of the ship, he saw a blaze of dark smoke where the grey hull opened up. And then he stopped, the shots only lasting for a single second, like a quick rip of fabric.

The gunners on the USGS ship attempted to acquire targets out of their confusion, and sprays of water opened across the surface of the sea in front of Mackey. He dodged left, then right, then left again. Looking back, he saw Thompson take an equally short run at the ship, his shots impacting further aft. They both circled around as the other two hovercraft completed their runs. The four fan-driven craft crossed paths, confusing the gunners again momentarily. The ships maintained course, expecting the hovercrafts to make another run.

"They're still moving!" Mackey shouted.

"Let's give them another pass!" Thompson responded. On the communications channel, Mackey could hear that the other hovercraft groups were engaging targets as well, though he couldn't see them in the confusion and stress of the battle.

On the second arc, Mackey placed the reticles quicker and opened up earlier, releasing a machinic flight of hornets at three times the speed of sound towards the USGS ship. But the force of the guns firing drove him sideways over some rough chop in the water, and with his hull knocked upward, the bullets rose above the deck, showering the superstructure of the cutter. He saw glints of sparks, smoke, and then brief flame as some superficial fixtures caught fire, and he quickly released.

The USGS ships moved apart, widening their footprint, to make the circle the hovercraft traveled wider, and slow down their radial motion. As Mackey and Thompson passed the other pair of hovercrafts on another loop, Thompson shouted over the circuit: "Delta group team, split and head opposite directions! Mackey and I will cut through the center!"

Before Mackey had a chance to argue the other two craft proceeded with the plan, each heading in opposite directions around the ships, drawing both cannon to follow them. Thompson turned rapidly, skipping across the surface of the water, and made a beeline for the space between the USGS ships. Mackey, inhaling deeply, turned to follow. As they entered the gap, the USGS cannons were turned outward, attempting to track the other pair of circling hovercraft.

"Get a good shot in on the port ship, Fred! I'll take the starboard."

Mackey watched as the gun turrets on Thompson's hovercraft swiveled to the right. Its thrusters pivoted, and the hovercraft slowed and swung around to the right, drifting left in a strafing pattern. Both guns had a full, uninhibited shot.

That is a good trick, Mackey thought. Then the guns opened up—protruding tongues of flame and a hazy cloud of ejected cartridges filled the air above Thompson's hovercraft. Before Mackey had a chance to see the damage, it was his turn.

He thought about that maneuver that Thompson had thrown, and tried to put himself into it. He thought about leading with his hip, and the craft began to turn and slide across the waves, facing him towards the ship on the port side. He pointed, the reticles appeared dead below the funnel of the ship, and he fired.

He was so close, he could see the grey metal panels buckle and blister, opening like the flap of an envelope under a knife.

Past the ship now, Mackey saw the USGS cannons begin to turn about towards him, and he corrected his sideways glide as he increased thrust, thinking with all his will about getting the hell out of there. He followed Thompson, skating out across the waves in a wide arc, putting distance between themselves and the ships, as cannon shots impacted the water around them.

"I think we got them!" Thompson shouted over the channel. Mackey turned and looked behind him, and indeed, it appeared that both ships were stopped—and there was a thick black smoke emitting from one of them, a different color than the thin grey vapor from the funnels when they had been underway.

"Delta group, if your targets are halted, rally to Beta and give support!" the Assistant Secretary ordered over the line.

A green indicator reading "Beta" appeared. It was Parsons' group. Thompson, Mackey, and the two other hovercraft formed a diagonal echelon and sped off across the waves in that direction. Mackey zoomed in his vision to get a handle on the situation. The group had been facing three cutters. One was disabled, but three hovercraft had been destroyed. The two active ships were taking erratic, evasive action, and it was all that Parsons and the other hovercraft could do to stay out of the automatic cannon fire.

"Let's give them some help, Delta group," Mackey said. "Thompson and I will take the farthest ship; you two lend a hand to Parsons on the near side."

They split into these two smaller groups, to give the USGS gunners more targets to track. Cutting out in an clockwise arc around the two dodging ships, Thompson and Mackey watched their target's heading, looking for an opening.

"Should we try and get in behind it?" Mackey asked.

"Let's wait until it turns towards us, and head straight in. At a faster relative speed we'll be harder to hit. Beta unit—" Thompson called to the other craft, still desperately trying to avoid the ship's cannon fire, "wait until it targets us, and then move in for the kill."

The ship was large in Mackey's vision, superstructure partially damaged from machine gun fire, but still moving quickly. The cannon on the foredeck was firing rapidly, spraying shells out across the water at the Beta hovercraft, which dodged the plumes of spray from the exploding rounds. Coming about towards them as the cutter attempted to reverse direction, Mackey saw their opening.

They were too far away for a good shot, but Mackey fired a quick burst across the bow of the cutter to get its attention. It worked. The ship made a line for them as they raced towards it, its cannon turning to engage.

"Well, it's seen us now," Mackey said. "Full speed ahead! Beta unit, now's the time!"

He watched as the Beta craft, now free of the fire that had been pursuing it, cut in quickly at an angle from the rear of the cutter. But there wasn't time to watch, as shells began to explode around him and Thompson.

Without needing to communicate, they split up, again forcing the gunnery crew to pick between targets. They slid side to side, oscillating their angle of approach, ducking back and forth amid the lines of explosions reaching out across the blue water, the shells searching for the rubber hulls of the hovercraft. The distance was rapidly closing.

Then, the Beta craft reached the target. Flying across the water in a white gust of spray, its guns let loose armor-piercing rounds in the hundreds and thousands. Ripping into the steel plate, the rounds found a fuel line. A blossom of orange flame jetted from the side of the ship, peeling back into a black cloud of thick, oily smoke. The ship quickly changed course, turning into the wind, and the hovercraft beat a hasty retreat back out to sea. Mackey and Thompson, also peeling off in their arcs, watched as the cutter heaved to, engines disabled. Crews raced about the cutter in order to battle the licking fire crawling up the side of the ship towards the deck.

The last ship, now surrounded by Parsons and two other hovercraft, had turned around and was headed back the way it came.

"It looks like they're breaking off," Mackey said over the channel.

"Same here," Ross' voice came over the air. "One ship disabled, one retreating."

"Excellent. All groups make your heading 190, form up on me. Let's get on with it."

There were only fifteen hovercraft that rejoined the box formation. Mackey wondered how many troops and sailors were on board each one. His various indicators told him many things—the location of each group, the heading, his targeting information, and how many rounds he had left for each gun. But nothing about the number of lives that were under his remote care.

As they approached the beach, the craft formed two columns, one behind Hopper, and one behind another craft labeled with the indicator "Able 2."

"Autopilots will now re-engage to put us in formation as we navigate the tracks," the Assistant Secretary announced.

The columns of hovercraft hit the beaches at speed, kicking up spray and sand as the down-drafted air propelled the craft over the obstacles. Mackey's view was blocked temporarily by the clouds of dust and moisture, a fog of particulate haze that shrouded the sun. A good thing the autopilot was in control, he decided. Soon, they were on tarmac, and the debris diminished. Mackey felt a bump as his hovercraft climbed the short concrete edge of a P-car track loop in the beach parking area. Felt was a misnomer—his vision jostled, and his body, disconnected and yet still present, reacted with a jolt. But there was no sensation, only awareness of the terrain his vehicle was mounting.

Soon, they were rocketing down the P-car tracks, past the large stands of Upper Peninsula conifers. The hovercrafts were slower perhaps than P-car travel, but impressive in their size, overlapping four lanes of tracks easily with the large black cushions as they raced in single file.

Where was the traffic? Mackey wondered. A four-track route would not simply be devoid of cars. It must have been shut down, somehow.

The area was rural, few buildings were visible along the route. The hovercrafts rushed past the apparent vacancies in a maelstrom of noise and dust. He saw no one—no P-cars, no pedestrian walkways, no windows that anyone might see through.

After some miles, the convoy of hovercraft hopped off the edge of the tracks, each massive craft sailing over the embankment of the raised track grade before coming down in a cushioned splash onto a graveled lot. Before them was a massive hole nearly a mile wide—a surface mine of some kind, possibly iron, judging from the blackish red color. This must be the National Mine that Hopper mentioned. It was abandoned, empty, a black scar in the wooded landscape. Looking across the gap cut into the earth, Mackey saw another hole, and another, extending off into the distance. Racing along the edge of the mine works, he peered down from the remote view into the angularly sliced depression, terraced with tracks for the giant ore trucks. Below, there was a collection of water in the bottom of the mine, colored an unnatural aqua, rich with mineral runoff.

Ahead of them were some collapsed warehouses and elevators, where the larger interstate automatic trains must have been loaded. They shot by, kicking up a brown-red dust, passing slag heaps nearly one hundred feet high.

There was an explosion. At the head of the column, two hovercraft flipped into the air, breaking into pieces as their metal frames landed on the ground again in uncomfortable angles, sending the shards of propeller blades flying back through the column.

Out of the pit in front of them rose a small helicopter, painted bright white. Very small. Too small to contain a pilot. The bulbous nose of the craft contained no windscreen, and the body was a mere thin strip of metal, holding two wings onto which were mounted the aircraft's only cargo: a pair of rocket pods.

The helicopter fired again. As the column of hovercraft speeding across the ground could not deviate from its course while on autopilot, the rocket easily found another target. Impacting a hovercraft's fan nacelle, the warhead exploded, sending a fireball skyward and the hovercraft spinning off course, to plummet into the abyss of the open mine on the right side of the column.

"Hello, Assistant Secretary and associated bureaucrats!" an new voice crackled out of the speaker behind Mackey's head, sounding over-modulated, too close for comfort, spitting through the electromagnetic signal in a wizened voice, tinged with accent. How could it be? But he knew it had to be. It was the voice of Nicholas Roerich, invading their channel.

Hopper ignored the greeting and spoke to the hovercraft group. "Prepare to take evasive action! Autopilots disengaging in three, two—"

Suddenly Mackey was no longer in the hovercraft. He was in a P-car—that is to say, above it. He was speeding through the commercial center of a small city in the rain. Looking to his left, he peered into a pedestrian mall, with busy shoppers hurrying to and fro with umbrellas. He blinked involuntarily at the drops of rain that were smeared across his vision.

Now he was in a different P-car, heading across a bridge. He knew this view—it was the Bay Area, and he was heading from Oakland across to San Francisco, in heavy traffic, cutting in and out of clouds of fog.

Now he was back in a hovercraft, but a different one. This one had damage, was operating slowly and shakily, cutting across a field of grass before looping around a small lake, orange with iron ore residue. He heard Hopper's voice again on the communication channel: "—trying to break into the data link, stand by for countermeasures! Those still in control, take your—"

And he was in a car again, approaching a residential block. But above it, as if he was on the roof. As if he was the radar sensor pod, installed above the ovoid bubble of the car. The trees in the complex were flowering. *Magnolias*, he guessed, judging from the large leaves. *What was going on?*

Mackey tried to gain control, looking around him for any sort of indicator. He demanded to stop, putting his entire will against any further forward motion. The P-car stopped on the track, other traffic rapidly reducing speed behind him. It was an odd thing, to see cars stopped on a track. Motionless, frozen, like a film paused on a single frame, while the rest of the world continued by. He looked down through the glare of the sun on the Perspex below him, and saw a pair of occupants below him, fiddling with the control console inside the car.

And he was in a hovercraft again, speeding under a network of high-voltage power lines, across the brush-covered right-of-way, cleared of trees. Looking behind him, he saw the white helicopter giving chase. He pointed, and to his relief the gun reticles came alive, a deep red, and he fired in the air, spraying bullets across the Michigan sky. The small helicopter dodged, banked to the left, and disappeared behind the pine trees.

"This never would have happened in a real aircraft!" Mackey heard Parsons yell, to apparently no one in particular.

Mackey was in a P-car again. He was traveling at high speed along a coastal arterial, rising above the floodplain on a constructed causeway. Which coast, he had no idea. He traveled in complete silence, watching the traffic coming in the opposite direction at relative speeds of what must have been five hundred miles an hour. On his right, the ocean side, waves broke against shattered rock piled against the causeway to minimize erosion. On the shore side, there were large oaks, green beasts with twisting branches, extending off across the floodplain as far as he could see. Such an extent of trees!

"Can anyone hear me?" Mackey tried the communications channel.

"I can hear you." It was the voice. Roerich. No one else responded. There was no other sound.

"I know who you are," Mackey hazarded. But not wanting to bet it all yet, "You're the old man, from the temple in the Sierras."

"Ah yes," the voice responded, not displeased. "And I know who you are. You must be our new friend in the fine grey suit."

Mackey was not displeased either, but buried it. "What is it you are trying to do?"

"Trying to reclaim some stolen property. My apologies for putting you in this strange place. It must be disconcerting. But we will soon be in a different place."

Mackey watched the surf spray lightly against the rocky embankment as he traveled rapidly along the ocean. Along the tree-lined side of the tracks, he saw rows of odd, ramshackle construction, tucked in among the overhanging branches. Plywood, shipping crates, tarps and other scraps too difficult for him to process at the speed that the P-car was moving had been hastily or shoddily piled into some sort of low, messy buildings. It appeared like stacks of palletized building material, left to moulder in the weather. It must be a Rooseville, Mackey suddenly realized. His father had always hated the name, and would not let him say it in the house even though it was commonly spoken. And then it was gone, and there were only trees, and the ocean.

"What is it," he tried, "that the Department of Commerce believes it has lost?"

"That is our business, my friend. But I am sure you will learn about it when it is time…when your superiors desire that you know about it. That is the business of all of us who work in government, is it not? We know what we are supposed to know when we are supposed to know it."

Mackey thought about the bodies he had seen launched from a disintegrating hovercraft into a high-speed impact with the water. He thought about the long knife that had been held at Thompson's throat on a hilltop in California. He thought about satellites snapping photos, about Parsons' strange tales in the Thermosphere Club, told while the most important technocrats in the world sipped cocktails nearby.

"There's more to it than that, though, isn't there? I think we both know that."

The voice chuckled, but suddenly sounded distracted. "There always is. But I'm afraid we must put that off for later. It is time for us to go."

Mackey was in the laboratory at the NATSB. He was looking down from a table at five bodies, in five tanks. With a sudden rush of discomfort, he realized that one of those bodies was him! He was in the remote, the one they had inspected before teleporting off into this strange network of hovercrafts and P-cars. There was no one else in the room.

"Why have you brought us here?" he asked.

But there was no response. Either the voice of Roerich had gone, or he was not answering. Mackey seemed to be trapped. No thought he made seemed to have any effect. On his chest, he felt a strange vibration as if something was crawling across him, and he squirmed in reaction, oddly watching his body in the tank squirm at the exact same time. It was the electromagnetic amulet that Hopper had insisted that they wear. It was under his suit, pressed up against his skin. Suddenly, he had become aware of its presence, in the way that someone might suddenly become aware of their heartbeat. But now the sensation had stopped. Perhaps it was only Mackey's imagination.

And then he was back in a hovercraft, slowing as it approached a low-slung building surrounded by a barbed wire fence, up against a cluster of very tall pines. Was it the same hovercraft, or a different one? Mackey wasn't sure how he would know. His craft stopped, deflated, and dropped to the ground. Doors opened on both sides, releasing a squad of twenty helmeted troops carrying submachine guns, dressed in Postal Inspector tactical uniforms. They rushed the fence, broke open the gate, and surrounded the building.

Another hovercraft pulled up, dropped, and disgorged more troops. And then another, and another. A total of ten arrived, and finally from the indicators, Mackey was able to see that Hopper, Parsons, Thompson, and Ross had all made it. Or, were at least back in a hovercraft.

"Is it over?" Mackey asked. "Is he gone?"

"I'm told it's over, but be on your guard." Hopper's voice came through the speaker, clear and distinct again. "There was an attempt to mimic the authentication of our projected consciousnesses, in order to get back into the NATSB computer system. The attack failed, and my techs isolated it and shut it out. But they might try again."

"I saw some weird things," Ross commented. "I was in the bottom of the ocean, and then out in space."

"I was trapped in a navigational buoy," Parsons lamented, "for what felt like hours."

"When they mimicked our authentications, the computer responded by routing your projections to other points on the network. By creating a flood of routing traffic, they were hoping to overwhelm the limiting safeguards, and convince the computer their authentications were one of our projections, and ride it back to the origin, so to speak."

"It seemed," Mackey said questioningly, "that my remote was being put into a number of different P-cars. Like, I was above it. In a place that seemed to be near the radar node. But P-cars do not have cameras in them."

Hopper hesitated before responding. "It is not widely known . . . but some do have cameras. It is a limited rollout, no more than ten thousand units, across the continental United States only. We are doing a test of remote video transmission to see if the Postal data systems can handle the throughput."

"These cameras are transmitting video from random cars, all the time?" Thompson asked.

"Without the owners of the cars having any idea?" Ross was incredulous.

"The security risk is low," Hopper explained. "The purpose is for safety only. The video feed is anonymized, and there is no way to tell who is in the P-car below the video camera."

Mackey thought about the occupants of the car he had seen below him, and how it seemed as if he might even have had control over the car. But he changed the subject, not wanting to bring up the further details of his experience speaking with Roerich quite yet. "We are at the site, correct? What happens now?"

"The Inspectors are securing the facility, and then we'll be released to enter."

Moments later, the call came over the channel, "Assistant Secretary, site is secured. It appeared to have been evacuated of personnel."

Mackey watched as the remote ball perched on the front of Hopper's hovercraft popped into the air and began rolling along the ground. "Follow me," she said.

Before he could form the question, he felt himself tossed upward, and he landed on the grass. He moved in the same way he had piloted the hovercraft, by thinking it. His vision was now only a foot from the ground—the images shook back and forth as the image feed passed from camera to camera, scattered across the surface of the remote as he rolled forward. It provoked a bit of nausea at first, but soon he was able to ignore it, just as he ignored the bounce of his footfalls while walking.

He caught sight of the other remotes rolling along, their triangular edges popping in and out in order to thrust them forward, following the remote indicated as Hopper. She bounced up the steps of the facility, through the door held open by a Postal Inspector.

Mackey tried to bounce the remote, and quickly discovered he could.

The five remotes rolled down a hallway inside the building, and into a laboratory.

"This is probably the control room for the ELF radio apparatus," Mackey realized aloud. "Those cabinets are step-up transformers. There will be additional transformers nearby, the size of whole buildings. The ELF radio requires *a lot* of power."

Parsons' remote hopped onto a countertop and moved along it. "Mary, look at these up here."

Ross' remote followed, and paused while she scrutinized the consoles. "This appears to be a data receiving station. It's getting some sort of downlink, and feeding it into a computer."

"There are astrological charts," Thompson said, his remote on top of a desk by the wall. "Printed out of the machine here."

"Well, those are the pieces of the puzzle so far," Hopper announced. "It seems that we can verify that they are receiving information in response to their use of the astrological charts, and then re-broadcasting it via ELF. But to whom?"

"It would have to be to a submarine," Mackey concluded. "We know the ELF can't reach satellites. And anyway, if it was any land station, there would be a hundred other better frequencies to use than ELF."

"But why transmit them to submarine?" Ross asked.

"Assistant Secretary," the commander's voice broke in on the channel. "You should come out to the hangar."

The remotes dropped to the floor and rolled out into the hall, down the passageway towards a pair of large double doors. Two Inspectors opened the doors wide. Mackey looked up at them, wanting to apologize for being a remote, for some reason. But the Inspectors didn't give the self-propelled shapes a second glance.

In the cavernous hangar, white lights on the ceiling illuminated a tiny squadron of small white vehicles. Each was without pilot, without cockpit, without even much airframe. Some had fixed wings, others had rotors. One type even had two pairs of rotors on separated vertical wings, not unlike Parsons' prized Vail aircraft. A few had obvious weapon mounts, but they all had small, teardrop-shaped pods hanging from the undersides of fuselages and wings.

"Well," Hopper said, "this explains the appearance of the drone."

"These are target aircraft," Parsons said. "For training fighter pilots."

"They've been used for more than that," the Assistant Secretary corrected. "They've been doing reconnaissance for years, taking photographs. We've also used similar drone vehicles for electronic conflicts. They can be used as countermeasures, for diversions. And as we've seen today, they can be armed. Although most of the time they are too small to carry much in the way of ammunition."

"I think I know what those small pods are," Mackey said, speaking of the small teardrops underneath the drones. "They are jamming pods, aren't they?"

Hopper's remote approached the drones for a closer look. "I believe you are right, Mackey."

"Do you know what they might be used to jam, Fred?" asked Parsons. "If the Inspectors open one up for you, could you tell?"

"I could look," he offered. "But I would really need my lab equipment back at the Electromagnetic Bureau to be able to say for sure."

"Who made these?" asked Ross. "I've never seen any of these airframes, and almost every military or Departmental design comes through Plant 42 at some point for testing."

"I know where they come from," Thompson offered, cautiously. "And I'll tell you. But first I need to tell you something about myself."

The remotes adjusted, each catching Thompson's remote with one of their camera lenses, though his remote showed no sign of emotions, or any other human indicator that would have given them insight into his cryptic pronouncement.

"I think," Hopper said quickly, "we've seen enough here. Commander—we're going to cease remote operations. Thanks to both you and your troops...very brave under fire. I'll see that the Secretary hears of your heroism here today. Please, secure these remote units, and maintain a security perimeter at this complex until you hear further from me."

"Yes, Assistant Secretary. Thank you, ma'am."

The view of the hangar area faded into static before being replaced by the NATSB logo, and then the white grid of the helmet. Mackey sat up in the tank, his back sore, skin covered in sweat, balance disoriented in the dark of the helmet. Pulling it off, he saw the others climbing out of the tanks, rivulets of saline fluid running off of them and onto the laboratory floor, stretching their limbs and jaws, getting over the sudden rush of muscle disorientation as their brains reoriented to their bodies.

Hopper put her glasses on, her white suit still shedding liquid. "We'll change, and meet in the adjoining conference room. Then we'll hear what Ranger Thompson has to share with us."

There was no conversation as they changed clothes, each merely conducting their own awkward struggle as they lurched out of the tank gear. Mackey's muscles were oddly sore, as if even in floatation they had been tensing and relaxing without his full awareness of them—or perhaps imbued somehow with the heavy motions of the hovercraft. He could still feel the odd, gliding sense of hovercraft motion, the lingering delay of effect between control change and motion change, the balance of weight necessary in a heavy, hovering vehicle, not quite airplane, not quite boat. His glasses, put back onto his eyes, helped a little to replace the missing sensation of the screen that had taken over his sense of space.

As he dressed, Mackey held up the electromagnetic amulet around his neck. It was motionless, still, like nothing more than a piece of fashion jewelry. He tucked it underneath his shirt as he buttoned it, smoothing down the wrinkles with his hands.

In the conference room they gathered silently, again around a table with Mackey and Thompson on one side, Parsons and Ross opposite, and Hopper at the head.

"I realize," Thompson began, "that telling you this might endanger my life once again. But I cannot keep silent, because I believe I have crucial information about what is to happen."

He continued. "There is no time for Mr. Mackey to receive the drones at his lab and analyze them. But I know where they come from—a private factory, called Rand Aeronautical, in San Diego. We must go there at once and determine what the drone will be used for."

Ross spoke up immediately. "I think I speak for all of us when I ask how you know this."

He nodded, his eyes low, and continued. "My name is not Gene Thompson. It is Evgeny Tikhonov, and I am an agent of the Russian Bolshevik Technocracy-in-Exile."

The faces around the table were stunned. Thompson—or Tikhonov—continued speaking into the silence. His voice was still a perfect American accent, his deep brown skin betraying no quiver, no panic. He looked exactly the same as he had, only now exposed as someone completely different than they thought him to be.

"You were right, Assistant Secretary, to suspect that the Anti-War may be a factor here. I am sorry to tell you that your problems are not simply with the Department of Commerce, nor simply with the URER, but with both. Your Department of Commerce has been, for some time now, funding certain aspects of URER technological development, and aiding them through the leaking of new technological patents. This is against your laws, of course, as well as it is potentially politically embarrassing for both the URER government and your own government. We Bolsheviks, enemies of all capitalistic exploitation of technological resources, sought to expose this collusion in Russia and abroad."

Mackey was completely unsure of what to believe. "Why would Commerce want to help the URER?"

Tikhonov folded his hands on the table. "The tensions of the Anti-War are largely viewed by Commerce as being bad for the Department of Transportation. Furthermore, your Department of Commerce believes in competition, to its very core. They want the government and corporations of the URER to be a techno-logical competition for the Department of Transportation. And through that competition, they believe they will level the playing field, and gain power of their own against Transportation."

Mackey was still unsatisfied. "So they broke the law to do it? Orthogonal Procedures are one thing, but leaking technological patents of the United States government is essentially treason."

Hopper spoke up. "If Commerce wanted to leak information on new technology to the Russians, they couldn't do it from the Patent and Trademark Service. That would be too obvious, and the information there is under high security."

Mackey nodded. "Ever since the Pykrete Scandals in the 1940s, Patent and Trademark have access to every technological advance made by any agency of government, but they are heavily locked down and tracked. Any suspected leak would trigger a full review of access."

"That is correct," Tikhonov responded. "But the Smithsonian Cultural Service has no such restrictions. Material in their archives can be accessed freely by any government."

Ross thought aloud. "The National Standards Service gets information from the Patent Service, in the form of proposed changes to scientific and industry standards, due to new technologies."

"Numerologists and free energy enthusiasts, respectively," Parsons said to himself.

"Suggested changes to the standards are then logged by the National Standards Service in the Smithsonian archives," Mackey said, ignoring Parsons, and fitting together the pieces proposed by Ross and Tikhonov. "They could track potential new technology, if they are watching the proposed revisions of standards. It would be difficult and cumbersome to work backwards from standards to the technology, but not impossible. Like, if there was a proposed revision of the bandwidth allocations for radio phones, one might suspect that a new technology involving higher throughput of radio phone frequencies was in the works."

"And each of these agencies have large liaison offices between them, which help to identify the most helpful material," Tikhonov suggested.

"It's true," said Mackey. "The Patent Service has a full Standards Communications Office, Standards has an equivalent office to communicate with the Patent Service, as well as one with the Smithsonian, who has one for communicating with Standards. That is something like four hundred bureaucrats, all for transferring information concerning proposed changes on scientific standards. That does seem bloated, even for bureaucracy."

"With four hundred personnel and some good computer analysis, it would be easy to look backwards through the standard revision information, and identify the most likely new patents under development. Reverse engineering, in a sense," Hopper concluded.

"Internally, they call it 'forecasting and foresight.' And not only that, but they embed reports of these technology forecasts within the standards data in the Smithsonian archive," Tikhonov completed the circle. "Some of it is embedded in code, other parts are in plain language. The pieces only need to be decoded and fit together once the URER accesses the archives, and then it is a matter of experimentation until nearly the same patent invention can be 'discovered,' as if independently."

"So they are communicating, without communicating," Parsons mused. "Like reading each other's minds, but through hundreds and hundreds of pages of bureaucratic documents."

"Technological advance is much easier if you know exactly what to work on, what materials to use, what industrial processes to try," Ross said. "It takes out months and months of guesswork. The URER would be getting hundreds of pages of these hints, giving them a shortcut to new breakthroughs."

Hopper turned to the now-revealed spy. "You can prove all this, Tikhonov?"

"We are on the verge of doing so. I was undercover with the Forest Service, doing reconnaissance on Roerich to determine his role, when I was discovered. That is when we crossed paths, thankfully for me."

"But other than to thwart the URER, why are the Bolsheviks interested in helping the Department of Transportation?" Mackey asked. "We're not as market-oriented as Commerce, but we're still part of a capitalist country."

Tikhonov smiled. "We seek to shut off the URER's exploitative access to free technology, first of all. But as well, we admire how the Technocrats run things, just not all of their aims. Your technology is, of course, the best in the world. If only you were interested in using it to empower the workers and allowing them to control their own technological destiny, rather than, say, sending mail to the moon. If your material and historical aims were only slightly different, perhaps we would be best of friends."

"Politics aside for a moment, what does all of this have to do with drones?" Parsons asked.

"That, I do not know for sure," Tikhonov admitted. "But I know of these drones and their manufacturer, because it was among information leaked to the URER that our agents intercepted. New models produced by a private company with very good remote capabilities, not unlike these remote tanks here at the NATSB. Those are the drones we saw in Michigan. That company must be linked to Roerich and his scheme with the satellites and radio waves, although I can't say how."

He turned to Hopper. "I realize you must arrest me now, as a Bolshevik spy. But you have saved my life, and I have no regrets about aiding you with this information. You must go to Rand Aeronautical in San Diego, and figure out what Roerich is up to before the satellite deadline, now—" he checked the clock on the wall, "only ten hours away."

Turning back to the rest of the group, he let his eyes come to rest on Mackey. "I'm sorry for deceiving you in this way. But you must understand that it was the only way for me. Our revolution, in which technology is owned entirely by those who use it, required my dedication. To that goal, I am completely pledged."

Hopper stood up. "We can debate ideology later perhaps, Tikhonov. But now, we need you. You have filled in a number of missing pieces here, but we still do not have the entire picture. We have yet to determine what the drones and the satellites are meant to do. And so there is work for us yet. If you are able to continue making your services available to us, I think the Department of Transportation could use a Bolshevik partner."

From the expression on Tikhonov's face, he had clearly expected handcuffs. "You don't want to arrest me?"

Hopper shook her head and, reaching for her briefcase, stood up. "Under unique circumstances, you've become a part of this team. You're an asset to me, and to the Department, and assets are things that I do not give up lightly. So, if you are willing—"

"You certainly proved yourself in the hovercraft battle," said Mackey.

"You ask good questions," Ross added.

"And what you don't know about the occult, you make up in knowledge of scaring off bears!" Parsons smiled.

"Well, if it seems that you are all of a single opinion about it, then I have no choice but to be of any help I can," Tikhonov decided, "at least until I am able to return to my country."

They all shook hands.

"If we're quite finished, we all have aircraft to catch," Hopper urged. "Mackey, Tikhonov, and I will be headed to San Diego on the PE-70. We will investigate Rand Aeronautical. Ross and Parsons, you get back to Plant 42 and ready a strike team. As soon as we find the location where this drone, submarine, and satellite scheme is to take place, we will move."

"Will you be dropping us off?" Parsons asked. "Because I've had quite enough astral projection for one day."

"There weren't any ballistic transports ready at Plant 42," Ross broke in, "but there is a unit kept at ready station on Wallops Island. If we take that, you can fly direct to San Diego."

"Fantastic!" Parsons slapped his hands together. "Can we take the Chesapeake Bay Tunnel? I love the Bay Tunnel!"

September 4, 1958

Dear Fred Jr.,

Just writing to let you know how proud your mother and I are of you, as you enter your final year of engineering school. I can't say that I have much faith in the rest of the world. Eisenhower, like the career HQ staffer that he is, has just fired Postmaster Truman. Your mother and I heard him on the radio this morning, saying how the "Age of Administrationism is at an end, and it is time to move on to new things." That's horse pucky. "New Things," like falling behind the Russians, and letting them have outer space all to themselves. New things like letting the damn Commercialists sell everything we've worked for off to the highest bidder. Same old thing, more like. If Administrationism was good enough for us in the Postal Squadrons during the war, I say it's good enough to take us to the stars. And yet here we are, with Idiot Ike selling us all short.

But enough about politics, you're probably tired of hearing your old man's rants. At any rate, I'm glad that you will soon be a fully qualified engineer. I hope you'll follow in your father's footsteps by providing service to your country as best you can, forever championing the cause of science against the interests of greed and avarice, taking your generation forward into the technological future.

We're very, very proud of you, son.

Fred Mackey, Sr.

10
Emergency Brake

HOPPER WAS ON THE SATELLITE PHONE THE ENTIRE FLIGHT TO San Diego, the white plastic handset pressed to the edge of her impassive face. Her agenda was unknown, but one of the tasks must have been arranging for a landing at Miramar Postal Air Station. The San Diego sun was beating down upon them from the moment they stepped out onto the tarmac, with the Pacific humidity meeting the desert dryness nearly exactly halfway. Not five minutes after coming to a halt, Tikhonov, Mackey, and the Assistant Secretary were in a Department P-car, spinning up the entrance track to the West Coast Arterial, heading north through the San Diego hills to the location of the Rand Aeronautical plant.

They discussed the upcoming task in the car. "From what I know, it is a private facility so the security will not be as good as a government site," Tikhonov told Mackey. "But that doesn't mean that the doors will be wide open."

Hopper was on the radio telephone in the car, as always, communicating with forces unknown out across an etheric abyss. Not an ether of electromagnetic radiation, which Mackey understood very well, but with secret government forces and nebulous offices of bureaucracy. She put her hand over the mouthpiece and spoke quickly to Tikhonov and Mackey. "It appears ownership of Rand has changed hands in the last six months. We can't say for sure, but it looks like the new owners could be a front for Megatherium."

"Megatherium, owning private companies? That seems like an obvious conflict of interest for Commerce," Mackey said.

"Megatherium isn't technically a part of the Commerce Department," Tikhonov explained. "It never was an official agency or part of a Service. It was more of an agreement between Commerce executives, especially those related to the Smithsonian. And that is the way it has continued to exist, very secretly, from the end of World War Two until now. As private individuals, the Commerce executives form empty companies, called shell companies. These, in turn, own interests that they could not hold publicly as executives."

"You know all about Megatherium and Commerce, it seems." Mackey eyed Tikhonov. "But you were asking all those questions about federal bureaucracy before, as if you didn't know anything about it." He didn't feel hurt exactly. But it was a shame that Thompson—Tikhonov—was one more myth himself. Another thing that couldn't be trusted to be what it seemed.

Tikhonov looked away from Mackey, out the Perspex bubble, to the residential complexes lining both sides of the arterial. The soft sounds of Hopper's whispers and Tikhonov's heavy pause were punctuated by the soft thumps of cars passing in the slipstream. "I am sorry that I've had to mislead you, Fred. I'm sorry that I had to mislead all of you. It's just that the time wasn't right to reveal who I really was. I had to feign a bit of ignorance in order to see what all of your motivations were. Please understand—I didn't lie to you because I thought you were gullible, or because I wanted to deceive you. I had to, in order to protect myself and my work."

The pieces of the puzzle did fit better this way. Subterfuge, at this point, felt more like truth. After Tikhonov's performance in the hovercraft battle, it seemed more natural that he was another one of these occluded government operatives, and not a civilian who had wandered into the scene. Tikhonov seemed a lot more comfortable as Tikhonov rather than Thompson, more able to speak freely about what he knew and did not know.

Tikhonov assured Mackey that everything he had told him about his life was true, just the names and locations were not those he had given. His parents had lived in Angola, but had moved to Russia to work on space program activities. Tikhonov had spent his childhood in the Kazakh foothills in Central Asia, which were not all that different from Idaho. He had learned English there, and perfected his accent while studying abroad in actual Idaho, while simultaneously constructing his back story. He had begun working as an operative for the Bolsheviks not because he enjoyed spying, but so that he could get out of the office apparat, and travel the world.

"What I can tell you truthfully is that we're on the same side, at least for now." He turned from looking out the side of the car to make eye contact with Mackey again. "Like you, I imagine, I have a particular set of ethics that guides my actions. I do what is best for my party, because my party and its members support my ethical goals. To have technology in the workers' control is the most ethical situation. So, our actions are defined by that end, and become ethical when they are in line with it. Right now, our goals line up, so I am allied with you and your Department. To stop this conspiracy between the Commerce Department and the URER is important. Just for different reasons, in your perspective and mine."

Mackey tried to judge what was really behind Tikhonov's eyes. "What if your commitment to your goals means killing people? That is what happens, when you define the means in terms of the ends."

"People kill for all sorts of reasons. For greed, for love, for anger, or for the inability to plan ahead and see it as an inevitable outcome. They arrive at that point, pretending to be unaware, powerless to change the outcome of what they call fate, and claim that violence was the only path for them to take. We can't pretend that the path to our ends merely happens to us. The path, the destination—it's all the same. To create any sort of society, planning ahead is crucial, in order to prevent deaths. That is the real challenge that we all face. To avoid what violence we can, through better planning."

Now it was Mackey's turn to avoid the other man's eyes by looking out the window. "I used to see both the path and the ends. I used to think I could trust what I saw. But now, I'm seeing ends emerge from behind the ends."

Tikhonov nodded.

"My father was the sort of person who believed in a definitive end," Mackey continued. "He believed in Technocracy. If it was a party, he would have carried a membership card. He was a partisan, I suppose. Working for the Postal Administration, he believed he was part of the end goal, and he was happy with that. I always thought that his dedication was overblown. Fanatical, even. I didn't think the difference between Administrationism and Commercialism could be so clearly accepted as a goal in and of itself. I looked at my day's work as an engineer and tried to focus on that as my challenge, to let the challenge of my work be the only goal I had. But now, that seems impossible. I don't know what my father would make of everything I've seen over the last few days. He would be surprised, shocked, I'm sure. But I think he would still know what side he was on. He would still have the end goal in mind."

"I wasn't born a member of the party, you know." Tikhonov let his hand fall onto Mackey's elbow. Mackey didn't move, just looked down at the hand upon his jacket sleeve. "It wasn't predetermined. I could have been just a citizen of the URER, and gotten a job in the bureaucracy somewhere. But at some point, I decided that I wanted to work towards something bigger than what was right in front of me. I didn't want to be a faceless bureaucrat, if you'd excuse me saying so. The Bolshevik end goal is not perfect. It is not the final goal that matters, but using the final goal as a tool to accomplish great things. This is the best goal I could find, and so I'm sticking with it, until they invent a better one."

Mackey thought about himself, and his life's accomplishments thus far. Was he a faceless bureaucrat? He certainly didn't have much to show for his life, except for his job. He had spent his entire life trying to fit in, trying not to stand out, for sake of his career. In that way, he supposed he was a faceless bureaucrat. Or at least, a bureaucrat unwilling to face certain facts.

He looked at Hopper and Tikhonov. They were a pair of spies. Behind every action was a hidden motive, and behind that motive, more hidden actions. They both convinced themselves that there was a deep motivation, a first cause for it all that proved itself with results. And that, they said, was the bottom line. But how could they really think that, if they didn't know who they were fighting against? Commerce, the URER, Megatherium, Roerich, or other unknown ghosts and spirits? If you didn't know your enemy, how could you know when you'd won? They didn't even know the real gods they thought they were fighting for. And meanwhile, people lost lives, and who knew why or whom to blame.

Parsons, on the other hand, saw everything as shrouded and hidden. The manic, mustached man accepted that everything was unknown, and reveled in it. It was all real and unreal, and everyone's contradicting motives were proof of that. So he threw himself headlong into that dark cave, seemingly willing to explode rocket engines, fly strange machinery, accept strange capsules and swallow them, taking the tweaks and holes in reality as part of the scenery. Or did he have some sort of deeper motivation? Was there a part of the conflicting, overlapping realities that he thought had value? Was there some sort of deeper truth that he was searching for—at least until one of his strange flying machines caught fire with him trapped inside?

What about Ross? What was her motivation? The woman had been working with Hopper for who knows how long, and yet she did not seem quite as dedicated to the Department. Despite her status with the Assistant Secretary and with the Department of Transportation, she was not an executive, but an engineer. The clandestine was a sideline. She was still an engineer, using programs to define ballistic motion and orbital patterns on a daily basis. Mathematics then, as she had said in her lab at Plant 42—that was her foundation, and bottom line. And yet, the woman carried a sub-machine gun underneath her flight jacket. How did she reconcile her equations and her guns? Then again, Mackey thought, her equations were meant to guide, among other things, the ballistic paths of nuclear warheads.

Hopper hung up the phone. "There is somewhere I must be, so you two will have to conduct this intrusion on your own."

Mackey thought of protesting, but couldn't see what good it would do. The Assistant Secretary had decided, and therefore, that was the way it was going to be. She produced a small box from her briefcase. It was brown, plastic like a cheap transistor radio, with an aerial and a button on the side. She handed it to Mackey. "Hit the button, and I will pick you up in five minutes on the dot. After you press the button, carry it with you, outside of your pocket. Try not to smash it—it is a bit delicate." He placed the small device in his jacket pocket without giving it much thought.

"What is your plan for entry?" Hopper asked.

"Sales interview," Tikhonov explained. "One of my people has arranged it. The person we have an appointment with has left early, but forgot to clear his schedule. That should get us in the door, and then we will improvise to find the drones."

"Stick with what works," Hopper said. "I'll drop you at the parking entrance."

The reception area of Rand Aeronautical was unfamiliar, an odd sort of space to Mackey's bureaucratic experience. Come to think of it, he couldn't remember the last time he had been in the offices of a private business. The decor was completely different than any governmental agency. There was a similar appeal, perhaps, but it didn't map onto any of the architectural dialects that government buildings spoke.

In the lobby, surrounded by a set of low receiving couches, an abstract sculpture piece formed from chromium parabolas denoted some sort of aerospace or scientific work. There was a phone booth, and a large desk where the receptionist waited for them to approach from the automatic revolving door. These were not entirely unfamiliar objects, and not an entirely unfamiliar space. It was a space for waiting, for the precursors to appointments, the fashionable outerwear of an institution in motion.

But the feel of the place was entirely minimal. The ceiling was low, confining, rather than magnanimous like the hall of a public building. There was none of the wood paneling, the polished marble, or other architectural features that spoke of institutional power. Instead, the trimming was in stainless steel, glass, and shining white polyvinyl. Instead of stone or tile flooring, there was spun-polyester carpet, in off-grey and black pinstripes, like the reception area was wearing a suit of its own.

It did not seem right somehow. Buildings were meant as gathering places for executives and employees, not meant to be one of them. Across the carpet their heels did not click, but were muffled, matching the hushed air from the HVAC system as if this bright space demanded silent apprehension, rather than cavernous awe.

Once they were cleared by the receptionist to go to their false appointment and given visitor's badges, they proceeded down the hallway to the elevator bank. There was no artwork on the walls. In any other building there might have hung photographs, paintings, or even marketing material. Here were only the smooth, polished surfaces of the architecture. As they waited for the elevator, Mackey commented on it to Tikhonov. "Maybe they haven't accomplished anything worth sharing yet." He shrugged. "Or nothing that they want to share."

They were directed to ascend to the second floor. But upon entering the elevator, Mackey saw that there were four sub-floors, and decided to do what he thought Hopper might have done. He pressed the button for the second lowest, and the elevator began descending.

"Did you see the layout of the building?" Tikhonov murmured. "It intersects a hillside. I would bet that on the extent of the building, the sub-basements emerge from the hillside."

"That would be a good place to remove aircraft from a lab or underground hangar," Mackey said.

The exited the elevator and walked quickly down a long hall, decorated in the same minimal style as the lobby several floors up.

"I can't believe they did the entire building out like this," Mackey commented, quietly. "Can you imagine working here? It feels like working in an empty closet."

"Your office—it's more comforting?"

Mackey wasn't quite sure what the Electromagnetic Bureau offered that Rand Aeronautical did not. "In public buildings, somehow, the chaos, the open spaces, even the older bits that need maintenance work—it reminds you of the public. That's what the world is like. You aren't cloistered from the world. You are part of the world you are building."

"And yet, you need a badge to get in. Your Bureau isn't a public library. The workers who build the equipment you design— they live, work, exist somewhere else, outside of your murals, atriums, labs, and large oak desks."

The offices were windowed, and they casually looked in as they passed, seeing workers at desks like any other office, albeit with a much more corporate color scheme. At least the work appeared the same, judging from the stacks of forms on desks, the boxes and filing bins stacked with paperwork, and the heads bent down over typewriters and drafting boards.

The offices gave way to larger doors, secured with security consoles. These must be the labs. To Mackey's surprise, the doorways were labeled with the name of what was contained within. They passed "Avionics," "Modeling," "Radar Cross-Sectioning," and "Materials." Would they simply find one that read "Drones"?

Tikhonov stopped in front of a pair of unlabeled double doors at the end of the hall.

"I have a good feeling about this one." He pointed.

Mackey gestured at the security console. "Do you have a good feeling about that?"

Tikhonov leaned his head close, scratching his chin. He felt around the outside edge with the tips of his fingers. Then suddenly, he stepped back, reared up, and planted a heavy kick in the meeting place between the two doors. They popped open with a crash. Mackey waited for the alarm, and heard nothing.

"Not even centrally wired," he marveled as they rushed inside. "Should have spent less money on carpet."

The room was not empty. Two technicians were behind a computer console, sitting on stools. They looked confused as the two men rushed at them. "What is the meaning of this?" one tried to ask.

"It's a sales pitch," Tikhonov responded quickly, producing the dazzle pistol from under his coat. Mackey suddenly remembered that they were armed, and wondered if he ought to have his weapon out as well. But it seemed as if Tikhonov had the surprised technicians covered well enough.

"Close the door," Tikhonov said to Mackey, "and find something to tie them up with."

He found some electrical cable and began doing the best job he could.

"What is it that you want?" one of the technicians asked, frightened.

"We want to see your drones," Tikhonov said.

"Why do you want to see our drones?" one technician asked.

"Shut up, Smith!" the other fired back.

"Well, apparently we've come to the right place," Mackey remarked, finishing securing each technician's hands behind their backs, and to the lab stools on which they sat.

"So." Tikhonov smiled, bringing the dazzle pistol closer to each of them in turn. "Where can we find these drones?"

They looked at each other. The one called Smith spoke first. "Well, it's not as if they won't find it, Habert."

"Because you clued them into it, you idiot!"

There was another set of doors in the back of the lab, and Mackey went to it. It seemed an obvious first guess. He opened one of the steel doors and peeked through. Looking back to Tikhonov, he waved him over. Making an obvious gesture towards the technicians with the dazzle pistol, Tikhonov walked back to the doors and stepped through.

It was one of the white drones, hung in a steel test rig suspended from the high ceiling, extending upwards some thirty feet in the air. Below it, on a test track extending the length of the long chamber, probably close to one hundred yards, was a P-car. The two men ventured forward to the control console at the side of the cavernous test space.

"Well, that was easy enough," Tikhonov murmured.

"Are they going to be okay in there?" Mackey gestured back towards the two technicians in the lab. "I'm not comfortable with the idea of having prisoners."

"They'll be okay if you tied those knots well enough. Beats being hit with one of these strange dazzle guns, I'm sure."

Mackey sat down at the console and began assessing the equipment. It appeared to be a test track control system, obviously enough. There were large buttons for power-up, emergency brakes, sequence countdown, and so forth. The computer console seemed equipped to run any number of routines. And then there was a stack of familiar-looking equipment, lined with grey scopes screens, plastic knobs, and output ports for Postal Standard RS-232 data cables. These devices would not have been out of place in Mackey's own laboratory.

"That's spectrographic test equipment connected to the computer," he told Tikhonov. "They were testing the jamming pods here, or some other radio function."

"Can you see how it is calibrated? To get any sense of the target for the jamming, or any other information?"

Mackey turned on the monitor set into the console, and pulled over a text entry keyboard. He wasn't sure of the computer's make, but a few attempts told him that there was a command-line interpreter running that appeared to function using a language not unlike FORTRAN. It was quite high-end, integrated with display and keyboard. He typed commands in line form, and the computer took his line of keystrokes and ran them without even having to compile first. After stumbling through a few commands, unable to check his typing before hitting the "run" button, he managed to get a few datasets on the screen. He wished the system was more like the terminal at NATSB for Eliza, where Dr. Willamette had been able to see her keystrokes appear on the screen as she typed. Those two interfaces combined would be one hell of a engineering platform.

"I don't know this system, but let me see what I can do."

Thinking of the lab back at the Electromagnetic Bureau, Mackey tried to imagine what sort of information might be accessible via this terminal. One thing test platforms always did was log the experimental data to a recording medium.

Without context, the responses to his garbled commands didn't tell him much, but it confirmed that this system had been testing the jamming equipment.

"See these? They are spectrographic plots over time or distance—not sure which. This here, these lines? That must be the jamming signal. It's wide band, blocky, and strong, like it's meant to knock any other signal off the map. And look at this—these holes here? That's band jumping. If you wanted to avoid our interference detection systems, that would be a good start."

"I don't get it," Tikhonov said, "but I'm glad you do."

"Okay, this must be the test cycle. It looks to be about ten seconds long, whatever it was."

Tikhonov leaned close, over his shoulder. "Keep gesturing at the screen while you talk, it makes you look very smart." He gave Mackey a grin.

Mackey blushed despite himself, and concentrated on the screen. "Let me see if I can bring back the last test cycle. Maybe we can replicate it." He tried a series of commands.

The screen printed a message. "System not powered."

Tikhonov read over Mackey's shoulder. "What does that mean?"

"Try the labeled button on the console. It must want the system to be powered up before loading the test cycle."

Tikhonov reached and pressed the heavy button. A series of lights and meters on the panel jumped to life. From the test track ahead of them, the P-car whirred into idle state as the track was electrified.

"That's odd," Mackey said, and tried his command again. The computer refused to respond, only displaying the message, "Start system countdown."

"That must mean this button here," Tikhonov said as he reached for the panel.

"Wait, maybe we shouldn't—"

Tikhonov hit the button. Yellow revolving lights lanced out from the ceiling, and a warning bell began ringing.

"Oh no . . ."

The sound of heavy, high-voltage current came crackling from the drone overhead, as the spectrographic equipment became ablaze with data. And the P-car began accelerating down the track towards the opposite end of the room.

Mackey furiously pecked at the keyboard, trying break in to the routine, but the car was already gaining speed, nearly sixty miles an hour as it made it through the halfway point. Tikhonov was watching a closed circuit view from the opposite end of the hall, displayed on a screen on top of the console in front of them. As the P-car sped towards the camera, he stared, captivated by the inevitability of it.

"Evgeny! Hit the emergency brake!" Mackey desperately pointed at the button on the end of the console.

"Oh! Of course!"

But it was too late. The P-car slammed into the barrier at the far end of the track, going close to one hundred miles an hour. The wheels derailed, snapping off the Perspex bubble of the passenger compartment, which impacted against the wall, crushed like a pop can. The heavy drivetrain and wheels came crashing through next, taking out the closed circuit camera, racks of test equipment, and crushing the bare cement bricks of the wall into a cloud of powder. The entire mess popped through the wall onto the other side, where California sunlight shined through the dust and smoke. An alarm was wailing, blazing electrical horn agony throughout the test chamber, turning yellow lights to red.

Mackey and Tikhonov didn't move for a moment, too shocked by the destruction to know what to do. Then, Tikhonov clearly remembered the technicians behind them. He dashed back and looked through the door.

"Shit! They're gone, Fred!"

Mackey just stared at the cloud of debris that had been the P-car, at the far end of the track. "That can't happen, it isn't supposed to . . ."

"What the hell is happening down here?" a voice shrieked from outside the door behind them.

"Come on!" Tikhonov snatched Mackey's arm, pulling him out of his stupor, and dragging him down the test track towards the wreck. Mackey remembered where they were, and began to run.

"Hey, stop!" Gunshots rang out down the test chamber.

Mackey and Tikhonov wheeled to see several security guards with weapons drawn. "Look away, Fred!" Mackey was already half-turned, continuing to run, when Tikhonov fired the dazzle pistol. A green flash, like a flat circle of lightning, appeared momentarily in the space between the guards and the two interlopers. Mackey looked back and saw the guards clutching the walls, hands to their eyes, screaming.

"Run!"

They dashed down the test chamber, closing the distance between themselves and the wreck of the P-car. Mackey looked over his shoulder again to see the guards starting to recover, looking around the room dazed, trying to find the two escaping men.

The wreck was even worse than it looked. The electrical motors that powered the wheels had cracked out of their heavy steel cases. Large capacitors from the power system had launched out of their mounts and pierced the remains of the passenger compartment like cannon shells, punching through the Perspex and then through the concrete bricks behind. Mackey caught sight of a bench seat, smashed into plastic fragments the size of potato chips, only recognizable by the scraps of vinyl that had been the cushion, now beginning to catch fire in the smoldering chemical blaze of a breached battery unit.

Shots rang out behind them again, hitting the concrete wall far above them, but Mackey was sure the next rounds would be closer. "Through the hole!" Tikhonov grabbed Mackey by the hand and pulled him through.

Stunned themselves by the bright afternoon sun, it took a few seconds to get their bearings. They were behind the Rand facility, as they expected. But where now? There was a stretch of tarmac leading to a dirt strip, like a small runway or test field. But that was an open space, hundreds of yards across. As soon as the guards emerged, they would be sitting ducks. Mackey looked to his left, and saw a chain link fence with a small access track for service vehicles on the other side, then another fence, and then the tracks of the West Coast Arterial, suspended forty feet above them on large concrete footings.

"Over the fence!" he shouted to Tikhonov.

They climbed, metal wire cutting into their fingers and feet, until finally they could throw themselves over the top. Then they ran a few hundred feet further down the service track, and began climbing again.

At the top of the second fence, Mackey risked a look back towards the building, where a thin trail of smoke was curling up out of the hole that they had made in the side of Rand Aeronautical. The guards had emerged, and caught sight of them. They chanced a few shots, which glanced off the chain link in a shower of sparks, and began climbing the fence after them. Mackey and Tikhonov dropped to the ground on the other side and dashed under the arterial viaduct, putting as much distance as they could between the guards and themselves.

"Hopper's transmitter!" Tikhonov yelled. "Press the button!"

Thankfully, it was still in his suit pocket. Mackey dragged out the aerial and jammed the button hard, clutching it in his fist as they ran over the gravel beneath the arterial. Above them, they could hear the rushing whirs of rush hour traffic shooting back and forth. It sounded like a river filled with wind. But above the sound, he also heard a strange gruff noise, like an animal growl. It was oddly mechanical, like a winch, or a saw. Looking behind them, he saw a bright light, getting larger and larger.

"What is that?" he yelled to his companion.

"I think it's a motorcycle!"

"A motorcycle?"

"With an internal combustion engine!"

Whatever it was, it was gaining on them, and there was no way they could outrun it. Ahead of them, in the center of the arterial, was a narrow staircase crawling up underneath the tracks above. A maintenance access way.

"Up the stairs!" he called. They dashed upwards, flat leather shoes banging against the metal slat steps. At the top was a door, and a small security console. Tikhonov threw himself against it, but the door held fast. Mackey looked down to see the motorcycle approaching the stairway, a two-wheeled vehicle with a bright light on the front, sounding like angry beast.

Mackey reached under his jacket and pulled out the electroblast. He folded out the stock and jammed it under the shoulder of his suit jacket. He raised it to the security console.

"Wait! The transmitter!"

Mackey gasped, and quickly handed the device to Tikhonov, who held it out as far away from them as possible, over the edge of the stairs. Mackey aimed, and pulled the trigger. There was a slight pop, like a camera flashbulb, and then nothing.

"Well that's just great!"

The security console light blinked from red to green. Tikhonov tried the door, and it pushed open. He pushed Mackey through and looked back down the stairs, to where two security agents were just mounting the steps. He pointed the dazzle pistol.

"Hey!"

They looked up on cue, and averting his eyes, Tikhonov released another disk of green lightning, sending the agents tumbling backward down the stairs as they tripped on their feet, temporarily blinded. Then he followed Mackey through the door.

There was another set of small stairs formed out of concrete, and another door—this one unsecured. They quickly pushed through, and found themselves in the middle of the arterial.

P-cars rushed in both directions, at speeds that might have been up to two hundred miles an hour. At the height of rush hour traffic, the cars were largely in formation, and the slipstream buffeted them back and forth across the thin concrete channel on which they stood, no more than six feet from the traffic.

They ran down the center of the tracks, bombarded by wind and noise from all sides. It was like standing on a highway of comets, each round shape blazing with the reflection of the afternoon sun, chilling them to the bone with rush of air and sound. The P-cars, from the outside, had the auditory presence of meteoric insects, engines whining with voltage, carving up the steel tracks with their wheels. It was impossible to focus on the sight of one as it passed by, it moved so quickly. Mackey looked up onto the tracks, and saw, for a split second, the eyes of a small boy sitting on the seat next to his mother. It wasn't even a fraction of a moment, more like a memory; real, but gone before it could entirely take shape.

The guards were behind them again, a few hundred yards back, dashing down the concrete drainage channel after them.

Tikhonov fired the dazzle pistol, but now wise to the game, the guards saw the raised weapon and hid their eyes, then kept running after the green flash had disappeared.

"Now what?" yelled Tikhonov over the noise.

Mackey pointed off to the right, across the arterial flow. "The exit track! If we can get to it, we can run down to surface tracks!"

Tikhonov gaped at him. "Are you crazy? It's across six lanes of track! We'll never make it!"

Mackey stepped to the edge of the channel, mounting the raised lip that led up to the tracks' surface.

"We can! Stopping distance is too far at this speed, but the cars will automatically emergency brake to reduce impact speed against a track obstruction. We should gain half a second to dash. Take off your coat! Make yourself look big to the radar so it can see us!"

Tikhonov looked skyward and mumbled to himself. "Just like chasing off a bear . . . "

They held their coats above their heads, and waited until there was a gap between the next approaching formation. It wasn't a big gap, but it would have to do.

"Go!" Mackey shouted. They stepped onto the tracks, waving their jackets above their heads. The rapidly approaching P-cars let out a grinding scream as the radar sensor triggered the emergency brakes and the motors reversed current flow, sucking the energy out of the electric drive, absorbing the force of inertia. The oncoming cars were slowing, but not enough, becoming larger and larger as the shining Perspex nose of the lead car came up onto Mackey and Tikhonov. Mackey felt the slipstream of a formation tear at his clothes as it passed them on the adjacent track.

"Go!" he screamed again, and they dodged forward on to the next line. The braking formation, now with the path cleared ahead of it, resumed acceleration, rocketing past them down the line. Mackey could just make out the bodies of passengers thrown to the floor by the emergency braking, looking around themselves trying to figure out what had happened. It was likely none of them had ever felt a P-car throw on its emergency brakes before.

The sound of the passing formation's roaring slipstream was quickly replaced by a terrible screaming as the next approaching line of cars engaged their brakes, still tumbling towards Mackey and Tikhonov, the latter desperately flailing his coat in the air. The next track cleared with a massive whoosh of air, and they lept onward, slowly progressing outward towards the exit track. The braking formation continued, again showcasing cars full of confused passengers picking themselves off the bottoms of the passenger compartments.

And again, the scream of brakes coming at them down the track. Mackey grabbed the back of Tikhonov's shirt, waiting to pull the man with him as soon as he saw an opening. But the bottom of his stomach dropped out. Coming up along the far side the braking formation was another formation on the next track, passing the slowing formation easily, its path unobstructed.

"Back! We go back!" Mackey screamed, pulling Tikhonov along with him as they leapt back the way they came. The two P-car formations passed them as the next approaching line on their track began braking, sending its electric squeal out on the air towards them.

"This is not what I would call progress!" Tikhonov yelled, waving the jacket in the air like a flag.

Mackey looked at the oncoming traffic, and made a judgment call. "Okay! When I say, we cross two!"

"You mean we skip one, or we skip two?"

The screaming brakes were fast approaching, the first P-car in formation looming large, bearing down on them with incredible speed. Mackey grabbed Tikhonov's shirt collar tightly.

"Just follow!"

The adjacent track was cleared with a gust of wind, and they leapt across onto the third lane, and then another gust, and they leapt again to the fourth. It took them longer than Mackey had thought, and another formation was bearing down on them fast.

"Again! Go!"

The mounted the fifth track, and then quickly, the sixth. Finally they made the exit, and began running. If only they could make it to the descending curve of the ramp before a P-car switched onto the exit, they could jump off onto the embankment. It was one hundred yards away.

Mackey heard the scream of braking. A P-car was approaching on the exit track. "Run, Tikhonov! Run!"

They dashed for it, but it was too far. The P-car was on top of them, brakes shrill like the cackle of a crow. Mackey turned and threw up his arms.

The P-car stopped. The gullwing doors popped open, and the car stood motionless. Music poured out of the open car, a popular radiophonic folk ballad that Mackey was somewhat familiar with. Panting, covered in sweat, he looked up and saw the Postal Bureau logo on the rounded bubble nose. The car was empty.

Tikhonov turned and saw the stopped car. "Is that our ride?"

Bullets glanced off the concrete and one careened off the logo on the car's nose itself as the Rand Aeronautical guards opened fire between P-car traffic from the drainage channel. Mackey and Tikhonov dashed for the P-car and threw themselves in, as the lyricist's voice made the plaintive case for track overpasses as an analogy for unrequited love.

The doors closed, the car sped up, taking the exit at speed, dashing across three lanes of traffic on the surface tracks without regard for the signals, causing a new cycle of shrill braking as the pattern was disrupted, before accelerating up the entrance ramp on the other side of the junction and rocketing into traffic on the arterial heading the opposite way. The men lay on the floor of the car, panting, while the ballad played at an unreasonable volume in the relative silence of the car's interior. It was like they had a glass dome slipped over top of them in the middle of a hurricane. Only with a teenage heart throb musical act somehow captured along with them.

"Hello, Mackey?" The Assistant Secretary's voice emanated from the console as the music, thankfully, automatically decreased in volume. "I hope the remote car got you both back, safe and sound without any collisions. Remote signal overrides tend to be a bit . . . unpredictable. I'm bringing you back to Miramar Station. Parsons and Ross think they have a target destination for us, so we need to meet them in Nevada, immediately."

"Anonymized video transmission, indeed." Mackey sighed, catching his breath. "Now I'll never be able to relax inside my car again without worrying that someone, somewhere, is watching me."

"As long as you can still adjust the radio manually, I'll be fine," Tikhonov gasped.

Lunar Post Card, Pre-Paid
Service via South Atlantic Anomaly Sorting Station

Julie Harrison
7002 Denison Ave
Unit 3145
Cleveland, OH 44102-6014-6478-8173
United States
Earth

Julie,

Only 6 months more until I'm back at home with my little girl! I hope school is going better for you, darling. Your mother should have a present from me to give to you. It's not from Copernicus Station, because we can't take anything back to Earth with us—but I think you'll like it. My work is going well, even better than we hoped. You know I can't tell you any details, but the Postal Bureau is very pleased with our digging progress. We've made a number of important discoveries. Be good for your mother, dear. I love you, and I'll see you soon.

Your father,

Harlan

Box 451-672
Copernicus Station
Montes Carpatus Route H
Luna

11
Primum Movens

Kicking out a sonic boom over the Pacific Ocean, the PE-70 Valkyrie rocketed northeast over the coast near San Clemente, speeding inland over the mountains, clear across the Mojave, and then over the small gambling resort of Las Vegas before slowing, circling down from the stratosphere to come in for a landing at Mail Sorting Area 51, deep in the desert of southern Nevada.

Mail Sorting Area 51 was one of the most notorious guarded Postal Bureau complexes in the world, because of a popular myth about the presence of alien technology kept there, recovered from a supposed crash in Roswell, New Mexico, in the late 1940s. After all that Mackey had seen of the real secret technology of the Postal Bureau and the Department of Transportation, he couldn't help but shake his head at these amateurish theories. If only the public knew the real secrets. And yet, when the Assistant Secretary had met them by the aircraft at Miramar and announced their destination, he did look at her askance, briefly.

Hopper, for her part, couldn't resist ribbing him a bit about it once they were on board the aircraft. From her desk, still deep among her files and with the telephone in her hand, she took a moment to turn to Mackey and offer a joke.

"Certainly you believed aliens would make an appearance at some point, Mr. Mackey?"

Tikhonov piped up, "If my guess is correct, we are going to Area 51 because it is the current base for the 106th Tactical Fighter Squadron, equipped with PA-111 Sleet ground attack aircraft."

"Everyone is more of an expert than me," Mackey said glumly, "so I suppose I'll just sit quietly and take whatever surprises come."

Tikhonov smiled and bumped Mackey with his elbow. "Come now, Fred. You are the star of our last mission! You confirmed that the drone jamming pods target P-car radar sensors, and then engineered our escape under fire."

"Some escape." Mackey shivered. "Running into traffic on the arterial. We're incredibly lucky we weren't ground to paste underneath the wheels of twelve successive P-car formations."

Hopper smiled at the engineer, dismissing his morosity. "Some of the most important missions have the most inelegant patterns to them. But if you discovered what you needed to find and no one got killed, that is what counts at the end of the day. And besides, with your information, plus what Parsons and Ross have discovered, we now know enough to take the final, decisive step."

"About that," Mackey suddenly said. "It just so happens that plot we have discovered focuses on P-car radar systems, as near as we can tell."

"You know that is correct," Hopper said, looking down to read the files in front of her at the executive desk, cradling the telephone handset against her ear.

"And it just so happens that I am an engineer who specializes in P-car radar interference issues."

"You are also aware of the veracity of that statement." Hopper continued turning pages of a report.

"When you came to my office at the Electromagnetic Bureau, you said I was the nearest engineer with a Bureaucratic Literacy Level of G."

"I said that."

Mackey folded his arms in front of him. "What I would like to know is how it was that you were so lucky as to randomly pull an engineer who happened to be a specialist in the exact nature of the plot you were investigating, which you supposedly did not know at the time."

Hopper paused reading, and stared out the window for a moment. Tikhonov and Mackey both looked at her, wondering how she would respond.

"Contrarily to what you are implying, I did not know that P-car interference was the central element we were searching for. There were a great many unknowns when I began investigating this case. It's not surprising that often there are more unknowns than knowns. Often luck has a great deal to do with it. But what is true is that in this case, my finding you was not entirely up to luck."

Hopper turned in her seat and looked directly at Mackey through her thick glasses. "As you've no doubt seen, some of the information that I use in my work comes from—unconventional sources. Some of these are very distinct, like Eliza. In its way, Eliza provides direct information. Others are not so distinct, and come from a variety of lesser sources, which are then collected, compiled, and collated together. I cannot tell you where or from whom I got the information, because in fact there is not a where, and there is no whom. But information came to me that suggested a person knowing about P-car radar interference might be useful at some point. I did not know if it was true, or in what way it would be true. But I decided to act on that particular information by way of recruiting you."

Mackey wasn't sure how to respond to this. "You can't tell me how you knew?"

"I can't tell you, because there is nothing to tell. The information was obscure and incomplete. I didn't have foreknowledge, I played a hunch. I merely acted on the information at hand as best I could, just as we all have. I could tell you the path and source of every bit of information that I've encountered over the last week, but frankly, that would be quite boring, and a waste of the very short time of this supersonic flight when I would be better off reading these Bureau reports from the Secretary's office which I am told I must sign today."

And with that, she went back to reading, listening to whatever voice or sound or silence was coming through the handset, leaving Tikhonov and Mackey just to look at each other. She also neglected to fill them in about what Ross and Parsons had discovered, assuring them that they would all get together for the briefing upon arrival.

Tikhonov was not off his mark about the reason for going to Area 51—upon landing, Mackey could see the Sleet attack aircraft lined up on the flight line, swarming with ground crew servicing and arming the machines. De-boarding the Valkyrie, Tikhonov and Mackey followed Hopper into the command building and directly into a crowded briefing hall.

At the back of the room, already packed to capacity with Postal Bureau pilots, the commanders of Inspector detachments, and a number of higher level Bureau executives, they found Ross and Parsons, whom they greeted with firm handshakes.

"Heard you had an exciting escape, Fred!" Parsons pumped his hand. "Wish I could have been there for the fireworks, rather than playing technician for Mary's computer gymnastics."

"You were happy enough to find yourself a new explosive toy," Ross reminded him.

Parsons' eyes lit up. "Wait until you see this! The Skunk Works chappies call it a Wizard's Hat, of all delightful names, and it—"

He was interrupted by the Assistant Secretary calling the room to order.

"Thank you. This is a secure, detain, and intervene mission, under the auspices of Executive Branch Procedural Violation Codes, defined in Title 53. I am in command. Everything that will happen here today is classified Top Secret, zero disclosure. In the event of Congressional or other legal inquiries that may occur in the future, you are to refer to these instructions, at this moment, as your Constitutional *primum movens*, and all culpability and justification from this point forward falls to me, Assistant Secretary for Innovation of the Department of Transportation."

Mackey blinked, swallowing the full meaning of what the Assistant Secretary had just done. She had put her entire career, and even her freedom, on the line. If there was to ever be a person to blame for whatever was about to happen, she had just declared that person to be herself. She had stepped out of the shadows of Orthogonal Procedures into the light of potential Congressional hearings, and whatever criminal charges might lead from that. She had placed herself on the prow of the ship.

"Here is the situation. The Department of Commerce has a technology under its control that allows them to jam the analog radar group-scoping functions of P-cars. When this jamming technology is applied, the automatic safety controls of any P-car are rendered null and void, with deadly consequences."

She paused a moment as the room filled with murmurs. What Hopper suggested took a moment to sink in. This room was full of pilots and armed Inspectors who risked their lives on a regular basis. But the idea that the P-car system—the technological basis of Transportation power in the world—was now vulnerable was enough to make them all feel the floor fall out from underneath them.

"This is true, Mackey?" Ross whispered. "You're sure?"

"We saw it," he whispered back. "I've never seen anything like it. Blocking all bands, completely masking projected images, and at the same time not triggering interference detectors. We saw a car slam itself into a track end barrier at nearly two hundred miles an hour."

"It is one thing to feud with another government Department," Ross spoke through gritted teeth. "But it is another thing entirely to put public lives at risk by breaking carefully engineered safety measures." She put a hand on Mackey's shoulder. "We'll make sure we put a stop to this. As engineers, first and foremost."

She looked back to Hopper with a cold expression on her face. Her words stuck in Mackey's mind. She was right. The Department of Commerce was, in a very literal way, destroying the work to which Mackey had dedicated his career. This jamming technology risked the very lives that he held in his hands every day at work. If there was a single fiber of professional ethics in his body, he needed to help put a stop to this. Perhaps, when it came down to it, he had more of an internal ideology than he thought he did.

The Assistant Secretary was pointing to the projection of a slide, showing a diagrammed map of the United States with a number of points marked. "We believe their intention is to identify particular locations to apply this jamming technology, and to do so simultaneously across various locations in the

United States. These locations will be identified on the fly using a deep space listening satellite, and relayed through their network via a ground station."

Now it was Mackey who turned to Ross for confirmation. "It's a bit more complicated than that," she explained. "Their tracking isn't meant to be done by the Crystals—that was just for their first round of reconnaissance, which you and Hopper discovered. For the actual run, working visually would require a person examining each Crystal photo to find the P-car targets within the photograph, after first rectifying the image to map coordinates. All of that would take far too much time.

"But when Hopper said you and Tikhonov discovered a P-car connection, it clicked. P-cars use radio waves to self-identify themselves to the track signals. The track signals then relay this information by radio to other nearby cars to aid in formations. These signals are also captured by Mass Transit Bureau monitoring systems, and then relayed to Postal Bureau satellites. The Crystals need to be in low earth orbit in order to take photographs, but the relayed P-car signals can be heard from anywhere. Just one high-orbit eavesdropping satellite could listen in on many of the Postal Bureau satellites that relay signal information for the Mass Transit Bureau. A single satellite can do that for the entire continental United States and then relay it to the ground.

"That is what is going to happen. That second set of birth charts, which translate to orbital positions all occurring at the same time—those will be the positions of particular Postal Bureau communications satellites, which then will be targeted for eavesdropping by a single deep space satellite."

"The Postal Bureau doesn't encipher the track signals?" Tikhonov frowned.

"Why would they?" Mackey shrugged. "The Mass Transit Bureau doesn't. It's anonymized, and the Postal Bureau figured the information was available to any P-car on the ground. No one ever thought there would be value in listening to every anonymous P-car signal at once. But when Commerce has tapped into all that data, they can mine it for specific information, if they know what they are looking for."

"Like the location of any particular P-car, anywhere in the United States, once they had already isolated its anonymous meta-identifiers," Tikhonov whispered.

"In this case, the meta-identifiers of the personal P-cars of various mid-level executives responsible for various functions of track network safety across numerous Bureaus," Parsons said. "Once they know exactly where these P-cars are, they can jam their safety sensors specifically using drones flying overhead. Not only do they make the P-car system look dangerous and vulnerable to accidents, they take out those responsible for the P-car system in a series of seemingly random disasters. That bit of analysis Hopper discovered with the help of Eliza while you two were breaking and entering."

"How did Hopper get to Washington DC and back so quickly?" Mackey asked.

"I have a feeling," Parsons spoke slowly, "that there is more than one Eliza. Maybe quite a number of them."

"If that's the case, why did we have to fly back to DC?"

Parsons sighed. "Sometimes with Grace it's better not to ask. She always has her reasons. Maybe the other instances of Eliza are secret. Maybe they are in places we can't go. Or maybe she just wanted us to be back where the astral projection tanks were, because she knew what was coming next. That's the thing about Grace—for as long as I've known her, no matter how much you think you see what she's up to, she's always making twice as many moves behind your back."

Hopper had been continuing her briefing while her team whispered among themselves. "The ground station relays to a programming station," she explained to the room, "which will equip local teams with the location information they require to make synchronized jamming attacks."

"Submarines." Mackey figured it out for himself. "They must send the information via ELF radio to submarines, and then program and launch the drones from underwater."

"Seems very haphazard." Tikhonov sighed. "Too many links in the chain, and one had to eventually give way."

"It's the only way to not be caught," Ross said. "If you had ground teams launching the drones, communicating over standard radio equipment, someone would be discovered."

Suddenly, Mackey could see it, clear as a bell. "If they aren't discovered, people won't know it was jamming. They'll think it was a failure of the P-car system itself. They won't blame unknown attackers, but the Department of Transportation."

"Whose fault it is, in a way," Parsons said. "The system was vulnerable. But there is a difference between vulnerability due to attack and vulnerability to accident, in the eyes of the public. If the Department suffered an unprecedented electronic conflict attack, that would give them a mandate for war. This scheme is designed to make Transportation look incompetent."

Hopper signaled for a new slide, showing a list of aircraft and attack group assignments. "Our strike will be two-fold. We will take out the deep space listening satellite with a High Virgo anti-satellite missile attack. Meanwhile, a strike team will land at the ground control station, to collect evidence of the plot and secure the site. The strike team will be supported from the air by the Sleet squadron. I'll let the Commander take over for the specifics of the strike."

She came and sat amongst the team while a uniformed Postal Flight Officer took over the briefing. "We'll be going in with the strike team, in vertical takeoff and landing aircraft. Not—" Parsons closed his mouth, as Hopper finished her sentence "in the Vail."

"Where's the ground station?" Mackey asked.

"In the end, that was the easiest part to discover. There's only one Commerce ground station with the equipment necessary to communicate to the high orbit that Ross concluded they must be using. It's at Mount Shasta, in Northern California."

In the white, blinding heat of the Nevada desert, the team made their way to the aircraft along with the hustling Postal Inspector assault platoon and the attack aircraft pilots. Although relieved to know they would not be in the Vail—which he had seen parked on the runway as they were coming in—Mackey was not much more convinced by their new conveyance, a PC-142. It looked enough like a normal cargo plane from a distance, except with shorter wings. But then he was informed that the ability of the vehicle to hover was enabled by the entire wing tilting backwards, until the four propellers were spinning vertically. The Vail's flight mechanism made it look like it was powered by a quartet of desk fans. The PC-142 at least had real turboprops, but Mackey would have much preferred the wing to be permanently attached to the airframe.

But once again, Mackey was onboard an unconventional vehicle, with Hopper, Ross, Tikhonov, and Parsons, and a complement of Postal Inspector troops, and they were lifting off into the sky above the hot dry lake bed, before forming up with three other PC-142s into a small flight heading northwest towards California. He supposed that at this point flight was no less safe than the P-car network with which Mackey was much more familiar. If there was technology that cast aside even the most relied-upon safety measures of the P-cars, then a tilt wing aircraft didn't seem quite such a gamble.

Out over the arid mountains of Nevada, the PC-142s were met by the squadron of PA-111 Sleets, to give them cover until they reached the target area. After the attack on the hovercrafts on Lake Superior, Hopper was taking no chances. Out of one of the small windows, Mackey could look up to see the cover aircraft overhead, flying in close formation some thousands of feet above them, keeping an eye out. The Sleets were slick, aerodynamic fighter-bomber aircraft, with variable-geometry wings that slid back and forth for different amounts of lift. They were a bit far away to make out clearly, but Mackey could see from the silhouettes that the undersides of the Sleets were loaded up with ordnance, bombs and missiles of various size and purpose.

The Postal Inspector troops on board their aircraft were all fully equipped, carrying assault weapons of various specifications that eluded Mackey. But his knowledge as a Department engineer, as well as a bureaucrat, informed him that if there was one thing the Postal Bureau designed for, it was specificity of mission. Not one for catch-all solutions, the many generations of minds behind the development decisions made in Postal laboratories looked for artful solutions: technologies that did one task better than any other alternative. Whatever it was that Hopper had in mind, these vehicles and the troops inside of them would be ready for exactly that. The dazzle pistol and the electro-blast had succeeded exactly, on his and Tikhonov's mission in San Diego. The hovering hybrid plane they were riding in would probably fit their landing site equally precisely. Certainly, a quick and dirty solution would work in a pinch, but if there was a weapon or a vehicle to be deployed by the Postal Bureau, it was more likely to come out looking like a scalpel than a mallet.

Unless, of course, it was a very large scalpel. Parsons was sitting in a jump seat, checking his new hardware, the so-called Wizard's Hat. Mackey wasn't sure what it was supposed to do, but he could only guess it involved large amounts of flame and smoke. It did appear to be a cone, which he supposed accounted for the name. But it was a dark green, three feet long, made of some sort of composite material, and yet seemed very light in Parsons' hands. There was a small control console on the outside of the cone, and the wide end, most certainly what might be called the 'business end,' showed a trio of dark holes, each about three inches wide, arranged in a triangle over the one-foot diameter of the wide end. Mackey was curious about what might come out of those holes, but also didn't really care to get closer for a look.

Ross was also prepping her weaponry, which at least appeared to be more conventional from the outside. Her custom-built cartridges looked quite different than the ammunition the rest of the Postal Inspectors carried, but the two sub-machine guns she had were not dissimilar. Although, now that Mackey was able to get a close look as Ross checked the action and disassembled and reassembled the various components, he did catch some very telling differences. The metal of the weapons was quite eye-catching: jet black receivers and grips, but with polished copper barrels and sights, and what appeared to be wrapped copper coils around the chamber and trigger area. She wore them now on a double set of retracting slings, over body armor plates, no longer bothering to conceal them under a jacket. Ross' silhouette, enlarged with the weapons, the armor, and the extra magazines positioned across her person, made her appear far more imposing than anyone would imagine a mathematics expert in her early sixties to be. Pulled back to her shoulder blades, the twin guns looked like metal, military specification butterfly wings. Her silhouette, cast against the interior of the transport plane, looked like a ballistic angel of death.

Hopper, the other member of the team with a dangerously disconcerting appearance, was consulting with the commander of the Postal Inspectors, over-ear headphones carefully placed beneath the brim of her omnipresent hat. She was accepting reports, and giving orders, which was as much her chosen ordnance as any projectile. However, Mackey did notice that she held her so-called 'transistor staff' in her hand, having handed off the role of carrying paperwork to a Postal Bureau assistant she had drawn into her wake.

The Assistant Secretary pressed one hand to her headset, as if concentrating to perceive events happening in some distance space. About at this time, Mackey had learned in the briefing, a delta-wing PB-58 supersonic bomber would be taking off from Mail Sorting Area 51, circling up through the atmosphere, accelerating to speeds over Mach 2. Then, it would launch the High Virgo missile, which would speed out of the atmosphere and into orbit, carrying a nuclear warhead. ASTB had performed high-orbit radar sweeps and identified the eavesdropping satellite. When the weapon detonated, the electromagnetic pulse would be more than enough to fry its circuits into a lump of distorted solder. The High Virgo launch would be timed to hit the satellite at precisely the moment they made the attack on the ground station.

His attention drawn back to his immediate surroundings, Mackey loaded their dazzle pistols with newly charged batteries he received from Tikhonov, and re-armed their pair of electro-blasts by changing the disposable capacitors underneath the panel of the flat, square, metal end. Under his shirt, he felt the electromagnetic amulet against his chest as he smoothed the holsters down under his jacket, making sure these strange weapons were secure about him.

Tikhonov seemed to be itching for something with a little more deadly force, but did not put his idea into words, perhaps wary of what Hopper might say in response to such a request by the Bolshevik. Mackey, on the other hand, was more than happy to be without the responsibility of any weapon firing actual projectiles. The ability to hang back behind any automatic weapons fire seemed like an ideal defensive strategy for him, regardless of what sort of protective ability the amulet might or might not have.

As they crossed over the aqua hues of Eagle Lake into California, with the peak of the volcanic Mt. Lassen visible out of the left side of the aircraft, the pieces of the plan began to fall into place. The Sleet escort sped off ahead of them, dropping in altitude. The flight of VTOL aircraft dipped low over the hills as well, as they approached the massive volcano of Mt. Shasta.

The Commerce tracking station was on a hill on the southern slope of the mountain. As Hopper had announced in the briefing, the Sleet fighter-bombers would take their runs to destroy any air defenses in the area, so that the PC-142s could land and deposit their troops without opposition. The ground assault would target a rear entrance, where the defenses would likely be less pronounced. And Hopper's team would be going in along with the first wave.

The craft circled wide, giving the occupants a view of the site, where several trails of smoke rose into the blue California sky, no doubt signalling the success of the Sleets' attack run. The PC-142 slowed, began to hang in the air as the wing swung vertically, and the plane descended in a hover. Touching down hard, the rear door swung open, and the Postal Inspectors streamed out, taking defensive positions around the fresh bomb craters kicked into the hillside. Hopper's team followed, taking cover in the tall pines that covered the site.

Mackey saw that the giant white radomes on the hillside had been thoughtfully left intact. But the airstrikes had done good work. Several emplacements of what appeared to be guided missiles were on fire, abandoned by their operators. There was no opposition on the ground. This site, it seemed, was deserted. Did this signify that their coming was expected? Or that they had targeted the wrong place? The advance Postal Inspector team moved towards the steel-enclosed entrance of the tunnel. That would take them below the surface of the earth, into the command center of the station.

A concrete shell, a wide, sweeping arch above the tunnel, kept the rest of the mountain back from the rear entrance way. Across the span of the half-tube into the earth, a heavy steel door was secured. Parsons sauntered forward, lighting a cigar that he produced from inside his tweed jacket. Holding it carefully to one side while digging in his bomb satchel, he said nonchalantly to the Postal Inspectors, "You all may want to back up."

The other members of the team and the Inspectors did so hurriedly as Parsons produced a tube of grey, greasy material, which he began smearing across the hinged edge of the heavy door. Affixing a small fuse to the pasty mess, he said, "Now you all may want to run," as he dipped the cigar ember to its twisted end.

From their points of hurried cover, they felt the air snatched from their lungs as the local air pressure expanded in a solid, exothermic thump. Looking back through the light grey haze that hung in the high mountain air, Mackey saw that the steel door had been severed from its mounts, hanging sideways across the tunnel, revealing a dark mouth heading downward.

The armed Inspectors rushed into the tunnel. Then Hopper's team moved forward to follow. Ross and Parsons took the lead, the rocket scientist's cigar glowing orange in the low light. Parsons carried the Wizard's Hat cradled under one arm, his bag of explosives over the opposite shoulder, while Ross held both her guns in ready position. Hopper was next, holding the transistor staff ahead of her like an unlit torch. She was followed by Tikhonov and Mackey, their dazzle pistols at the ready.

The tunnel was dark and crowded, lined on either side by pallets of unidentified equipment: computer terminals, industrial winches, large cylindrical power supplies for unknown components, and other unidentified material. The Inspectors spread out, not wanting to be caught lumped together in an ambush. Ambush—although no one had said it, it was what was on everyone's minds. Why was there no defense? Why did the site appear deserted, even after an air strike? What were they approaching, as they advanced down below the surface of the earth? For some reason, a saying of Mackey's father popped into his head at this moment: "Check the mail slot." He used to say it when Fred was putting on his shoes. "Check the mail slot" was what they used to say when dressing in Postal Administration flight training. Fred Mackey Sr. had been stationed in Arizona, along with an endless battalion of scorpions that had a habit of crawling into their boots at night.

The tunnel grew wider and steeper, with inlaid steps cut into the raw igneous rock in places. Then the concrete and metal panels disappeared, giving way to stone, dark, wet, covered in serpentine swirls across its surface, with loose sand deposits on the floor of the tunnel. The passageway grew tall, narrow at the roof, bent together like a dark sleeve, held horizontal by the cuff. In the gleam of the tactical lights from the Postal Inspectors ahead of them, Mackey could see the ceiling glowing with tiny points of light, like the Milky Way.

Hopper saw Mackey looking upward. "It's a lava tube," she said. "Mt. Shasta is a volcano, though it hasn't been active in two centuries. Those are microbes, living off the minerals in the rocks."

"Don't lava tubes normally travel just underneath the surface?" Ross whispered.

"This one is taking us down underneath the mountain," Parsons said.

They must have traveled nearly half a mile under the rock, sloping downward on the smooth, sandy floor, before the tunnel began to widen. It opened into a chamber hundreds of yards wide, and what might have been a quarter of a mile long. Out in the open area were more crates of equipment, a number of modular shipping containers, and three odd-looking aircraft, apparently in different states of repair. How did they get these vehicles into the cavern? They were too large for the tunnel they had just descended. Above them, the ceiling was not visible in the gloom, though a strange light, blue like the bottom of a mountain lake, cast an eerie illumination over everything.

In the distance, an animalistic roar filled the air. Everyone froze. It sounded primordial, deep and guttural, as if forced from the lungs of the cave itself.

"Spread out," Hopper commanded. "This is where it happens."

And she was right. From across the chamber came a rushing wall of grey fur. Massive beasts, shaped roughly like bears but as large as elephants, with large flat noses and long curved claws, came thundering out from behind the obstacles scattered across the hall. They could smell them—a soggy, matted stink of dried saliva and sweat, musty like a zoo, grimy with the congealed filth of the underground. They charged, long tongues wagging in the low light. The ranks of the prehistoric monsters were a surging sea of animal rage.

The Assistant Secretary looked at the scene, open-mouthed surprise showing on her face. It was the first time Mackey had witnessed any such emotion come over her. "My goodness— ground sloths," she breathed. "Actual, literal Megatherium." But her astonishment lasted for only a second, and was instantly replaced by the culination of decades of command. "Open fire!" she barked.

The Inspectors opened up with their weapons, sending the shrill chatter of automatic fire rebounding off the distant ceiling and walls of the volcanic gallery, a machinic roar to challenge the extinct herd in bestial supremacy. Dusty clouds revealed hits bursting over the charging ground sloths, but the rounds were like mere fly bites, angering them, focusing their rage into a bloodlust.

Behind the charging horde, a group of tall, pale men wearing long cloaks stepped out, carrying staffs. Their skin shone a sickly white in the blue glow of the invisible cavern roof. They gathered together, chanting, holding their staffs in the air. Between the upturned points a shining silver cloud gathered, as if drawing moisture from an invisible depression in the air, rolling it over and over like atmospheric dough, gaining in size, in opacity, in luminous malice.

"White shamans," Ross muttered, spitting onto the ground.

"Parsons!" Hopper ordered. "Break up that sloth charge!"

Parsons needed no second order. Biting his cigar in the corner of his mouth, he dropped to one knee, pointing the bottom of the Wizard's Hat up at a forty-five degree angle, right in the direction of the leading sloth, now just one hundred yards away. Quickly tapping on the control console of the weapon, he sighted loosely one more time, and mashed a fat red button once, and then twice.

Two spherical rounds popped out of the Hat, sailing upward like corks from a champagne bottle. Completing their lobbed arc, they impacted on the sandy hall floor just in front of the forward Megatherium. After single, low bounces, they popped open, squirting a blanket of flammable gel in a radius of five feet, which then was ignited by central blasting charges. Twin fat mushrooms of solid orange petroleum flame gushed upwards, blotting out the darkness and blue gloom before fading into thick black smoke. Three of the giant sloths caught fire about their narrow faces, and in shock and pain gave up the charge, catapulting outward through the ranks, causing confusion among the giant prehistoric beasts, slowing their progress. They shook their heads in the hail of fire from the Inspector troops, as if trying to decide whether to proceed or retreat.

"Ross!" Hopper ordered next. "Cancel that shaman party in the back!"

"With pleasure," she muttered, releasing a magazine from one of her guns into her hand and slamming another home. She chambered a round and raised the weapon to her shoulder, aiming high at the ceiling of the cave. Looking upward, making some mental calculations, she punched digits into a keypad along the forward grip of the weapon, then squeezed off a quick burst. Mackey watched in amazement as tracer rounds cut upward, and then with a shower of sparks in the air like fireworks, rebounded down again towards the group of cloaked figures, impacting at their feet. The figures did not react, continuing their chant as the silver cloud between their raised staffs grew thicker and darker.

"Just another few microseconds should do it," Ross said, keeping her feet carefully still and entering a new calculation into the gun. She squeezed off another longer burst. The rounds arced upward over the Megatherium, then released the same shower of sparks as secondary charges redirected their flight downward, scattering bullets down across the group of shamans. Mackey watched amazed as six of their number fell to the ground.

The silver cloud between them shivered, but continued to glow, cracking with electric light, and beginning to rumble loud over the noise of the sloths and the automatic weapons. The cloud condensed, clenching like a fist, and then arced out with a lightning bolt, illuminating the hall with blinding blue light in the same instant as it impacted in between a number of Inspectors, blowing them sideways, sending the smell of charred flesh across the squad.

"Smoke!" Hopper shouted. "Then forward, into the sloths! Don't give the shamans a clear target! Use fragmentary grenades if you have to, but watch your crossfire!" Inspectors rolled smoke charges out into the floor, creating a veil of grey fog that obscured the incursion force from the shamans in billowing curtains of blue and black. The Postal Inspectors moved forward as the sloths found their collective rage again, and continued their mad, frantic run through the smoke towards the human beings.

Ross changed ammunition in one gun and opened fire, laying a row of incendiary rounds across the Megatherium, causing minor fires in their fur that glowed like candle points in the thickening haze. Parsons dug into his bag and pulled out a small length of pipe, then used his glowing coal to set the fuse before tossing it overhand out into the fog. As the Megatherium charge galloped over top of the pipe bomb it exploded, sending the animals shrieking, slipping in great flows of blood, but not sapping their fury.

Hopper stepped to the fore, raising her walking stick ahead of her, pointing it towards the leading sloth galloping towards her with furious thunder. Mackey turned to Ross, pleading, "Do something! She'll be trampled!"

Ross turned, the Megatherium now only yards from being on top of the Assistant Secretary. Hopper knelt to the ground, looking up through her glasses at the prehistoric monster, tongue outstretched, feet raised to crush her small form. Mackey heard an odd ringing cut through the melee, like a mechanical mosquito's whine. And then, with an overhand motion, the Assistant Secretary forcefully smacked the tip of her staff into the sand of the cavern floor.

A dry crack rang out in the cavern, like the shatter of a tree trunk broken by a gale. The floor ahead of Hopper split open, dropped by the force of the resonant harmonic vibration into a wide rift, the rock shedding sand into a dusty cloud as it fell downward, impacted as if by a vast, oblique spearpoint. The Megatherium was instantly sliced in two as if by an invisible scythe, like time and space were ripped in half with a single, sudden yank of a thin piece of paper along the edge of a desk. The halves of the sloth's carcass plugged the rift that had opened below it with a sickening thud, as its blood and entrails sloshed out into the sand.

"She always does manage to take care of herself," Ross said to Mackey, as the engineer stared through his eyeglasses, forehead wrinkled and jaw agape.

Hopper looked back at them and gestured with two fingers. "Ross, Parsons—on the left. Tikhonov and Mackey, find the control room, it has to be nearby. Find it and see what you make of it. Wait for us there."

In the burning fog enveloping the cave, the four made their way around to the wall as the Inspectors began engaging the Megatheriums with machine gun fire and grenades. The beasts seemed easy enough to wound with explosives, but the tough part was keeping them at a distance. Mackey watched in horror as a giant sloth loomed out of the fog and, swiping upward with a set of razor claws over a foot long, caught an Inspector under the armpit, sending both Inspector and limb flying through the air in opposite directions.

Ross laid down covering fire with incendiary rounds, setting small wildfires in the fur of the animals, which caused them to rub themselves against the floor as if stuck with a burr or a thorn. Parsons tossed small bombs when he could get a clear throw, each lit with his cigar and lobbed through the air at the animals. Through the smoke, Mackey couldn't make out the shamans at the other end of the hall.

Sneaking around one of the disassembled aircraft, the group looked for a clear path, but only found more sloths. Ross turned to Mackey and Tikhonov. "You two hug the wall and head forward. We'll cut in from here and cover you."

"What was that advice about bears, Tikhonov? Just don't back down!" Parsons grinned, puffing his cigar.

Suddenly, a Megatherium cut through a wisp of smoke, carrying one of the shamans on its back, waving his raised staff, purple flame gathered across the point. The animal reared, and Mackey, in reaction, fired his dazzle pistol. The green bolt missed the shaman, but hit the sloth dead on. It stumbled wildly, screaming that deep prehistoric groan, its long tongue lashing like a whip. The shaman lost concentration and fell to the ground, the flame vanishing from the tip of his staff as if quenched in water. Reaching within his cloak for a weapon, the shaman struggled to his feet, only to find Ross waiting, gun at the ready.

"I could touch the moon with a stone skipped on the sea." She smiled. "Your stolen thunder is no match for me." Grimacing through his thin lips, the shaman pulled out a pistol, but there was no time. Ross' shots hit him three times in the chest, and he dropped forward, his robe bursting into flame. Mackey and Tikhonov ducked as an explosion went off a bit too close. The Megatherium was wounded by the bomb blast, sending it crawling back into the smoke.

The mustached scientist shrugged his tweed shoulders, pushing a cloud of cigar exhaust into the surrounding mist. "Sorry."

Over the noise of automatic weapons fire, they heard the zinging crack of Hopper's transistor staff once, and then twice. Purple light crackled, diffused by the smoke.

Three shamans appeared out of the smoke. Two held pistols, and the third's staff bristled with purple light. "Fred," Parsons spoke slowly, "run."

Ross whipped up her opposite gun, turning it to an awkward 90-degree angle. She released a burst of rounds into the nearest shaman. Knocked backward by the force of the bullets, but before he could fall to the ground, his chest exploded in a sparking nebula of blood and bone, as the secondary charges on the rounds sent them out of his torso and into the body of the shaman next to him, taking them both down to the sandy floor of the cave. While the third shaman turned towards her, Parsons lept forward, pulling up the Wizard's Hat, connecting with the underside of the shaman's jaw. "Now!" he yelled at Mackey. Bullets whistled out of the smoke, impacting on the rocks behind them. Tikhonov grabbed Mackey's arm, and they dodged away, into the gloom.

They moved quickly and quietly around the stacks of material and equipment in the cavern. "What do you think we're looking for?" Tikhonov whispered.

"Not sure," Mackey responded. "A room large enough for computer and radio equipment. Chairs for technicians, consoles to operate the gear."

A thundering sound was approaching, and they dodged behind a stack of crates just in time, before a wounded Megatherium crashed past, apparently not seeing them in the thin remains of the fog. The smoke was clearing now as they got further away from the height of the battle. The sound of explosions and automatic fire still echoed across the cavernous area.

"Look." Tikhonov pointed. Ahead, a tunnel cut into the rock, and two shamans stood guarding the passage. "Seems likely, no?" Mackey gripped his dazzle pistol. "We have to take them out, after we blind them," Tikhonov whispered. "Otherwise they will chase us. Do like you did back in the Sierras. Shoulder to solar plexus. That'll knock his wind out."

"Ready," Mackey said. "Three, two, one—"

They leapt out, hitting a full run, side by side. The shamans saw them coming and began reaching for weapons. Tikhonov and Mackey fired at the same time, delivering a green wave of light. The shamans grabbed for their eyes, screaming. The blaze was so bright it rebounded off the luminescent cave walls, causing Mackey to briefly see spots. But he was already leaning into his shoulder, ready to deliver his entire weight to the man's chest. Dizzy though he was, his aim was true. The shaman crumbled backward, smashing into the rock with his head.

Tikhonov had also hit his man, square on. "Get their pistols," he said to Mackey. "And whatever that staff is, throw it away. I don't know what it is, but I don't trust the stuff." Mackey kicked the staffs out into the gloom, and handed the pistol that had been knocked to the ground to Tikhonov.

"Are you sure?" Tikhonov's dark eyes looked questioningly.

"I think it is better off in your hands than mine," Mackey reassured him.

Tikhonov nodded. "Very well. Then you take this." He handed his dazzle pistol to Mackey, giving him two fists of laser light to strike out with. "Quickly, before someone sees us." They dashed into the corridor.

It wasn't long before they found it. This underground site was for a particular purpose, and that purpose was clearly the central hub of the cave system, though it seemed they were now impossibly deep within the mountain. The two men stayed hidden behind the door frame in the dark tunnel as they sized up the situation. The control room was a gigantic dome shape, hollowed from the solid rock of the volcano. Far larger than Mackey had suspected, a hundred yards across, the room was built in a semi-circle around a giant projection screen on the wall, showing a map of the planet overlaid with wave-form orbit tracks. The room was also crowded with personnel, nearly twenty technicians, each busy at their station, focused on operating the computers and other paraphernalia. Around the far side of the room stood a squad of the elite Smithsonian Guard, well armed from what Mackey and Tikhonov could see. Many other passages led out of the control room in all directions, to points unknown within the mountain.

"More computers." Tikhonov sighed. "How do we get you on a machine with all of these people in there, not to mention the Smithsonian Guard?"

"I have no idea," Mackey said, nervously. Then he heard rapid footsteps coming up the hallway behind them. He wheeled around with the dazzle pistols ready, only to find Parsons there, covered in dirt, his plaid jacket burned on both sleeves. He waved wildly, a brilliant smile around the cigar in his mouth. Mackey motioned for quiet. Ross followed him, then Hopper, and then a small group of Postal Inspectors.

"Are these all of our people that are left?" Tikhonov whispered.

Hopper signaled no, and leaned close to the group. "The rest are back guarding the remains of the shaman squad, and forming a defensive position in case the sloths return."

"Where did they go?" Mackey asked, worried.

Hopper shrugged. "The last of the herd took off down a side tunnel. Who knows to where, or why."

"Those fools in the hoods are from the Indian Affairs Service, I have no doubt," Parsons whispered. "They always leaned towards wholesale appropriation. Communication with animals, on the other hand, is more of a Fish and Wildlife Service thing. I'm guessing the shamans were using that technology somehow, putting the fear and rage into them. When we broke up the bigoted parlor games, they probably lost control of them, and they scattered according to their natural senses again." He turned to Ross. "How about those wannabe medicine men, eh Mary? You sure were dropping them left and right!"

Ross shrugged him off. "What goes around comes around, as we say in orbital mechanics. But what sort of animals were those?"

"The namesake of our friends, the Megatherium Club," Hopper said quietly. "An extinct species of megafauna last alive during the late Pleistocene. Where they got them from, I haven't a clue. But that's what they were, sure enough."

Tikhonov gestured at the control room. "Sloths aside, what do we do now? Too many in there to take all at once!"

Hopper checked her watch, and motioned to one of the Inspectors, who approached, carrying a small telephone set attached to a reel of very fine wire that he was spooling out behind them.

"The High Virgo should impact in just a few minutes. That should take the station out of action. We'll confirm, and then call for reinforcements." The Assistant Secretary took a headset from the Inspector and put it on. "Radios won't work underground, but this line runs back to a mobile surface antenna."

She listened to the words coming over the air. "Ninety seconds until detonation," she whispered.

"Why is it called High Virgo?" Mackey asked. "It's just an anti-satellite missile, right? No occult functionality?"

Parsons shrugged. "You tell me, Fred. Some of our equipment just has funny names. Maybe whomever signed off on it happened to be a Virgo. Or loved a Virgo, maybe."

"Thirty seconds!"

They crouched in the tunnel, watching the scene in the room intently. Mackey tried to make out what the various screens might indicate. A lot of telemetry data, to be sure, but for what? Other than the course of what must be the eavesdropping satellite, marked with a white sine wave upon the map of the earth, he couldn't identify anything.

"Detonation!"

They all braced for impact, but of course, there was none. A five megaton warhead detonated hundreds of miles beyond the thick earth atmosphere. Gamma rays from the fusion blast impacted with stray atoms in the upper atmosphere, causing a tsunami of free electrons speeding through space. The electric fields from these accelerating particles reverberated through the circuits of anything nearby, generating a surplus current in any standing wire, frying transistors, microcircuits, and motors in the fusion's electromagnetic surge.

All that they saw below in the ground station was one column of telemetry cease scrolling across the screen. The small circle placed upon the sine wave of the orbit line disappeared. Technicians began furiously punching at the screen.

"That's it." Mackey smiled. "Got it."

Hopper held her earpiece, listening carefully. Tikhonov nudged Mackey. "Are you sure? Are you sure it's completely gone?"

Mackey looked at the staff of the ground station running frantically about, checking machines for any sort of fault or error. He imagined that the realization would be immediate, but certainty would be slow in dawning. They would be checking every other conceivable failure, looking for bad connections, faulty terminals, or logged errors. Even though they already knew what the problem really was. They would want to replace every wire and cable in the system, one by one, before they admitted that their satellite was suddenly gone.

But they weren't doing that. They were sitting back down. Commands were being given, and a new sine wave had appeared on the screen. What were they doing?

Ross pointed. "It's another satellite, isn't it? They have a backup."

Telemetry data had started running across the screen again. The curve of the sine wave was shifting. "They're running a burn," Parsons said. "They have another functional satellite in orbit, and they are burning fuel to change the orbit and bring it into position."

"Another eavesdropping satellite?" Tikhonov asked. "So they can still run the jamming program? Can we hit it again?"

Hopper was conversing rapidly with whomever was on the other end of the long wire. She removed one earphone from the headset. "It's no good, there's no time to prepare another High Virgo shot. And even if we got it, they might have a third satellite. We have to take the command room—now."

She turned, exchanging furious hand signals with the Inspectors, one of whom started running back up the tunnel. "We'll get reinforcements, and then we'll try and make a—" She was interrupted by a loud, primordial roar.

"Oh no." Parsons sighed.

"Which direction, which direction?" Ross spoke quickly.

"I don't know, there were too many echoes!"

The technicians in the control room heard it as well, looking around, trying to get some sort of a sense of what the sound was and where it was coming from. And then it sounded again, louder, like a deep brass trumpet, filled with rage.

The Megatherium stormed out of one of the side tunnels into the control room. Next to the computer terminals, it looked even more gigantic, three times the height of a human, perhaps the biggest of the lot. Blood streamed down its legs from a large wound on its side. And as it reared up onto hind legs, tongue wagging out, eyes bulging, it sprayed blood from its mouth across the room as it let out once more its furious cry. With one wheel of its claws, an entire computer cabinet was crushed into scrap metal, launching streamers of magnetic tape across the room.

"As soon as they open fire," Hopper said, "go!"

It took mere seconds for the Smithsonian Guard to get their wits about them and their guns in hand. The technicians ran out into the tunnels in a panic, the last of them getting clear just as soon as the automatic fire rang out like tearing canvas, echoing in the dome-shaped chamber.

"Take out the Guards!" Hopper yelled. "Leave the animal to me! And make sure you don't destroy the equipment!"

Parsons ran right, and Tikhonov followed. Hopper dodged left, with Mackey after her. Ross took one step into the room and reloaded her weapon. She raised the gun to her shoulder, sighted towards the ceiling, and punched in her timing on the keypad. She let loose shots in a wide arc, up across the top of the dome, rotating the barrel of the weapon as she panned across. She painted a wide rainbow of tracer and secondary charge sparks as she did so, raining down bullets onto the heads of the Smithsonian Guard. She felled all but two.

One of the remaining Guards was hit by Tikhonov as he cut across the room from the right, firing with a pistol. It was a good shot, just over the rows of monitors and consoles, dropping the Guard to the control room floor. "The equipment! Mind the equipment!" Hopper screamed.

Seeing Tikhonov's motion, the giant sloth lumbered towards him, crushing desk chairs and tables. Hopper tried to get its attention, but could not. Instead, she was confronted with the last of the Smithsonian Guard, raising his gun. "Look out!" Mackey screamed from behind her, uselessly. He fired his dazzle pistol, but the green light was absorbed by a computer cabinet between himself and the Guard.

Hopper stopped, pointed her staff at the Guard, and sank to her knee, touching the point to the concrete floor. The zing-crack of the transistor staff rebounded off the walls of the control room like a thunderbolt. When Mackey peered around the computer cabinet, he saw a crack emanating from where Hopper stood, through the concrete, and up into the wall beyond. On one side of the rift was the body of the Smithsonian Guard. On the other side was his right leg and right arm, still clutching his weapon. His blood ran into the massive crack opened up in the concrete, down into the mountain below.

Mackey gaped in shock. "What is that thing?"

"It's a type of ultrasonic knife," she said. "But no time for an engineering lesson now, we must help Parsons."

Across the room, Parsons was cornered by the Megatherium. He dropped his cigar and, without looking, quietly rubbed it out with his foot. He had put down the Wizard's Hat and had both arms extended, palms down. The creature was up on its hind legs, long claws swiping left and right, closer and closer to the rocket scientist.

"Jack!" yelled Ross from across the room, switching magazines. "When I fire, run!"

"No, no!" he responded calmly. "Don't shoot."

He closed his eyes, raising his palms so that they faced the giant sloth, elbows at right angles. The behemoth roared, spitting blood and hot, steamy breath all over Parsons, blowing his hair back. The smell of the wounded beast was thick in the room, like compost in a summer heat. Parsons did not move.

Hopper moved forward, to get an angle on the creature that would not catch Parsons in the crossfire. Mackey followed along, more for wanting to stay near to Hopper than any constructive plan, but he held the dazzle pistols ready, meaning to give the Megatherium a double blast to the eyes if it turned their way.

The sloth dropped to all fours and began licking its claws. It bellowed, a sound like the foghorn of a cargo ship, echoing off the walls of the room.

"What is happening?" whispered Mackey.

Then the Megatherium lumbered off to the left, past Parsons, and out one of the side tunnels, trailing blood and smacking a desk chair across the room with its giant, fur-covered tail. They all converged upon Parsons.

"What the hell were you doing?" Ross demanded.

"I was feeling its pain." Parsons sniffed, wiping away a tear. "I took its wounds into me, so that it might be relieved. Poor thing. Out of its time. It's meant to roam a jungle the likes of which we no longer know. It is a vegetarian. It loves banana leaves and yucca, and would eat avocados the way we eat blueberries."

Mackey looked at Tikhonov, who looked at Ross, who looked at Hopper, who rubbed her eyes. "Well, that's lovely. Now, what's happening here?" She gestured at the screen, and they moved to the computer terminals as the Inspector reinforcements from up the tunnel arrived, securing the entrances and exits.

"We could try and disable the information transfer between the satellite and the ELF transmitter," Mackey suggested. "But we have no idea how that is done, or where those control programs are running. It would probably be easier to seize control over the satellite directly."

Ross was examining the screens of the various stations, wiping away sloth blood to see what was displayed.

"This one, here," Parsons said, still wiping away tears.

"How do you know?" asked Mackey.

Parsons pointed to a sign mounted above the terminal, reading GUIDO. "Guidance Officer," he said, deadpan.

Ross came over and sat in the chair. All the screens were dark. There was an arc of bullet holes across the face of the console. "Well that's just great," she said. "The Smithsonian Guard must have got it."

"Look for GNC," Parsons said. "Guidance, Navigation, and Control. We should be able to fire the guidance rockets manually, and if we're lucky, put it enough out of orbit that it can't function correctly."

Tikhonov found it, one row back. "It appears to be functional!" he called.

Ross quickly took a seat, letting her guns retract on their slings, a smoking pair of fully-automatic wings. Mackey found some paper and tried to wipe as much of the sloth blood off the console as he could.

"Good, good—" Ross said, entering some commands. "This isn't too unfamiliar. Looks like they borrowed most of their system tech from ASTB."

Her fingers flew over the keyboard, and the screens printed out lists of data. "Goodness, there's a lot of satellites under control here. I don't know which one we want."

Mackey read various numbers off the big screen, where the trajectory of one satellite was plotted. "Any of those correspond?"

"Nothing."

Parsons began clearing a place on the floor. "We'll locate it," he said as he emptied an inbox from a desk and placed it on the ground, "the old-fashioned way." He took some of the sloth blood from a computer terminal onto his hand and began drawing a large circle on the concrete with the thick red liquid, smearing it like paint.

"What are you doing, Jack?" Ross looked down at him.

"No time to argue, Mary. Come sit in the circle."

"I told you, we're never doing that again."

"It's nothing like that, no summoning, I promise. Just a quick clarity spell. It will be over before you know it. No demons, no lightning, no portals this time, I promise."

She pushed back from the chair and sat inside the circle on the ground. Parsons was scribbling characters in the blood on the outside of the circle, some sort of symbols that looked to Mackey a lot like overlapping triangles. When he finished, Parsons grabbed a handful of paper and shredded it into the metal inbox he had placed on the ground in front of Ross. Then he took a seat opposite her.

"Does anyone have a sword?"

They looked at him.

"Well, I suppose a knife would do."

"Sergeant!" Hopper called to a Postal Inspector nearby. "Your knife, on the double." He delivered it to the Assistant Secretary, who handed it to Parsons. He held it aloft, pointed it to the four cardinal directions of the circular room, and then pointed downward. The paper in the inbox burst into flame.

"Just close your eyes, Mary. Everyone, close your eyes."

They did so. Mackey wanted to see what would happen, but he was too worried about getting in the way, somehow doing something wrong. He had absolutely no faith that this would work, but at the same time, he wanted it to. There was no time, and they were out of ideas. This had to work, as there simply wasn't anything else.

Parsons began to chant in a language that Mackey had never heard, squeezing sloth blood and saliva from his hands into the fire. He could smell the smoke of the burning paper wafting through the room.

"I feel our sloth friend with us still," Parsons said. "He will help you. Follow the beast across the sky. He joins the constellations of his ancestors. His animal gods, which they worship, not unlike us. And those angels will deliver the address on a flaming arrow."

Mackey could taste the acrid smoke curling into his nostrils, but at the same time, he felt calm. He imagined the sloth as Parsons had described it. A thick jungle, in another time, another climate. Trees with lush, wide leaves, fruit and flowers dripping from the foliage. In the distance, a snow-peaked mountain. And through the trees, a group of humans, digging in the earth. Planting something? No—burying something. Something important. A plan set in motion now, for the good of the future . . .

"Enough, enough now." Ross stood up, brushing off her hands, waking Mackey and the rest from their impromptu daydream. "I know what to do." Parsons' eyes trailed her, satisfied, as she sat back at the console, leaving Parsons alone in the center of the blood circle, as the paper smoldered into ash in the tray.

Hopper smiled. "Go for it, Mary. Burn them."

Ross was busy typing commands into the console. She looked back at the Assistant Secretary, who nodded once, her hat impeccably on her head as ever. Ross hit the "run" key.

A red warning light jumped into place on the large command screen as the sine wave orbital path began rapidly changing shape. Then another warning, then another, and another. The screen flashed red as blood, message texts running into and over each other on the screen, as the alerts surpassed their ability to be understood. Klaxon horns wailed, echoing throughout the mountain.

"That's it, then?" Hopper asked.

"That's it."

"You didn't?" Mackey asked, unbelievingly. "You deorbited *all* of the Commerce Department's satellites?"

"Not all of them," Ross said, crossing her arms and leaning back in the chair. "Just all the ones that could be accessed from this console. Just over two hundred."

"NOAA won't be able to issue weather reports," said Tikhonov. "Fish and Wildlife biological tracking, USGS climate studies, all of it will be set back by years. I can't believe it."

"Worse has happened," Hopper said. "And worse would have, if the entire transportation system of the United States had come to a grinding halt."

"Assistant Secretary," one of the Inspectors interrupted. "There is an older gentleman who has just arrived outside by aircraft. He says he is expected. We have him secured, but he insists on speaking with you."

"Come," she said to the group. "Let's get out of this mountain."

As they exited the tunnel, dusk was well underway. Looking up, they saw points of light streaking across the sky, white lines curving through the atmosphere as they dropped to earth. Thin hairs of brilliant starlight, quickly replaced by wisping brown trails of smoke, condensing into light paths of moisture that hung pink in the sun retreating over the eclipsed edge of the planet. They watched the artificial meteor shower, as the majority of the satellite constellation of an entire Federal Department burned up on re-entry. Across the continent, the daily activities of millions of government employees were vaporizing in the friction of the earth's thick atmosphere.

Mackey thought of the white grid from the inside of the helmets in the astral projection tanks. He felt light, as if his feet were weightless, his body suspended in the cool mountain air like a clear liquid. He thought about all the data, all the electronic components, all the technology on board those satellites that was being consumed. It was countless hours of effort on the part of so many people. And yet, down here on earth, factories were currently churning out more of the same. That new technology, forever condensing from the technological systems of the nation, would soon rise, like clouds after the falling rain, to replace those human-manufactured stars that had fallen to earth.

"Make a wish," Parsons mused.

The old man was surrounded by Inspectors, all holding their weapons tightly.

"It's all right," Hopper said. "Give him some room to breathe."

Nicholas Roerich did not look exceptionally happy, but still managed to stand casually. "Assistant Secretary!" he called. "Thank you so much for your assistance in this matter."

"Assistance," she said, not so much questioning as repeating his word.

"Yes, of course. Rogue elements within Commerce, conducting this terrible, terroristic scheme. With help from foreign agents, if I'm not mistaken. I would have been here in time to stop them, naturally. But I am so glad that they could not put anything so nefarious past the Secretary and yourself. Alertness has always been one of your most outstanding qualities."

Mackey moved forward, about to say something, but Parsons grabbed his arm. "Time to let the executives chat it out, Fred," he whispered.

"Nicholas, I have to say this was quite a bit of an inconvenience." Hopper tilted her head ever so slightly.

"A very gracious favor to give up your time, both on your part, and that of the Transportation Secretary, and that of your talented experts here." Roerich smiled, his entire face breaking into sharp wrinkles. "Consider it a return of the favor for that time with the National Airspace Transit Bureau, and the case of the UFO sightings in Texas—I was not there, but I am sure you remember, of course."

"Of course."

"Well! In that case, you may withdraw your Inspectors, and my security team will handle things from here. I'll call them by the VHF in my aircraft. Our satellite communications seem to be down just now."

"That's a shame. My apologies." Hopper signaled to the Inspector in command, and the troops hustled to their aircraft and began loading up.

Roerich took a step towards Hopper and extended his hand. She shook it. "Lovely to meet you as well, Grace. Until next time. I suppose the Postmaster will keep the pig for now."

They parted. Hopper turned without speaking and headed towards the aircraft at her usual rate of speed. Her team followed, and Roerich returned to his aircraft.

"That's it? And it's just over like that? Swept under the rug!" Mackey said, awestruck. "What about Major Briggs? What about the sacrifice on the hill, the hovercraft crews, the Inspectors killed by the sloths, the—all the . . ."

"That's how it works, my friend," said Parsons. "No one wants the mess to get bigger, because next time, everyone could be standing on the opposite side. So back into the shadows it goes, until the next time things go Orthogonal. The occult must remain occult. Or else, of course, it would not be."

Mackey couldn't believe it, but at the same time, he could. It was stalemate, and always would be. This was how they managed to keep it secret, throughout the years. No one would ever win. No ideology would ever triumph, as long as the sides were evenly matched. Mackey looked around for Tikhonov, to see what he made of all this. But he was gone.

"Where is Evgeny?" They all looked around. "When was the last time anyone saw him?"

"I don't think he ever came out of the mountain," said Ross. "He was behind me while we were walking, but then he just wasn't there."

"Don't worry about Tikhonov!" Hopper called back. "I'm sure he has places to be. As do we!" She gestured at the aircraft, and they hustled to follow her on board.

As they took their seats, Mackey remembered another question, in a long line of questions. "What did Roerich mean," he asked Ross and Parsons, "by saying the Postmaster will keep the pig?"

Ross nodded. "It's old executive branch lore. About the rivalry between Wallace and Roosevelt. They had a figurine of a pig which they traded back and forth. Like a college mascot stolen by a rival school—some sort of East Coast fraternity boy game. It became a metaphor for the feud."

"It wasn't a literal pig," Parsons interjected. "It is a massive crystal, found beneath the earth. They called it the Pig. It belonged to Roosevelt, but Wallace wanted it. They argued over it. Now the Secretary of Transportation has it, so we have the upper hand, but—"

"Mackey!" Hopper approached as the aircraft was lifting off, its four propellers pulling it off the earth and into the darkening sky. "This is for you."

She handed him a small ring, set with a dark black stone. She showed her hand, and on her finger was the same ring. Parsons and Ross showed their hands, also with identical rings. Mackey put his on his finger. Engraved into the stone were the initials OTC.

"Welcome to the Order of the Technological Crystal." Parsons smiled, pumping his hand. "You're one of us now."

"It doesn't stand for that," Ross said dismissively. "It's Office of Technological Countenance. Top Secret, naturally, perpetually Orthogonal."

Parsons began to argue with her, but Mackey shut his eyes, listening to the engines roar as the wings tilted horizontal and the Postal Bureau aircraft lifted off into the night.

Author's Invocation

This novel is fictional. But many of the persons, places, and events mentioned are based on reality, or in some cases, absolutely real.

The saying goes that truth is stranger than fiction. I'm not certain of that, but I do believe that truth inspires the most interesting fiction. The history of the United States government over the course of the 20th century is one of the most convoluted, complex, mysterious, and still-often-secret epics we have. It is also a series of stories that directly affect the present-day lives of American citizens, and all those lives the American empire touches, perhaps as much as anything can be said to directly affect the lives of human beings today. I could write a work of history to argue this point, but there are many good ones already written. So I'll try a different tack. And so I present to you a story tangential to history.

This is a story inspired by the way that the United States government works, and has worked over the last one hundred years. It is not so much a story of a different United States government in a fictional timeline as it is the story of our actual government told through the contemporary language of rumor, drama, analogy, conspiracy, and speculation. In this story, you will meet actual members of the pantheon of American government—but wearing masks, disguises, clad in ghostly apparel, channeling fantastical possibilities normally concealed behind the cosmological plane. Within these pages, I declare a holiday from the bounds of reality, of fact, of authoritative history. With my usurper's authority as author, I direct that for the span of this tale, all real characters shall appear in new guises, with obscured countenances and a dramatic mission, as if we still celebrated the wild, chthonic religious carnival of old. May we slip on our Erismann inversion goggles, so that the world may be turned upside down, as the nature of our eyes' lenses dictates, in order to see with new eyes for a brief time.

All festivals are temporary, and that is their power. When this festival comes to an end, the spirits evaporate, the magic ceases, and cosmology of history returns to its daily business. However—when this play is over, remember that although the conjurers have departed and the masks are put away, those gods invoked within the sacred theater still roam invisible.

If you are interested, here is a list of names. Every name on the list existed once, in real life. You may invoke them according to your own will, because that is both the right and the curse of those who find themselves on the cusp of history we call the present.

May those who have come before us be the lights along a path to a better future than the present that they gave us.

If you are curious about the actual history that inspired this book, let these names start your search.

Grace Hopper
Mary G. Ross
Jack Parsons
Nicholas Roerich
Werner Von Braun
Theodore Vail
Franklin Roosevelt
Henry Wallace
Alf Landon
James Webb
Roy Johnson
Charles Walcott
Joseph Weizenbaum
Wendy Carlos
Charlotte May Pierstorff

Summa Corporation
Megatherium Club
The Explorers Club
The American Miscellaneous Society
Project Mohole
Project Azorian
Scientology, re: Operation Snow White
Operation Paperclip
Manhattan Project
Spear of Destiny
Szilárd petition
The Great Game
Project Sanguine
Stargate Project
Project MKUltra
First Earth Battalion
ARPANET
ELF (Extremely Low Frequency)
Bell Labs
Greenbelt, Maryland
Mount Weather
Ames Research Center
Vandenberg Air Force Base
San Fernando Valley Superfund Sites
Santa Susana Field Laboratory
Plant 42
Skunk Works
Fairbanks Highway Research Center
Marine Corps Air Station Miramar
Ryan Aeronautical
Area 51
Pykrete
Sputnik
High Virgo
Saturn rocket family
The Apollo Missions
IBM S/360

BAL (programming language)

COBOL

FORTRAN

RS-232

Celestial Navigation

Keyhole Satellites

KH-1 Corona

KH-11 Kennen/Crystals

PRT (Personal Rapid Transit)

AGT (Automated Guideway Transit)

Ithacus VTVL Ballistic Troop Transport

MGM-1 Matador Missile

Objective Individual Combat Weapon

MK285 smart grenades

XM25 CDTE System

Exacto self-guided bullets

ELIZA

Air Mail Scandals

Teapot Dome Scandals

The Baltimore Freeway Revolt

California Aqueduct

Outer Space Treaty

United States Resettlement Administration

Works Progress Administration

National Recovery Administration

United States Post Office Department (now the United States Postal Service)

The Census Office

Weather Bureau (now the National Weather Service)

The United States Geological Survey

General Land Office (now the Bureau of Land Management)

Reclamation Service (now the Bureau of Reclamation)

National Advisory Committee for Aeronautics (now National Aeronautics and Space Administration)

United States Railroad Administration (World War One era)

Federal Radio Commission (now the Federal Communication Commission)

The Bureau of Air Commerce (now the Federal Aviation Administration)

Advanced Research Projects Agency (now Defense Advanced Research Projects Agency)

National Reconnaissance Office

The Smithsonian Institution

The United States Patent and Trademark Office

The National Bureau of Standards (now the National Institute of Standards and Technology)

The Indian Affairs Office (now the Bureau of Indian Affairs)

The Forest Service

The National Parks Service

The Fish and Wildlife Service

The Department of Commerce and Labor (now two separate departments)

The Department of the Interior

The Agricultural Division (now its own department)

The Department of Transportation

Bell-22 VTOL Aircraft

Sikorsky S-64 Skycrane Helicopter

Vought XF8U-3 Crusader III Fighter Aircraft

F-82 Double Mustang

XB-70 Valkyrie Supersonic Bomber

LTV XC-142 VTOL Aircraft

B-58 Supersonic Bomber

F-111 Fighter-Bomber

Firefly/Firebee drone family

. . . and other things we don't know about yet or aren't allowed to say . . .

About the Author

Adam Rothstein is a writer and theorist on tactical and strategic uses of technology, focusing on historical deployment and social effects. He's keen on the Future Weird, and has been spotted experimenting with radio waves, media waves, and the rift between institutional and insurgent technological approaches.

Currently, he's researching anthropocene landscapes, infrastructural aesthetics, and material ecologies.

Orthogonal Procedures is his first novel.

CPSIA information can be obtained
at www.ICGtesting.com
Printed in the USA
LVOW03s1914161117
556459LV00006B/14/P